THE ART OF FALLING IN LOVE

HALEIGH WENGER

LITERARY CRUSH PUBLISHING

Literary *Crush* Publishing

Sweet Romance. Forever Love.

The Art of Falling in Love

© 2019 Literary Crush Publishing

Published by:

Literary Crush Publishing

PO Box 451

Springville, UT 84663 USA

Cover design: Blue Water Books

A CIP record for this book is available from the Library of Congress Cataloging-in-Publication Data

Ebook ISBN: 978-1-950344-04-8

Paperback ISBN: 978-1-950344-01-7

For Mark, Bennett, Silas, Nolan, and Drew. It hasn't escaped me that I'm insanely lucky to have a built-in cheering squad.

ONE

My head pounds as I suck in a breath.

Okay. Focus.

Across the room, my laptop is open, cursor blinking on a blank screen. Despite my aching skull, today is the day I figure out what I'm going to do to get into Flagler College. I've always thought of myself as an artistic soul, but truthfully, I haven't ever stuck to—or mastered—any one medium. Still, art school is the only place I've ever wanted to go for college. And in order to do that, I need to create a project that shows my true talent, but I'm stumped. Maybe I have no actual talent?

No. I have to stop thinking that. This summer was supposed to be about Opa helping me figure it all out. This was going to be our Summer of Art. Opa said it'd be special.

He always made everything so special.

I choke off a breath and push thoughts of him away. I click over to another screen, eyes glazing over as I do.

I'm only a few bullet points deep into my list of possible entry projects when a shadow in my doorway interrupts me.

"Claire, there's someone at the door. Do you mind?"

Mom's hands rest on her hips, and her eyebrows rise in my

direction. Judging by the dark circles under her eyes, she's in no shape to chat with strangers. The distance from the front door to my bedroom doorway is so short that anyone standing outside could hear any word spoken, so I mouth silently to Mom. "Who is it?"

She throws her hands up and shakes her head, loose dark curls left over from the funeral yesterday swinging. "No clue," she mouths back.

I quickly run a brush over my own stringy hair and go to solve the mystery. When I open the door to find the porch empty except for a rectangular package, I sag against the doorframe. I'll admit part of me hoped to see Opa, here to announce that the past week was all a big, sick joke, but after seeing his body at the viewing, I know this isn't a joke.

It'll never be a joke.

I heave the package up with both hands and shut the door behind me. Mom has already disappeared, probably back to her room with a washcloth over her eyes to nurse her headache. I don't need her to tell me where to put the mail, though. All of Opa's papers always go straight to his study. I haven't even peeked inside since we got here yesterday. Too many memories. Too hard to look around and realize he isn't there in the black-leather swivel chair, one elbow propped against his mahogany desk.

I suck in a breath in preparation and swing the door open. Peppermint stings my nose as soon as I step through the doorway. It's all the same as it's always been: neatly organized chaos. Stacks of papers line the back of the desk, leaning against the wall. Clear plastic containers, one on top of the other, sit in rows against the other wall, and each of them contains even more paper clippings, important documents, probably a lot of my early art projects. My hands itch to grab onto all of it and take any piece of him that's left. His desk is smooth and cold under my touch as I run one hand along the dark wood and drop the package on top with my other hand.

Opa never minded me wandering around his stuff before, but now that he's gone, I glance around like he'll pop up from behind the mess to yell at me.

I turn quickly to leave, but something flutters behind me, and a mountain of papers slips off the desk, the top pages taking their sweet time gliding to the ground. I stoop to gather them. Then I cross my legs underneath me and sit in defeat amongst the mess. My hand hovers over a brightly colored paper at the bottom of the pile, and I bring it closer to my face to inspect.

TEEN SAND SCULPTING COMPETITION, the flyer reads in bold rainbow-colored print. It's promoting a competition at the beach, hosted by the recruiting team at Flagler. My eyes roam the paper for the details, which include a scholarship prize to the winner. Another paper is stapled to the back, and when I flip it over, I recognize Opa's small penmanship immediately.

He's written my name at the top of the page. My hands smooth over the other paper. It's a registration form for the contest, and it's completely filled out, down to my name, birth date, and high-school graduation date. But why?

My fingers crumple the edges of both papers as I fight the equal desires to smash them into a paper ball or hug them to my chest in lieu of the person I miss so much.

Opa did this for me. He believed this was something I'd be good at, or at least have fun with. Knowing him, he was probably planning on turning in the entry on my behalf and then luring me to the beach, where he'd spring the news.

My wet eyes find the registration form again, which I'd let fall to the ground in my uncertainty. I pick it up and fold it until it's small enough to fit into the pocket of my shorts. I back out of Opa's study and zombie-walk to the kitchen, my head buzzing.

Mom wanders in from her room, eyes trained on me like she can smell the secret simmering inside. We sit at the kitchen table after she grabs some grapes and sets them between us. I pop three in my mouth before I can work out how to tell her what I found. She stares me down while I chew, making it harder to concentrate until I unfold the registration form and slide it across the table to her.

She wrinkles her nose. "What is this?" I would roll my eyes if it hadn't been my exact response, too.

I've talked enough to Opa about my interest in art for him to know that I'm passionate about *serious* art. Not people making mermaids out of sand. Not fun-touristy contests on the beach. And I honestly don't have a clue what my dream school is doing hosting a contest like this. It has to be one of those things for kids or amateurs, something to fill the summer. Not for real artists.

Opa wanted this for me, but why? And is this really what I want for my portfolio, even if my dream school does host the contest? A bunch of sand castles won't impress next to the other applicants' inventive self-portraits and bold paintings.

I bury my head in my hands. If I thought my head hurt when I woke up this morning, it's nothing to the brain-numbing thumping I've got now.

"Opa wants me to enter this contest, apparently." Mom starts to say something, but I hold up a hand. "I can handle this. I'm going down to the beach tomorrow to ask around. Maybe it's not as dumb as it sounds."

Not likely. But, I can at least give it a shot.

She considers me for a second. "Okay. Let me know what you find out."

We sit in silence as we crunch juicy purple grapes. If Opa wants me to do this contest, I should at least try. Maybe I can find some way to enjoy this summer after all, doing something he wanted for me.

My heart suddenly feels a little less tight, and I almost smile. Almost.

From across the table, Mom makes a deep throaty sound. I don't know what she's thinking about, but she's frowning to herself and shaking her head like she's in the middle of an argument with an invisible enemy.

I pat her shoulder. This is awkward. "Forget about the flyer. It's not a big deal," I mumble.

She flashes me a blank stare and rubs her head. "It's not that."

"Oh." I bite back relief that she isn't planning on obsessing over the contest. The last thing I need is her hovering over me while I fling sand in honor of Opa. "You look worried."

She massages her temples while she talks. "It's everything. The funeral. Your sister..."

Yesterday after the funeral, I caught Livvy out in the church foyer leaning against the wall, staring at her phone and pretending not to see anyone else passing by as they whispered condolences. "You're not still texting that guy from last summer, are you?" I'd asked her.

I'd only met him once, but she's barely shut up about how 'epic' their time together was. Like three months out of the year justifies a real relationship. Especially when you're only fifteen. She even used her birthday money to see him over Spring Break. Not that she told my parents *that* part of the story.

She shot me a death glare and clutched her phone closer. "None of your business."

That's how she's been ever since we found out about Opa.

"She'll be okay, Mom." I reach across the table and squeeze her hand. Hers is soft and small while mine is calloused from holding a pen daily to sketch. I'm not sure Livvy will be okay, but it's what Mom wants to hear, even if we both know I can't promise anything on my sister's behalf.

TWO

The beach is empty, just like it always is this early in the season. The schools in Texas let out a few weeks earlier than the schools here, so we always have a window of time where the shores are clear of crowds. Opa used to call Jefferson Shore "his" beach, even though it's accessible to the public. Mom never understood why we wouldn't want to go to the beach behind the house, a small, rocky patch of sand privately owned by the neighborhood Homeowners' Association. Opa's beach is better, but no matter how much we tried to explain that, she didn't get it. No one ever questioned Opa to his face, though; he was right about most everything. Even when he was wrong, he was right. I used to argue with him for hours, trying to explain why cell phones have made the world a better place, but he was anti-technology, and nothing I said could ever make him budge.

"You'll miss out on the rest of the world," he'd say.

"It's part of my world," I'd respond.

And round and round until all that was left was to stare at each other in frustrated silence.

And he'd always end with: "The world's always gonna be bigger than what you can fit in your hands. Being connected to the world around you is how you see all the art it has to offer." If he had his way, we'd get rid of all our phones and computers and spend 24/7 outside.

He almost convinced me, but I'm too loyal to my cell phone to just give it up.

I slide myself down onto my butt on the nearly abandoned beach as I use my hands to smooth the patches of sand on either side of me flat. One hand bumps against something under the sand, and I fish out a small blue flashlight. *Huh. Boring.* I put it back down next to me and resume playing in the sand like a toddler at the park.

There's something therapeutic about letting handfuls of grainy sand wiggle through my fingers. The beach at sunset is my second favorite time of day, closely rivaled by the super early morning. Daytime hours are too blindingly hot during the summer, and there are way too many tourists sweating it out for it to be worth the trip. Strolling a couple hundred feet from where I sit is a couple holding hands and walking so closely they almost look like one big over-sun-screened blob. They move in and out of the edging tide, whispering things I can't hear. There's no one else around besides the homeless man napping on the steps by the parking lot. I stretch my arms out again and scoop up fistfuls of warm soft sand and let it filter out of my hands in slow streams.

"Hey, man, that's my flashlight."

I spin to see a guy about my age with his hand outstretched. My arm automatically shoots upward, light in hand. My eyes widen.

Careful not to brush my fingers with his, he pulls it from my grasp and pockets it. "Thanks." Instead of the smile I expect him to be wearing, one eyebrow's cocked and his mouth is a lopsided line. "Oh. You're a girl." He slowly moves his gaze from my loose tank top to my too-tight shorts, causing my cheeks to burn hot. So embarrassing.

"Yep, I am definitely a girl."

I've never had to clarify it for anyone, and the words are sticky and foreign on my tongue. He points to my hair and rubs the back of his neck with one hand. The implication washes over me.

"I'm so sorry," he says.

I let my hands go to my ultra-short locks. A new haircut for the summer, and a first for me. I've always had shoulder-length brown hair, but the day that Opa died, I found myself in my bathroom with a pair of kitchen scissors and a shaky YouTube tutorial on DIY pixie cuts. I've avoided looking in the mirror ever since but reading my mom's tight-lipped expression every time she sees me is more than enough to remind me of her opinion on it.

The guy still hovers over me, eyes darting between me and the parking lot. He clears his throat a few times like he's going to speak and then swallows, his Adam's apple bobbing. I wouldn't blame him for running, truly. He makes a movement that I'm sure means he's going to walk away, but instead he drops down onto the sand next to me and stretches his legs across the sand.

"I mean, I can totally tell that you're a girl now. I'm just dumb. Don't feel bad about your hair. It's really cool, actually."

He looks sideways at me with puckered lips and furrowed brows, concerned over the misunderstanding. I almost can't help the smile pulling at the sides of my mouth. Some of the embarrassment fades away, and I finally let myself breathe enough to really look at him. He reminds me of a teenage surfer from a Disney movie. He has sun-bleached blond hair, perfectly unbrushed strands that come down to his chin. I peek at his eyes, which are classically blue and framed by dark lashes. He's gorgeously tan, obviously. But his chill surfer vibe is compromised by how hard he works to apologize for offending me, and I have to admit it makes the corners of my mouth turn up in spite of myself.

"My hair is not cool, but thanks anyway."

He shrugs, and I mentally kick myself for doing that thing where I can't take a compliment.

"So, what's the flashlight for?"

The beach usually clears once the sun sets, and anyone who sticks around is most likely there for a bonfire or lighting up a pipe. My breath catches as he pulls something plastic from his shorts pocket because if the only reason he's sitting next to me is to sell me crack, I'm so out of here. Thankfully, all he brings out is an empty trash bag. From his other pocket, he pulls a wad of blue latex gloves.

He grins as I let out a long breath.

"You're cleaning up the beach?" It's nearly impossible to keep high-pitched skepticism out of my voice. No way this hot seventeen-year-old is here by himself to fish trash out of the ocean on a Friday night.

"Yep."

I tilt my head. "Just because?"

"Come with me. It's easier if I show you." He waves his hands towards the darkening skyline and clicks his flashlight on. The small light shrouds us in an eerie halo, and I'm reminded that I'm sitting alone on the beach at night with a complete stranger. I stand, my legs unsteady on the uneven sand.

"Maybe some other time, but you have fun with that. I have to get back home."

I half-wave and turn to walk away in slow motion. Part of me wants to stay. I love this beach as much as anyone and maybe more. If there's so much junk here that this guy has taken it upon himself to clean up, maybe I should too. But the part of me fueled by years of Mom's paranoid warnings wants to get out of here before he suffocates me with his trash bag.

"What's your name?" His voice calls from behind me, and I stop and turn again despite Mom's nagging in the back of my head.

"I'm Claire. You?"

I can barely see him from this distance in the dark, but I think a smile spreads across his face. It shouldn't matter, since he's a stranger, but I wish it were lighter outside, so I knew for sure. I'm a sucker for a cute smile.

"Claire." He turns my name on his tongue like it's brand new to him. "I'm Foster. Thanks for not stealing my flashlight."

He steps toward me and reaches to shake my hand. A breathy laugh escapes me as our fingers brush before I snatch mine away.

"Yeah, sure," I say. "Will you be back to this part of the beach again?"

He grins, and I'm graced by an up-close version of his ultra-watt smile. Not too bad.

"I'm here every night, Claire. Come back any time to pick up trash and save the beach with me."

He waves his trash bag in the air again and I laugh. I shouldn't reward him for that kind of line. But honestly, it might be working. Cute smile and cares about the environment? It's at the very least a positive change from the other boys in the upcoming senior class at my high school. I'm tempted to bring up the time I was ten and spent the entire summer break scouring the beach for soda bottles to trade in for cash. Opa was so proud of me that he retrieved his wrinkled leather wallet from his jeans pocket right there in the grocery store and paid me double what I got in can money.

And there it is. The heart wrenching *pang* again. When it

leaves me, it doesn't stay gone for long. All it takes is one stupid anecdote or memory and I'm back to full-time mourning.

"Maybe I will," I tell him. I swallow the lump forming at the back of my throat and turn quickly away from him. Seriously, I can't cry here.

Once I reach the parking lot, I check my phone. The familiar blue-lit screen shows that my parents have been working overtime to get a hold of me. I slip my phone back into my shorts and drive home without reading any of the messages. I'll be home in a few minutes, and there's no point in starting the argument five minutes earlier.

When I pull into the driveway my parents are standing in front of the beach house with their arms around each other's shoulders. I snuck away to the beach for an hour tops; this seems a bit overkill. My mom is wearing her crying face, her eyes so squinty they look like slits, and even Dad is kind of red-eyed. I get out of the car and jog over to them. Maybe this isn't about me.

"What's wrong?"

Mom shakes her head and starts crying again. She looks up at my dad, but he can't seem to find words either. A pit forms in my stomach, and it grows larger with every silent second. Head-lights creep along the street, and a car I don't recognize stops in front of the house. We all turn our heads in sync to watch Livvy appear from the passenger side. A boy is driving, but he doesn't look at any of us as he screeches away much faster than he arrived. Livvy pretends like she doesn't see us huddled together on the perfectly manicured St. Augustine grass. When she reaches the front porch, she folds her arms in front of her. Mom sucks in a breath like she's been punched, and I look between my parents and my sister, waiting for someone to fill me in on what's happening.

Livvy responds to my panic with a half-smirk. "What? They haven't told you the whole sob story yet?"

I manage to shake my head but everything is buzzing, the same disconnect from reality I felt when Mom stumbled into my room a week ago to tell me Opa was gone.

"Everyone's just going to have to get used to it," she says. She glares at my parents' faces before turning back to me.

"Get used to what?" I'm almost begging at this point. *Please*, make it, whatever this is, stop.

And then my sister holds up her left hand, the slight twinkle of a gem dancing off her index finger, and all hell breaks loose.

THREE

The voices coming from behind my parents' bedroom door don't even resemble whispers anymore. Full-out war echoes through the beach house's thin walls as soon as breakfast ends. They're supposed to be at work—the family-owned gift shop that used to be Opa's is a big part of why we're here every summer. They took the day off to *discuss*.

Livvy and I wait outside the door, ears perked up like it's a radio show. Words I've never heard either of my parents say are flung with abandon, and they bounce off my ears like tiny rocks intent on shattering whatever semblance of a peaceful summer we had left. My mom starts sobbing, and I move away from their door because her tears are contagious. The deep vibrato of Dad's voice overpowers her crying.

"A promise ring...are you kidding me?"

Livvy's cheeks are red like she's been slapped. I'm surprised to see her show any emotion at all, since she's been too cool for virtually everything lately. Mom whisper-screams something back to my dad, but it's unintelligible. This argument could go on all day. I inhale and turn to where Livvy's buried herself in a pile of pillows on Opa's reclining chair. Maybe she misses him as much as I do. She hasn't said much, but maybe apathy is another part of her new personality.

"Do you want to head to the beach?" I'm not in the mood for the beach, but I'd rather be anywhere else at this moment.

She nods, and I don't wait for her to change her mind. We leave behind our parents' echoing voices and hurry out to my car with our swimsuits tucked under our arms. I scrawl a note letting our parents know where we are and to call us when it's safe to come back and slip it under the starfish welcome mat before we go. We drive in complete silence. I'm too distracted to turn on the radio, and for once Livvy is too.

The parking lot is nearly full. It shouldn't be this busy. I gaze out my window at the beautiful day outside—a rare breeze, not too humid, but hot enough that everyone's dying to go swimming to cool off.

"Perfect. I can't believe I didn't realize it was Saturday." I slap a palm to my forehead and groan.

If this summer were normal, I wouldn't even be here today. I'd be hours away with Opa in a museum by now. Since last summer, he and I had been mapping our trip to as many semi-local art museums as we could find. He was going to help me find my niche. Now the trip is off, obviously.

I sneak a glance at Livvy, but her eyes are glued to the window. She doesn't care if I never find a parking spot because it's not her problem. If I have to be at the crowded beach with my sister and all her drama, at least I can't deny it's a nice day. I reach behind the driver's seat for my swimsuit and beach bag, but a loud hiccupping stops me. Livvy's arms are wrapped around her head, but it's still not enough to hide the fact that she's a tropical storm in progress.

"Liv?"

I tread carefully because she may explode any minute. She lifts her head and a cascade of dark-brown curls falls over her face. Agh. I can't believe I'm still jealous of her hair with everything else going on.

"I'm sorry," she says. Her voice is hoarse, even though she's barely said a word since last night. "I didn't mean to make everyone so mad. Now Mom and Dad hate me."

I blink. I've never heard Livvy apologize unprompted for anything before. And here she is crying in my car and actually taking some responsibility for the mess she's caused.

"Do you hate me too?"

She meets my eyes, and I forget to hate her for a second because she looks like my little sister again and not the self-absorbed teen queen she's turned into. Her lip quivers as she watches me. She's waiting for me to fix everything for her, like I always do.

"No one hates you. We're just worried about you."

It's true. I've caught enough of my parents' latest argument to understand the root of their anger lies in their all-consuming worry about my sister. What if she runs away or gets trapped in an abusive relationship? I obviously don't want any of those things for her either, but she won't listen to me anyway, so I keep it simple.

I take a deep breath and try to flash her my most supportive smile. "You can be in love. But be in love in a normal way. Be fifteen. Don't get engaged or...uh...promised."

She rolls her eyes so far back all I see is white instead of her normal blue. The spell is broken, and she adjusts her self-granted, invisible tiara with a scowl in my direction.

"You don't know anything about love. You've only ever dated like one guy."

I glare at her, but I don't say anything because she's so obnoxiously right. Met by only my silence, she gets out of the car and prances towards a group of teenagers crowded around the beach. I jog after her but come to a quick halt when I see she's running toward her boyfriend. *Typical.* Now I'm stuck chaperoning when I should be at home working on my college entrance essays. I drag my feet as I approach her group and wait for her to acknowledge me. She's by far the youngest person there; everyone else looks like they're my age or older. Someone in the circle reeks of pot, but I can't pinpoint who, which means it's probably all of them. Livvy ignores me until I scoot closer and bump her with my hip.

"Claire! You know Evan, right?" She smiles up at him as he reaches a lanky arm around her waist and squeezes until a playful screech comes out of her. I wouldn't believe the categorically happy sound came from her at all if I hadn't seen her turn from sulk to flirt right in front of my eyes.

He doesn't smile at all. Instead, he nods at me without even bothering to focus his eyes on mine for longer than a nanosecond. *Awesome choice of boyfriend, sis.* I nod back, a barely discernible jerk of my head that hopefully conveys exactly how much he disgusts me.

After another minute of lurking behind her new friends, I turn to tell Livvy that we need to go before Mom and Dad see the note and freak about us leaving. But she's gone. I twirl like a manic ballerina until I spot her and Evan heading toward the tide. He's strutting behind her, staring at her butt while she practically floats across the sand. Hiding at the beach is supposed to make things better, not exasperate them. I groan, nearly tripping over myself to catch her before she disappears entirely. Exhausted, I stop, hands on my hips, and channel my best Mom impression.

"Livvy! Meet me back here in an hour so we can go home, okay?"

She turns and grins, walking backward while swinging hands with her zombie of a boyfriend. "Okay. Sure."

I'm not buying her glittery smile, so I trudge back toward

the parking lot and plop down onto the sand. I choose an area as close to the pier and parking lot as possible, so I can monitor everyone leaving, just in case Livvy decides to run off. I pull out my phone, since it's all I have with me, and go to the notes section to jot down my art-school essay ideas. It's not the same as really sitting down to work on them like I wanted, but I can make a little progress while I wait.

Maybe I should be working on contest ideas, per Opa's brilliant plan for me. But like every other time I've sat down since we got the news about Opa, my mind is a frustrated map of grief and ideas are hard to come by. My mind wanders to summers at the beach with him and how different this one will be.

Two summers ago, Opa surprised me with a new set of pens for sketching. We drove across the bridge to Anastasia Island and parked ourselves on the sparkling sand for hours. Opa napped on a giant towel under his umbrella, tan hat propped over his eyes while I sketched the mountainous dunes and the waving sea oats that dot them. When we went home that afternoon I'd excitedly pulled out my nearly full sketchbook to show my parents. They'd flipped through the first few pages before commenting how 'nice' and 'cute' my drawings were. When Opa found me in my room after dinner that night, he'd spent an hour devouring my work and pointing out his favorites. Then he'd put both giant wrinkled hands on each of my cheeks and held them there, looking at me like I was the most amazing thing he'd ever seen. Like I was art to him.

"Hey, are you okay?"

I don't realize how engrossed I've become in my memories until an unfamiliar voice snaps me back to the present.

I squint up at the voice and shield my eyes from the sun. The boy from last night bends down toward me; he's wearing a frown. Right, his name is Foster.

"Oh…uh…yeah, I'm okay. I'm just waiting for my sister."

I am waiting for her, but she's not the reason my eyes are beginning to water. My face must be too easy to read because Foster raises his eyebrows and shakes his head a little.

"Want me to wait with you? You look kind of sad."

Before I can answer, he sits down next to me, stretching his bronze legs out in front of his body. Maybe he'll be a good distraction, because it's hard to want to cry over Livvy and Opa while he's lounging next to me wearing nothing but swim trunks and flip flops.

He nods toward my phone. "What are you working on?"

My digital notepad is blank, even though I've had the app pulled open for a while. Unless I can somehow make an art project out of the stinging pain of how much I miss Opa, I don't know if I'll ever finish by the end of the summer.

I sigh and tell Foster as much. He shrugs. "You can do it." Something small and black peeks from the underside of his arm. A tattoo. A pang of jealousy slices through me. Mom would never let me into the house alive if I showed up with ink—even something small like that.

Talking about Opa isn't helping. The next best thing is talking about Livvy, but it's not great either.

"If my sister isn't back in thirty minutes, I'm going to have to hunt her down." I lean forward with my face in my hands, mouth turned down.

He raises an eyebrow. "Oh yeah?"

I nod. "We're only here today because she…"

My teeth find my lip as I shake my head. "It doesn't matter, but she's in big trouble and my parents are flipping out. But now that she's run off again, they're going to completely lose it if I go home and she's not with me."

Mom's face flashes across my mind, her eyes stretched to the limit, her mouth a grim slash across her face. Dad's silent disappointment. And it'll all be on me if Livvy's not there to bear the brunt of it.

He bends his head over the sand. "I can relate. Your sister sounds like a few of my family members. A little too much sometimes."

My first reaction is to defend her, but I can't anymore. I choke back whatever lie I was about to spew on her behalf. "She totally is."

He nods. "I'm sure you love her anyway."

"I do, but sometimes, it would just be easier without her. Today for example." I spit the words out much too fast and sharp, and I'm sure the heat creeping along my neck and ears is a visible pink.

He raises an eyebrow, his lips pinched. "Oh."

I've somehow said the wrong thing, because his shoulders stiffen at his sides.

Seconds tick by like weeks until I think of something else to say. I point to his pocketless swim trunks. "Where do you keep all your cleaning supplies in those, anyway?"

He throws his head back and laughs even though my joke is dumb.

"I only clean the beach at night. During the day I work, and sometimes when I have a break—like today—I surf."

I smirk. "I *thought* I had you pegged as a surfer."

He laughs louder. We're both overcompensating for my awkwardness, but who cares? How many times have I smiled since Opa died?

"You don't surf?"

I lift a shoulder. Just the thought makes my stomach turn over. "I stick to safer beach activities."

He sees right through me. "Not a great swimmer, huh?"

I shield my eyes from the blinding Florida sun and squint back at him. I could keep lying, but I'm afraid the conversation will end if I keep cutting him off, and I need the distraction more than I'd thought at first.

"How'd you guess? My Opa, um—that's what I call my grandfather—tried to teach me to surf when I was five and I got sucked in by the tide. He had to swim after me and pull me out. Ever since then I've spent all of my time at the beach on the sand, far away from the water."

"But the ocean *is* the beach. There'd be no sand without the water."

I roll my eyes and try not to wince at the stab of memories. It sounds exactly like something Opa would say. "My Opa felt the same way about the ocean. But we still did other things together. Like walks on the beach and bonfires and stuff." It's not like I'm scared of the water. My parents even made sure I took a few summers of swim lessons after the incident. But after that experience of getting sucked into the ocean, I realized I'm more of a sitter than a swimmer when it comes to the beach.

I stop and hope he doesn't pick up on my sudden mood change.

Foster frowns. "Is he still around, or…?"

My throat is dry. I'm not smiling anymore, and my words crash from my lips like a thousand bricks. "He died last week. He was sick for a while, though, so I guess in a way it was good. He had a heart attack. It was his second one, so he didn't make it."

Hot tears slide silently down my cheeks, and I turn my head quickly to keep him from seeing. The weight of his arm pulls along my shoulders, and through my blurry eyes, I smile, just a little.

"Sorry. That's tough."

I nod. It is tough. I wipe my tears with the back of my hand, hyper-aware of Foster still touching me, his arm warm and soft but still foreign. I scoot away and run my hands through the sand. I don't want him to think I'm giving off mixed signals. Or any signals at all. Being a nice guy is one thing, and flirting is something completely different. But I barely know the guy, so it's hard to tell the difference. I don't want to get his signals mixed up either.

I heave a sigh and look around the beach. A quick glance at my phone tells me it's past the time Livvy and I agreed on. Out of the corner of my eye, Foster follows my gaze.

"Who are we looking for?" The "we" is not lost on me, but I don't have time to dissect it because I don't see Livvy anywhere, and that's not a good sign. I shake my head and push myself up to stand. I almost fall in my hurry to run across the slippery sand, but Foster's hand catches me and steadies me. I should stop to thank him or at least fill him in, but I don't have the luxury of maybe-flirting with Foster while Livvy runs off and gets into even more trouble. I shrug him off as I bound across the beach for the pier lookout. While I'm climbing stairs to the lookout, I call Livvy's phone, hoping she'll answer and give me a reason to end my stress-filled rampage. The empty ringing serves as a backdrop for my frantic running as I push teenagers and small children out of my path. I almost trip again. This time it's over a toddler's Barbie towel, wadded up in a damp heap near the boardwalk. Livvy's voice picks up right before her phone switches to voicemail. My fear evaporates, and my blood boils hot under my skin.

"Hello? What the heck!"

Her voice is all cold indifference. "Hello? You can stop spinning out of control. I'm fine."

I stop where I am and swivel. I'm hoping to see her standing behind me like the crafty villain in a Bond movie, but there's no sign of her. "Liv, where *are* you?"

Instead of answering, she giggles away from the phone and whispers something unintelligible and not meant for me.

"Liv!" She needs to snap back to reality before she gets us both in trouble. "We need to go back before Mom and Dad drive down to the beach to drag you home."

I can practically hear her eyes rolling over the phone. "I'm not at the beach, so they can't drag me home, okay?"

Oh no. Is she seriously doing this to me? "Where are you?" I copy the voice Dad used when Livvy stole his credit card a few months ago and charged five hundred dollars worth of clothes from the mall. Cool, steady, and so quiet it's chill-inducing. Unfortunately, it didn't scare her then, so it does nothing now.

"Evan and I went for a drive to get away from all the negativity. But don't worry; I'll be back by tonight. Oh—gotta go! See you." She hangs up on me before I can cuss her out like I'm dying to.

I glance behind me to where Foster's still leaning against the railing of the pier. I walk to him and sigh. "Sorry I kind of freaked out. My sister is..." I point to my phone and exhale again. I'm so done with Livvy and the whole situation that there aren't even words to explain.

Foster frowns, his eyes wide. "It's okay," he says. "I get it."

I look past him. "Thanks."

He shifts his feet and frowns again. "I'm not trying to, like, stalk you or anything. You just seemed upset, so I wanted to come make sure you were okay. But it seems like you've got everything under control."

His cheeks are pink as he rubs the back of his neck. "You seemed upset," he says again.

I open my mouth to joke that I'm sure we'll run into each other again, maybe somewhere other than the beach this time. But nothing comes out before my parents jog toward me, worry lining their faces.

Crap.

"What are you guys doing here?"

I bite down on the words as soon as they slip out of my mouth. My parents are so worked up they don't even notice Foster leaning against the pier. He shrugs his hands at me while he backs away down the beach. I eye him, but I don't dare move.

"What are *we* doing here? I think you and Livvy better answer that first. You, we don't worry about, but your sister needs to tell us where she's going as long as we're within one hundred miles of that *boy*."

She spits the word out like she's talking about a poisonous snake. Never mind the fact that I'm pretty sure it takes two to decide on a teen engagement. Or promise ring. Whichever.

"I brought Livvy to the beach, so we didn't have to hear you guys freaking out all morning." I shrug. "I left a note."

I don't mention the fact that I've already lost my flighty sister, but my parents are already scanning the beach for her, their heads swiveling.

"She's gone," I say. I rub a hand over my eyes as their mouths hang open. After the way Livvy's acted lately, I can't believe I didn't see this coming. This summer is looking worse by the day.

———

Loud giggles sound from the front door, jolting me from sleep. Blindly, I reach toward my nightstand and click on my phone. 3:24 A.M. Open palm rubbing over my eyes, I groan into my pillow. Burglars don't giggle, and neither do my parents. I'm halfway relieved to recognize one of the voices as Livvy's. At least she made it home. But the other half of me—the part that's awake hours before I want to be—makes me wish I was close enough to throw something at her. Stomping to the door, I hiss through a tiny crack.

"Shut. Up. Mom and Dad are going to kill you if they hear you, and some of us are trying to sleep."

I don't stay awake long enough to determine whether or not she stays here or goes out again once the giggling stops. But in the morning, Dad pokes his head into my room to let me know she's back, sleeping soundly. How nice for her.

FOUR

Now that's it's officially June, the qualifying round for the contest is only a month away, and the most I've ever done with sand is shovel it into a bucket to make an embarrassing excuse of a sandcastle. And that's when I was seven. I try not to think about my lack of experience when I go ultra-early in the morning to practice at the beach. The cool humidity of the early morning is better than the sticky afternoon, especially when sand is involved. I've done some online research, watched a few YouTube videos, and gone over the rules listed on the back of the flyer. I'm as prepared as I can be, considering I have no real experience. I refuse to do anything halfway, so if I'm going to participate, I have to start taking this thing seriously. It's what Opa wanted.

Another perk of practicing in the morning is that there are fewer people around to see me epically fail. My shovel sinks into the damp sand, and I try to lift another scoop of the stuff. A muscle in my arm that I didn't even know I had screams at me. Heaps of sand line each side of me, sitting in lumpy white piles. And in front of me, deep enough to cover my legs to my kneecaps, is a cavernous hole—the result of all my digging. That's just the pre-work.

As I'm working, Opa's right here, dominating my thoughts. He was the first person I confided in about how much I wanted to go to a college like Flagler after high school. He loved to watch me sketch every summer evening from the back porch of the beach house. Would he have enjoyed watching me struggle to pack this sand together?

With aching hands and what I'm guessing is going to turn into a blister by the end of the day, I scoop from my sand stash, squeezing the grains in my fingers until they're molded firmly. Two hours later, I have a not-so-terrible sculpture of a cat. It's dry and starting to crumble on all of its sides. The cat looks more like it has a flower coming out of its butt than a tail, but it will do for now. The trench I've dug is way too wide, and it hides my sculpture from view of anyone standing more than a foot away. Sculpting isn't as satisfying as watercolors or sketching in ink because I suck at it. My hands ache from beating them against wet sand, and my forehead is hot to the touch from an epic sunburn, but still, my lips curve into a smile at the pathetic sculpture. I made something out of nothing, and that's always a win.

The beach is starting to fill up, so I dump the rest of my bucket of water on top of the cat rendering and head to my car before my pale skin burns any more.

This is the first time I've been to the beach this summer that I haven't happened to run into Foster. Yet, anyway. If I can just make it to the parking lot, I'll be home free. Definitely do not look toward the pier. He's probably not even there. But out of the corner of my eye, his shaggy golden hair is unmistakable, his torso leaning against the railing on the pier.

Crap.

My feet make the decision for me and propel me forward

until I'm too many steps in to change directions. I pick my way through the crowded beach-towel jungle to the pier, eyes trained on the bag slung across my shoulder like it's just so dang interesting I can't possibly look away. I stop a few feet in front of him and drag my gaze to his face. His eyes flit over me like he's been expecting me. Given our track record, maybe he has.

"I'm about to leave," I say, "but I saw you and wanted to say hi."

He nods and one eyebrow shoots up, but his expression doesn't change otherwise.

I stand there, mute and grinning like a clueless little kid while he takes his time responding. I squirm in the silence. Both of my hands are in front of me, dancing with each other, and I can't seem to decide whether or not my tiny tufts of hair should be behind my ears.

"Hi," he says.

I bite my lip. "About the other day with my parents..."

He winces. One eye closes as his mouth stretches in a red line against his tanned skin. "Yeah. What was that about?"

"I should have warned you about how intense they are." I blow out an unsteady breath. "They're just trying to help my sister. I don't think they realize how crazy they're acting, to be honest. But I blame it on Livvy."

He nods. "Yeah."

"Yeah," I echo.

He's smart enough not to keep the awkward conversation going any longer. "So the other day you were working on an application essay. Where are you applying?" He straightens against the worn wood at his back.

"Flagler." Opa took me on a tour the summer I was twelve, since he had a friend who was a professor there. The tall orange-and sand-colored architecture, the original stained-glass windows, and the old Spanish heritage swept me away. I knew I loved it even before I got to sit in the back of one of the beginner painting classes.

Foster raises his eyebrows. I can't tell what he's thinking, but apparently, it's amusing because his lips curve into a smile. Finally, I sigh. "What?"

He shrugs and smirks. "I'm applying to Flagler, too."

My mouth hangs open as I try to think of something to say.

"I didn't really think you were interested in the arts," I finally spit out. I don't mean anything bad by it, but he's more of the surfing type, not the modelling-clay-and-paints type. And I know artists because I've idolized them my whole life. Fellow artists are easy to pick out. We're easily distracted— always dreaming up a new project or concept. Most of the time we have paint plastered across our shoes and glued under our fingernails. Foster is Adonis, not whoever sculpted his statue.

He frowns, his dimples disappearing entirely as his whole face pulls downward. "Well, I am." He turns away from me to stare out over the railing again, frown lines still etched across his mouth. Apparently, running away from him pales in comparison to insulting his artistic abilities.

"Okay," I say, with a shrug that's just a bit too forced. Should I apologize or keep the conversation going? I swallow the pool of spit forming in my mouth, turning my taste buds watery and sour.

"So, what are you into, um—artistically speaking?"

He licks his lips and holds up a hand. I wait with my hands clasped together in front of me. No way am I going to say anything else. Then he steps to the other side of the walkway to grab a bulging bag of trash in each hand.

At the risk of offending him again, I opt for just a nod. It seems like we have pretty different interpretations of what art is, if that's what's happening here. That, or I've been right all along and he's a serial killer who stores his unused body parts in bags. I mean, it's unlikely, but the art thing is just as iffy.

He exhales loudly—a big sound like an exasperated elephant about to lose its cool—when I don't say anything and sets the trash bags on the ground in between us. I wrinkle my nose as the smell of mold and wet dog fills the space between us. If he thinks I'm diving elbows-deep into trash, he's got another thing coming. Or maybe this is part of his Save the Beach shtick.

"Is this your art?" I finally ask. My lips pucker like I've been sucking on a whole lemon.

He narrows his eyes and pulls open the red drawstrings on either side of the bags. I step closer to see that it's just as I suspected: trash. I put one hand on my hip and throw the other in the air. "I give up," I say. "There's no art here. Just garbage."

Now I've really made him mad. His eyes grow twice their usual size as he watches me with growing frustration. "I'm an outdoor artist," he says. Like it's obvious. Like everyone's mind connects art and garbage. Like I'm the weird one.

"Oh, right." We're not on the same page about art at all, because there is no way he can turn these black plastic bags full of stuff he found on the beach into anything that makes me feel the same way as "Starry Night" or "Mona Lisa". I *cried* when Dad and I saw "Water Lilies" at the Met in New York City. Whatever Foster's doing is so drastically different from those pieces it's not even funny.

He must sense my skepticism because he pulls out a clunky black flip phone, one of those pay-as-you-go ones, and slides next to me. Handing me the phone, he tells me to click through his camera roll.

"Look at that and tell me it's not art," he says.

Giving someone control over your phone pictures—even on a device this primitive—is a level of raw trust I'm not sure we're ready for, but I take it anyway and start scrolling. Every single picture, minus an admittedly adorable one of him nuzzling noses with a tiny grey kitten, is of his outdoor trash art. And after about the fourth picture, I have to admit I've been a total snob.

It's like when sunrise-colored waves crash across white-and-cream sand and the sun catches it all just right so the miniscule pieces of broken shells dotting the beach dazzle like tiny chandeliers. Except replace the waves with seashells, sea glass, and old bottles and trade the shells for copper wire, twine, and sticks. I'm not sure how it all works together so well, but it does.

And it's art.

"Okay," I say. "I was wrong. This is actually amazing. It's just not what I'm used to."

Here I am hauling around half-filled notebooks and expensive pens while I play pretend at fancy art-school applicant, and he's making things that *move* me, all with trash. My shoulders tighten at the sad truth.

Foster slips his cell phone out of my fingers, pockets it again, and raises an eyebrow. "Thanks. Maybe you can come with me next time I go scouting for materials."

My lips twitch. "Maybe I will."

If he can confidently swing around bags of garbage without living in constant fear of someone calling him out as a complete fraud, maybe someday I can too.

He rubs a hand across the back of his neck, pulling his fingers through his golden hair. "So, I guess this makes us rivals."

I blink. "What?"

Foster nods. "Yeah. You know, since every year Flager only has so many spots for new artists in each medium."

Something cold trickles its way through my chest. There's only a few spots. And I'm up against *this*?

Swallowing, I smack my tongue.

"I guess so," I say.

FIVE

"Pleeease?"

Livvy is standing in the middle of the living room, eyes wide and fake-watering, while the rest of us look on from the couch. She's been begging all week for someone to take her to the beach, ever since she got herself grounded and is forced to spend her days trailing Mom and Dad or sitting at home.

Mom and Dad watch the news, their attention glued to some story about a local election they've been following. I try to tune out all three of them as I open my phone to an album of pictures from last summer. Using my fingers, I pinch the screen and zoom in on my face in the first picture. My cheeks are cracked with a smile so wide that a flash of my pink tongue is visible between both rows of teeth.

"I've only been once so far this summer." Livvy's voice hovers one octave away from whiny.

The next picture is of Opa sitting in his chair, both of his hands steadying a dark green watermelon on his lap. One hand rests on the uneven yellow spot he taught me guarantees juicy pink fruit once cut open. I inhale and half expect to smell the grassy, soft floral scent of the rind.

Mom's voice carries over the TV, carefully, like she's trying hard to explain something difficult. "It was a pretty memorable beach trip, though, Liv. There's a reason you haven't been back."

There's a picture of Livvy and I with our arms slung around each other, her smiling so hard her cheeks take up most of her face and me angling my head toward her and laughing. Opa insisted on taking it last Fourth of July; we were wearing matching American flag T-shirts and a kaleidoscope of red, white, and blue fireworks sang above our heads against a sky of midnight black.

When he took the picture, he said we'd thank him later.

"Let's make a family trip of it. We can get something for lunch afterward. Sound good, Claire?"

Dad's voice is distant, like I'm underwater and the rest of my family's half a mile away on the shore without me. They could be screaming my name, and all I'd hear is a soft mumbling if I strain hard enough.

I shake my head until I surface enough to think clearly.

Dad repeats himself. "Claire? The beach and lunch after. What do you think?"

I look around, and everyone eyes me like I'm really the deciding factor here.

"Sure. Sounds good." I force a smile for my parents' sake and bite my tongue when Livvy squeals and wraps her arms around Mom and then Dad.

We're out the door within fifteen minutes—a family record. Obviously, Livvy's not leaving our parents any room to change their minds.

The beach is cloudy enough to scare away most of the tourists, so Livvy and I lie on beach towels while Mom and Dad take a walk down the shoreline, hand in hand. I close my eyes and inhale the coconut scent of the thick layer of sunscreen I've just applied. Livvy does what she does best lately and makes everything about her.

"Where are my sunglasses?" Her voice is so loud you'd think sun in her eyes was a national emergency.

My eyes still shut, I shrug one shoulder.

Her voice gets shriller a few inches from my ear. "Ugh. Mom still has them in her purse. Can you go get them from her?"

Blood boils in my ears as I prop myself up on an elbow and stare at her. "No way, Liv. I'm not your servant. You go get them."

She grumbles into her towel and rolls her eyes. When she gets up to chase after our parents, I walk down the beach in the opposite direction, grinding my teeth.

An abandoned pink sand bucket with a crack down the middle juts out of the sand. I bend to pick it up and hurl it across the sand. I'm so not in the mood for sculpting today. It lands further out than I meant for it to, and all that's left as evidence is a tiny pink speck. *Good riddance.*

"Hey." Foster's voice stops me cold. My hands tighten into fists at my sides as I turn.

"So, what did that bucket do to you?" He nods in the direction of the hunk of plastic now swallowed up in sand.

I shrug. "What do you mean?" Maybe if I pretend nothing happened, he will too.

"I saw you launch it across the beach."

Crap.

"I was hoping no one else saw that." But of course, he had. And he'd seen me run across the beach in a panic to find Livvy. Not to mention refusing to believe him about his art and Flagler. But he's still talking to me, which is more suspicious than flattering.

He smiles and holds up his hands. "I promise not to tell

anyone else as long as you don't start throwing things at me, too."

Great. Now I'm the girl with an anger problem. But anyone would look like they're mad next to him. He seems to always be around, always cool with whatever chaos is happening. My ears burn.

"Fine. Then I promise not to tell anyone you collect trash." It's a stupid comeback, but I've got an inexplicable need to catch him in the act of something embarrassing like he has me.

His expression doesn't change. "I told you I clean up the beach at night."

"It's not nighttime now," I point out, gesturing to the fiery orange sun currently baking through multiple layers of my exposed skin.

"And during the day, I sell my pieces. It's a good way to make some extra money." His voice softens and cracks a little on the word 'money' like he'd rather not say it out loud.

News flash: I'm an idiot. A mortified idiot whose ears are so hot I wouldn't be surprised if they burst into flames and dissolved into a pile of black ash right on the spot.

It's his turn to stare me down, a well-deserved smirk lurking under his calm smile.

"Sorry." It's a pitiful way to apologize for accusing someone of being a creep when they're actually doing their job. I squint at him with a smile that comes nowhere close to reaching my eyes. "I guess I just wasn't expecting anyone to see me throw a fit out here."

He shrugs. "I was just kind of thinking it's lucky we keep running into each other."

Lucky. The word slams into me. I need to escape—now. If I don't get out of here, who knows what terrible thing I will say or do next. I don't need any more awkward in my life.

"Are you really out here every day?" I've always looked

forward to the break from school during summers. It's hard to imagine working full-time instead of sleeping in and wandering the beach whenever the urge hits me.

Foster nods. "Yep. I work here seven mornings a week, and then I clean the beach seven nights a week."

"Where do you work?" Looking around us, there don't seem to be many employment opportunities. There aren't even lifeguards.

"I sell my stuff out of a tent I set up."

I'm not sure what the appropriate response should be, maybe somewhere between surprise and sympathy because it's never occurred to me to get rid of the things I create. I'm not sure I could do it. I settle for a frown. "Wow, that sounds so busy."

Foster shrugs. I'm trying to wrap my head around a summer without freedom, but he's smiling. "I take afternoons off, which is more free time than I have during the school year."

My cheeks grow warm again as I consider how busy I feel during the school year. None of my friends have jobs. We're all too busy just going to high school.

"Why do you work so much?" I ask. He'd better not be one of those guys who's obsessed with expensive cars or something. Livvy had a huge crush on a guy in my grade all last year who was so busy waxing his Porsche that he wouldn't have noticed her even if she wasn't way too young. Does Foster even have a car? I haven't seen one.

He wrinkles his forehead. "College is expensive—or didn't you know?"

Right. I'm not an idiot. I know that college costs an insane amount of money. But, I've never given it too much thought. Maybe Opa did, though, considering the scholarship given to the winner of the sand contest.

"Oh, college. Duh." I hit my palm on my forehead like I just had a momentary lapse of memory. Like we totally understand each other. But suddenly Foster's art and his dedication to his beach clean-up project seem more important than anything I'm doing this summer. I shrink into my sand-encrusted shorts and T-shirt, my grip tightening on the expensive leather bag I got for my birthday just a few months ago.

He's watching me closely. "You don't have to feel bad for me," he says.

I blush because it's true. All of my friends at school have the same background, same kind of home life, same stuff I do. We all got cars on our sixteenth birthdays, albeit junkers. In my small town back home in Texas, everyone is the same—or at least we pretend that we are for appearances' sake.

Still, I'd rather lie than confess I have no idea what it's like to be financially independent. "I don't feel bad. It's cool that you have your own money. And you get to share your art with other people."

And at the mention of his art, a lightning bolt of recognition jolts its way through my body. Foster practically lives at the beach, and I've already committed myself to a strict schedule of sculpting practice, so I'll be here too.

And he reminded me how badly I need this. The precious spot at Flagler. I need to do this contest for me *and* for Opa.

"Actually, maybe you could help me with something? There's a scholarship involved, if that helps." Contest rules state a team made up of partners can split the scholarship prize in the event of a win. Seeing as I don't *need* the money, I don't mind sharing if it will convince Foster to teach me.

His eyes widen, probably anticipating the worst.

We're both competing for a spot in the art program next year, but Foster might be the only one capable of helping me. I square my shoulders. "My Opa wanted me to enter this sand-sculpting contest. He was always helping me with these kinds of things when I came for the summer, trying to inspire me, you know? But I seriously know nothing about this kind of art, and it seems like you do." There. A good old compliment sandwich. Who doesn't love those?

Apparently, Foster doesn't. He frowns at me and taps his fingers together while I give him my best puppy-dog eyes. "I could watch you and see if I have any tips," he says, "but I'm no expert either."

"It doesn't matter. I need all the help I can get. Even if we are rivals, we'll be applying to Flagler with different mediums, so I swear I won't take your spot. This contest would give us both a leg up." I need more than Foster's help if I want an actual shot at qualifying for the final round, but it will be a good place to start.

"Okay," he says. "I could probably show you a few things."

My chest thump-thumps double time when I look up and see his ocean-blue eyes smiling into mine. If this were a different summer, a different set of circumstances, maybe I'd be looking for something more than art lessons.

SIX

Livvy and Dad are in the middle of the world's most intense staring contest during dinner when I interrupt and tell my family about my plans for the contest with Foster, clearing my throat and then rushing right into it.

It's better to tell them now before they start nagging me for spending the rest of the summer alone at the beach. They'd much rather I tagged after Livvy or helped at the gift shop. But Opa left me this contest. It was his last gift to me, his last art lesson. If nothing else, they should try to understand that.

"And it's a really great way to branch out with my art. I might even use the experience as the topic of my application essay for Flagler. I even made a friend who agreed to help me out since he knows a lot more about this kind of thing."

"That's fine, Claire. I'm glad it's working out for you. I'm sure Opa would be happy for you too." Mom drags her eyes to me and says the right things, but her real focus is still on Livvy.

Dad nods. "Yes. We're glad you're trying new things." His eyes cut back to Livvy. It's like I'm a puppy begging for scraps under the table. Except it's not food I'm after, just my parents' attention, just this once.

"Now, Livvy, like we were saying—that boy is no good for you. What can your Mom and I do to help you see that?" Dad narrows his eyes, his game face fully in play. He's not bluffing about being willing to do anything to get rid of Evan.

And then Livvy, even though I saved her from Dad's wrath a few minutes ago, flashes me an evil smile: nostrils flared, teeth showing and ready to go in for the kill. Whatever she's thinking, there's no time to stop it before she butts in with a little too much fake excitement ringing across the table. She leans toward me, elbows digging into the tabletop.

"Why don't we worry about Claire for a little bit? Right, sis? I just hope you're being careful while spending all that time with the creepy guy who, like, lives at the beach."

My mom gasps so loudly we collectively flinch because we're afraid of the yelling to follow. Livvy's officially bought herself the distraction she was after. And, for once, Mom is speechless. She opens her mouth and closes it twice before settling into a deep frown, lines marring both sides of her down-turned mouth. No doubt she's picturing me with a more degenerate version of Evan, thanks to my sister.

Dad clears his throat and bobs his head in my direction. "What's she talking about, Claire?"

I shake my head at Dad and then at Livvy. "He's just this boy—who isn't creepy—who works on the beach. Like I just told you—he's helping me with the contest because he's also into art."

Dad shrugs and glances over at Mom, a little less shell-shocked after my explanation, though her mouth still hangs open slightly.

But Livvy has it in for me. She throws her head back and tries out a legit villainous laugh. "Into art?" She's practically sneering at us. "Your sand thing barely counts as art, but at least it comes close. This guy collects trash." She waits for my parents to air their disgust. Which of course they do. *How* does she even know that about Foster? I'm starting to get the sense Livvy has been paying more attention this summer than she lets on.

"Trash, Claire?" Mom is holding both her hands in the air near her face, just in case she needs to use them to start yelling at me. Dad was ignoring Liv up until she threw out the word "trash." Now he's eyeing all of us in turn with his fork paused in mid-air.

I sigh loudly. Am I the only one aware of just how ridiculous this conversation is? "It's not dirty diapers or anything, guys. It's recyclables, like bottles and newspaper." There's no easy way to describe Foster's modernist art, but I have to try. "He takes all of the plastic bags and water bottles people leave behind and turns them into sculptures. Add some spray paint and detailing with a brush, and they look good as new. Then he fits them all together with copper wire and when he's done, it's not trash anymore—they're colorful abstracts."

To my surprise, Dad is the first to nod. He waves his fork at me. "I actually know exactly what you're describing."

I open my mouth but come up with nothing. Instead, I point back to him and turn wide eyes on the rest of the family. They could take a cue from him for once.

"I've seen that kind of project on the news, actually. Very interesting. Good for the environment too." He winks at me while Mom and Liv both stare in my direction with shocked expressions. Dad is usually the last one among us to stick up for the arts, but he's the first to stick up for me when it's me against Mom. Maybe it has something to do with the fact that Dad and I are alike, and Mom and I are as opposite as two people can get.

"Thank you," I mouth to him as silently as possible.

Mom nods too, but her forehead wrinkles and unwrinkles at an impressive pace. She's probably still trying to decide whether or not art made with recyclables—dirty recyclables—is okay. Liv is glaring into her dinner, poking the food on her plate with random stabbing motions. A muscle in my jaw twitches with the need to kick her under the table and rub her face in the fact her tattling failed. The only thing stopping me is the too-sharp eyes of my parents on me.

But I can't help myself so I smile sweetly at my parents. "Anyway, Liv is just trying to distract you guys from the fact that some random guy is trying to turn her into a runaway bride—"

"He's my boyfriend!" Livvy leans across the table, shaking, as her voice rises.

My parents' eyes widen. They've completely forgotten about Foster, refreshed in their concern for my sister. The rest of the dinner is silent as my parents communicate via parental telepathy as they plot how to save Liv. I smile into my food while Livvy watches from across the table, burning me with a glare so fierce that my face flushes like I've gotten a real sunburn. It's a momentary victory—one she'll make me pay for later.

Like Christmas three years ago when she peeled the tape from her stack of waiting presents under the tree and then tried to re-tape them so no one would notice. I told Mom in exchange for a lighter punishment for failing two calculus tests, so Livvy unwrapped some of my presents too. Our parents made us donate all the unwrapped ones to a children's shelter. Then there was the time Livvy tattled on me when I tried to sneak out of my bedroom window last fall to see a concert with my friends from school. She didn't even do it to get out of her own trouble; she just enjoys being a brat.

When it comes to subtle forms of revenge, I'll take what I can get. I stab my fork into my meatballs and savor the warm, salty bite.

SEVEN

The very worst part about sculpting with sand is the digging. It's not like scooping up little bucketfuls of sand to make a cute sandcastle. No. This is intense digging like I've never experienced, or seen really, except for in that movie where Shia LaBeouf steals someone's shoes. I'm sweating before I even start digging, which is impressive for 6 A.M. By the time a small sand mountain accumulates behind me, the sweat drenches me, running down in rivers and puddling in my armpits and the waist of my shorts. The dark, wet smudges across the back of my shirt have to be super attractive. The lapping lukewarm waves call to me, but I'm determined to keep going until I've gotten at least half of my sculpture completed. If I meet my goal, I'll let myself take a break and cool my feet off in the water.

I've got something a little more complicated than a cat planned this time. If I complete all of the steps correctly, it should turn out to be pretty cool—at least for an amateur. I crouch near the edge of my rapidly expanding hole and scoop out more sand with my metal shovel. Just as I'm about to fling the sand onto the second pile behind me, a bucketful of warm, salty water crashes over my head and runs down my body. My mouth flies open, letting more of the overpowering saltiness wash over my tongue, and I spring to my feet. Foster stands behind me with a grin as wide as the Cheshire cat's. I want to yell at him, but the water feels so good as it drips down my body that I can't hold onto any anger. I pick up the bucket and toss the remaining drops back at him with a breathy laugh. He rewards me with a smile as he crouches next to me, still holding the shovel he brought. He leans it against his shoulder, smirking.

"The only reason I'm not killing you is because I was about to pass out from the heat." I flick more water from my fingers onto his nose.

"Your neck was bright red. I was just trying to help cool you off." His eyes crinkle at the edges, though his mouth remains solemn. His mouth—specifically his lips—captures my attention for a second too long. If he notices how pink my face is, he doesn't say anything. He turns and shoulders his shovel to start digging. I copy him.

We stick our shovels deep into the hole and work silently for several minutes. I don't hate working with Foster, because he knows when to talk and when to keep to himself. And he's actually an impressive artist. But even if he wasn't growing on me, I need him to help me prepare for the first round of the contest, because it's much more intense than I thought it would be. I push the shovel in for one final push before I allow myself another break.

Thunk! My forward motion comes to an abrupt halt as my shovel slams into something solid beneath the sand. Foster drops his shovel, stepping up beside me, eyes trained on the packed sand.

I nudge the spot with the point of my shovel. "There's something hard down here." The ten-year-old part of my brain entertains daydreams of a treasure chest full of gold doubloons and strung pearls, but my more rational side douses the hope in favor of the more likely scenario of an enormous rock or hunk of trash.

Foster picks up his shovel, and we both scoop sand from around the object until it's cleared. I crouch into the shallow hole until I'm close enough I might inhale sand if I'm not careful. At first glance it seems like my guess of large rock was correct. Foster comes closer to inspect while I pour a little water over it and rub it with the corner of my beach towel. Under the grime, a pattern emerges. Once it's cleaner, I can see that it's more of a dark green than the black I'd originally guessed.

"A turtle shell?" I arch an eyebrow and look to Foster. I've unearthed awesome things at the beach before, but this might be the best.

Foster frowns at the shell, his mouth crooked. "Weird." By the time we've finished digging it out, my breath comes in shallow wisps of air. I lean back and tuck my legs crisscross under my body while Foster lifts it up and places it in between us.

"You don't think this was, like, a sinister turtle murder? Maybe someone buried him alive?" I'm mostly joking, but part of me worries about handling the literal skeleton of such a beautiful creature. I trace a light fingertip across the shell's pattern.

Foster squats across from me. "I don't know. I think we should cover him back up. Maybe this was supposed to be his final resting place."

Thankfully, he's not laughing at me. He might actually be serious. I narrow my eyes but smile, still unsure if he's making fun of me or not. He picks up the shell and hands it to me, his hands careful and steady. I place it back in the hole, and we scoop sand over it in turns. After we're done, I lean back on my elbows and groan. I should say something else about the turtle. Or thank Foster for not teasing me about caring so much, at least. Instead I deflect.

"I don't even like swimming but getting in the water is all I can think about right now." I let my shovel slip from my fingers and fall to my feet. I shrug off my tank top, unbutton my shorts, shimmy them down to my toes, and then kick them aside. I'm wearing a stretched out black tankini I've had for too many summers, a fact that now embarrasses me for the first time.

He arches an eyebrow and then pulls his shirt off, too. As usual, he's already wearing swim trunks in lieu of real shorts, so he runs full speed into the water, his body sloshing through the waves. He's completely in his element. I was too hot to care earlier, but now I'm overwhelmed by a flash of self-consciousness. I tuck my arms lamely by my sides, my toes burrowed into the sand like I've decided to glue myself to the spot.

"Come on. We deserve a break." He mistakes my hesitance for work ethic. Sure, I'll take that. Pretending it has nothing to do with my dislike of swimming in the ocean is fine by me.

"I'm coming," I yell back. I inhale and charge into the ocean after him while doing my best to channel some sort of graceful water creature. A dolphin, maybe. If dolphins are afraid of drowning and other creatures biting their toes. Once I'm fully submerged in the water, my skin prickles against the lukewarm waves and my nerves dissipate with the cooling sensation. I dunk my head backward to wet my hair and hopefully wash away some of the greasy sweat near my neck. Foster does Olympic-worthy backstroke moves while I splash around, hoping no one notices the stark difference.

"Hey. Remind me to take you surfing sometime." Foster's only a few feet away from me—close enough to see my lip curl at his suggestion.

"No thanks. Don't you remember the story about my last surfing experience?" Why am I reminding him of humiliating things I've said?

He chuckles. "I remember."

I nod once. "So, we agree. No surfing."

He shrugs. Foster sucks in a breath, plugs his nose, and dives down under the water. I stay very still in the same spot where I bob, awkwardly waiting. Roughly twenty seconds later, he pops up and shakes his hair, spraying me in the process.

"Agh, gross." I swipe my hand against my cheek to wipe away the stray droplets.

"Sorry. But look what I found." He offers me a palmful of white shells. I wade toward him and choose an ivory one in the center of his hand. It's almost completely solid except for a small blob in the middle that looks a little like a heart. When we're ready to wade back to shore, I slip the shell into the pocket of my shorts while I wait for my swimsuit to dry.

I stretch out across the sand, cringing as tiny granules cling to my skin, turning me into a sentient piece of sandpaper. But the scratchy pieces dry almost instantly, and I'm able to brush them off with a swipe of my palm. The air's so humid and thick there's barely a difference in and out of the water. "This air is so sticky I can't move." I groan.

Foster glances sideways at me. "You sound exactly like a tourist right now, you know that, right?"

He's right, which is annoying and slightly hilarious. The easiest way to pick out a pack of tourists is to find whoever's bemoaning the humidity. I start to laugh, but a huge drop of water sloshes across my nose, catching me by surprise. In three seconds flat, hundreds more follow and we're soaked from the pounding rainfall before we can even register what is happening.

My arms and legs freeze, stunned under the pressure of the rain. Next to me, Foster rolls to his side, bends to scoop up his clothes and supplies, and then darts across the beach. My legs are rubbery as I sweep my things together and follow. I start toward the parking lot, planning to hide in my car until the downpour ends, but Foster doubles back to grab my arm, pointing toward the pier. I follow him because I'm already soaked, so it doesn't matter if I get wetter. He crouches under a corner of the pier and I stop too, hesitating.

"Come here." He motions me closer. I squeeze next to him, relieved. Somehow the small corner seems to be the only space on the entire beach that has managed to stay dry. Aside from the occasional stray raindrop, we're protected from the storm.

My back presses against Foster's chest. We're still in our drenched swimsuits, so everything sticks together. The more I try to smoothly un-squish my suit from his swim trunks, the more Velcroed we seem to be. I finally give in and settle against him again. Not that I necessarily mind the body heat he's giving off. We watch the rain in silence. Even if we wanted to talk, the water pouring into swimming-pool-sized puddles around us is deafening. My senses are so maxed out I almost don't notice when Foster slides his arms around my shoulders and pulls me all the way into him, closing the mere inch-wide gap that was there before. I inhale, and my heart pounds so loudly in my ears that I swear it's threatening to drown out the storm. I look around the pier in hopes of finding something to distract me from the warm buzz under my skin—the one that wasn't there the last time Foster and I were together—but the only thing under the pier is an army-green backpack and a tightly rolled blanket secured with a fraying rope.

"Do you think homeless people sleep under here?" I nod in the direction of the gear as my throat catches. It's hard to distract myself from Foster when, with each breath, every muscle in his arms tighten against mine.

Foster shrugs his shoulders. His breath burns onto the side of my face when he speaks. "Probably, but they're mostly harmless."

Not according to my parents. They consider homeless

people one of the biggest blights on our society. Lazy, unemployed, a burden on the backs of the hardworking people of the world. Especially here at the beach, they're Dad's favorite thing to complain about.

But Foster's right. I've never heard of any of the local homeless men or women hurting anyone. They mostly just hold up their homemade cardboard signs with pleas for money or food scrawled on them. Or, like the man I saw my first night back at the beach house, they sleep on the beaches and under the piers when everyone else is gone for the day, probably just thankful for a soft, quiet place to rest.

I quickly forget about the homeless population as the rain slows and my senses return. It's easier to feel like we're safe from prying eyes wrapped up like this under the pier, hidden away from the world. But the heavy rain is reduced to drips, and the sun is already sliding out from the disappearing dark clouds. The rest of the world slips back into focus, and this doesn't feel safe or secret anymore—just awkward.

I duck out into the soft sprinkles and turn to face Foster for the first time in fifteen minutes.

"Thank goodness that's over," I say.

What a stupid thing to say. Foster frowns and blinks in response before glancing away. If I didn't know better, I'd think my comment hurt him somehow. Should I pretend I have somewhere important to be and run? But he's holding half of my stuff, including the tools, so I keep my mouth shut.

He must think I'm an idiot, because he barely looks at me as we walk from the pier to the parking lot. I speed-walk so fast that I reach my car in record time, though nearly out of breath. Leaning against my car door, I watch as Foster makes his way to me, still wearing a frown.

A homeless woman passes. She's got a cardboard sign tucked under her arm as she trudges across the parking lot in faded, ragged leather boots that look like they were made for a very large man. She looks only a few years older than I am. I wonder if the army bag and blanket under the pier belong to her. Hopefully, her gear didn't get too wet. As she walks by, Foster raises a hand and nods at her.

When she's gone, I whisper, "Do you know her?"

He shakes his head. "Just trying to be nice."

I've never even considered waving at a stranger. Once, when I was nine, my family and I went out to dinner for my birthday. I wore a baby-pink T-shirt with the words 'Birthday Girl' written across it in rhinestones, and I matched the ensemble with my brand-new baby pink pleather coin purse. After we'd left the restaurant and I'd just barely gotten over the embarrassment of the teenage employees singing to me over my slice of chocolate fudge cake, with the nine glittery pink candles my mom had whipped out of her purse, I'd spotted a homeless woman slumped against the back door. I thought about how I'd just eaten so much food that my stomach was seconds away from rejecting it. Dad must have seen sympathy etched in my wide preteen eyes, because he'd taken me and Livvy by the shoulders and scooted us to the car so fast anyone else would have thought the lady was handing out poison apples.

And then there are people like Foster, just trying to be friendly. It's enough to make me think, but not right now. Not when my attention is still mostly focused on the golden-haired boy who's jut reached me.

It's been twenty minutes since the downpour, and the rain has completely cleared. The sun beats down on us again, working overtime to dry everything and making me sweat even though I'm still just in my swimsuit and flip-flops. I turn my face up to the sun and let my skin soak in the intense warmth. Foster's eyes follow mine, but he doesn't say anything.

"Thanks for your help today," I tell him.

I wish our closeness under the pier had never happened, because now I'm finding it so hard to say anything to his face. I blush at the image of us huddling so close, hidden away from the torrential rain. I could have sworn I felt something between us a few minutes ago, but now things are complicated.

Foster nods. "It was fun."

His voice is lower and softer than normal. We're standing side by side with our backs resting on my car door, but he turns to stand right in front of me. He's almost a foot taller than I am, so I have to crane my neck to meet his eyes. As soon as I look up at him, he bends down toward me. Before I can work out whether or not I want him to kiss me, he ducks his head and steps away, tucking his hands behind his back in tight fists and mumbling some sort of half-hearted goodbye. My doubt washes away as I bite down on my tongue in regret. I can barely breathe, but there's still enough room for one tiny desperate thought.

I guess I *did* feel something after all.

EIGHT

"Has it ever occurred to you I might know something you don't?"

Livvy's taunting voice snaps me out of my daydream. I'm lying on the sofa with my eyes closed. I'm trying to take a nap, but visions of Foster's arms around me in the rain keep interrupting me. Not that I'm complaining.

I open my eyes and prop myself up on an elbow. "What are you talking about, Liv?" I try not to encourage her too much, but the fact that she knows anything I don't has actually never occurred to me, so now I want her to spit it out. She walks around the sofa and plops down into a plush chair across from me. All of our conversations now are arguments, but I can remember a time just last year when we actually liked spending time together. Last summer we built a fort in the living room and watched romantic comedies until 3 A.M., at which point we crashed and slept until noon the next day. Then we used Opa's cookbooks to make German pancakes and gorged ourselves until our stomachs ached from a combination of too much food and laughter. All that seems so far away now. Before Opa, before Livvy and Evan, before me and Foster. Maybe too much has changed to ever allow us to get back to the way things were before.

But now she's doing her best to get under my skin. Does Liv know something about Foster? Maybe she was spying on us at the beach and she's trying to blackmail me by holding it over my head. Opa would never let us fight like this in summers past because he said we needed to be there for each other and we couldn't if we weren't speaking. Maybe that's why Livvy's gotten so distant all of the sudden. Opa isn't here to remind us.

"I just know things." She shrugs and twirls her hair around a finger. If I weren't too far away to reach her, I'd slap the smirk off of her face. I'm almost positive she doesn't actually know anything. She's just bored and trying to mess with me. I ignore her and walk into the kitchen for a snack. She follows me and grabs an apple at the same time I do. "Opa's beach is not as private as you think it is, Claire." She gives me a pointed look. She's obviously dying for me to explode and beg her to spill her secrets. I bite my tongue and suck in a breath without uttering a word and then storm to my bedroom before she can follow, shutting her out with the slam of a door.

I sit cross-legged on my bed with the shell I took from the beach today. I turn it over and over in my palm, rubbing it like a charm. Foster's hot—I've known that from day one: the first night after Opa's funeral, when he'd just appeared and flashed his lazy smile and stared at me with his too-blue eyes. But I'd never imagined us actually together—not until now. I've spent the entire morning analyzing everything—him leaning into me, putting his arm around me under the pier, meeting my eyes for a second longer than normal. Do those things mean anything? And then the way he stalked off afterward because I had to act like a total freak. Is it all in my head? A one-sided sort of thing?

Thumping against my bedroom door shakes me from my own head. I tuck my shell under my pillow where the photo of

Opa and me lives now. I don't know why, but hiding it seems like the right thing to do. I expect to see Livvy, but instead my mom's face appears in the crack of the almost-closed door. "Hey, Mom." I sit up and scoot to the side of my bed to make room for her. She tucks her hair behind her ears and watches me from the doorway with the same too-warm smile I've seen a thousand times before. The one that says she wants to talk. "What are you looking at?" I touch my hair in case she's getting ready again to complain about me not consulting her before cutting it.

She sits next to me on the bed and touches my knee. Her touch is soft and reassuring. No matter how old I get, I think I'll always need my mom in some way. It's been so stressful here since Opa died and Livvy went crazy that I've almost forgotten what it's like to sit together and not be upset about something. No yelling, no arguing, just Mom and me. She turns to me and breaks the silence.

"So, are we going to talk about this guy Liv was trying to tell us about?"

I groan. It's like my sister was born with a vendetta against me. I can picture her now, smirking to herself as she eavesdrops on this conversation.

"Mom," I keep my voice low in case Livvy really is lurking in the hallway. "It's nothing. He's just a guy I met at the beach who's helping me with the sand-sculpting contest."

I squirm under my mom's poorly suppressed grin. We talk about a lot of things, but boys are not one of them. The only boyfriend I've ever had was the son of my mom's best friend. There was nothing to tell her about him because she already knew everything there was to know. I'm not even sure I can count him as a real relationship. Unless we're counting relationships that are practically arranged.

She tilts her head up at me in an attempt at gravity, but her dimples give her away. "Do you like him as much as you liked Grant?"

Her question freezes me. Although what I had with Grant was devoid of privacy because of our moms, it wasn't fake. I remember the first time we kissed. I made the first move while we were saying goodnight on his parents' front porch after a night of board games on the couch. He drove me home afterward and I couldn't look at him the entire drive because I was so afraid of messing up what I later decided was a perfect moment.

But when Foster and I are together, things are more *real*. I barely know him, but I feel like myself around him, even though things have definitely gotten awkward. I don't have to try to be something I'm not. With Grant, the fear of saying something that might get back to my parents overshadowed us, and that hanging paranoia ensured I never told him much about me. Mostly we just kissed. It was nice, but just thinking about Foster and me under the pier, surrounded by a blanket of rain, makes my body tingly. I don't realize I'm smiling to myself until my mom opens her mouth in surprise. The high pitch of her words shakes me back down from the cloud I was floating on.

"Wow! You like him even more, don't you?" I don't answer her question because I can already see the wheels turning in her head. She bites her lip and mumbles something to herself while her eyes drift up to the ceiling.

"Dad and I have a few late nights at the shop this week, but we can do a game night and dessert this weekend."

"Mom, no. He's not coming over." I shake my head. But, all the humor has gone out of her face, and I know I'm going to lose this argument.

She holds up a hand to stop me. My mind races with possible excuses, and some of them are pretty legitimate. Like the fact that Foster isn't my boyfriend, and I'm not even sure he sees me in that way. Even though I might, possibly, maybe have a crush on him, I don't know anything about him besides our shared interest in art. You can't just invite someone who's basically a stranger to play Monopoly with your parents.

But Mom's steely eyes tell me that she doesn't want to hear any of those things. She just wants me to agree with her.

"I'll ask him, Mom. But he might be busy."

She sighs. "I understand this time around you want more space. That's normal." She pauses to think. "We kind of lucked out that you're our oldest and you're a rule-follower." I roll my eyes. I'm not sure if I'm being complimented or ridiculed. It feels like a little of the latter, though. "Your sister—we're realizing we may not have done all the right things with her."

I decline the blatant invitation to agree. I catch the drift of her disjointed thoughts. I'm pretty sure she's not trying to torture me—at least not on purpose. Mom wants to protect us so badly that sometimes it's suffocating.

"It seems like you really like this guy—"

I nod. "I might. I'm still trying to figure out how I feel."

There's no point in trying to hide my feelings now that she's dragged them out of me. She smiles, signaling her own victory.

"The next time you two are together, tell him your parents want to meet him. Tell him it's mandatory." Satisfied, she claps her hands together.

I, however, am not so confident. If I weren't already nervous to see Foster after our close encounter, I am now.

NINE

When I invited Foster over in a temporary and painful moment of insanity forced on me by Mom, I didn't expect him to agree. Similarly, when I brought home tall, gorgeous, and scruffy Foster, I didn't expect my parents to act so normal, despite Mom's earlier insistence on meeting him.

"Claire won't tell us much about you, Foster, but we've noticed you two have been spending a lot of time together," Mom crows from across the table.

"We have been super busy working on our sculpting plans." I try to butt in quickly enough that Foster isn't obligated to say anything.

He flashes his dimples, pulling Mom fully into his magnetism. "I'm really lucky she's letting me work with her," he says.

She insisted Foster stay for dinner and even though I was making definite 'no' signs behind my mom's back, he ignored me and accepted. I should feel betrayed, but it's freaky how easily he fits in. Even Liv, who is quarantined at home after being caught parked down the street with her boyfriend, is being really nice to him. And I know Livvy well enough to tell when she's making fun of someone instead of when she genuinely likes them. She's actually smiling versus the fake-smiling she does when company comes over.

Mom side-glances at Dad, who nods back at her. Color them impressed, I guess.

"Thanks for keeping our Claire Bear company." Dad winks at me across the table. I sink into my chair, wishing there were a way to pull the entire tablecloth over my face without anyone noticing.

Livvy coughs into her plate, buttered broccoli spewing in tiny pieces from her mouth onto the table. She grins from behind her hand, her shoulders bouncing in silent jolts of laughter.

Meanwhile Foster pretends he's not trapped in a room full of circus performers. He chews bites of broccoli and grilled chicken carefully, takes a sip of water from his glass, and smiles at each of us. Like everything's just great.

After dinner, Mom excuses herself and comes back two minutes later with a stack of board games. All of us, except for Foster, give her crazy eyes. She ignores us and asks Foster to pick the game. He picks Hungry Hungry Hippos, a game so old that I didn't even remember we still owned it.

"This game is for little kids," Livvy complains. My sister is annoying, but I have to agree with her. I mean, I *would*, if it weren't Foster's game of choice.

There are only four hippo heads, so Livvy gets to sit and watch. She pulls out her phone when Mom and Dad are focused on the game and sends her boyfriend a string of emojis that either mean she's really hungry (not likely, right after dinner) or something else really gross. Foster gets this intense look and he squints his eyes so they're only tiny slits. All of the sudden marbles are flying. Mom whips her hair around like a head banger as she tries to capture the most marbles in her hippo head. Dad and I just watch and shoot each other worried glances. Mom likes to win, and from the looks of it, Foster might give her a run for her money.

We cut them off at five rounds. Liv rolls her eyes at the end of every round, which stops me from doing the same. No matter how weird a Hungry Hungry Hippo showdown between my mom and Foster is, I can't bring myself to be annoyed. Seeing everyone, minus Livvy, happy like this reminds me of Opa. He would have loved seeing us like this.

It's dark outside by the time my parents let Foster leave. Birds scream at each other to go to sleep and fireflies float past our heads as we wave to my parents. We drove over together, so I have a good excuse to leave with him. Mom makes sure to remind me that she and Dad will wait up for me to get home. In other words: make it quick.

I stare straight ahead through the windshield as I pull out of the driveway. "Where should I drop you off?" It's weird to think that Foster exists anywhere outside of the beach, but he's got to live somewhere, I guess.

He waits a beat before answering. "Just back to the beach is fine."

We pull up to a red light. The streets are empty except for the shadows cast from the looming streetlights. Without the radio on, we can hear cicadas chirping into the night like an unwelcome chorus. I turn in my seat, facing him as much as I can within the constraints of my seatbelt.

"It's ten-thirty."

His shoulders straighten. "I've got some stuff to do still. I haven't collected yet today."

I shake my head. "It's too late for that, isn't it? Don't you ever sleep? Your parents must be super chill."

The light changes, and he doesn't respond. When I pull into the beach parking lot, he unbuckles, his jaw twitching.

"Thanks for the ride. And tell your parents I said thanks again. It was cool."

I run a hand along the curve of my steering wheel, the worn leather familiar under my grip. "I'll tell them. Thanks for putting up with my family today. I could tell they all liked you."

His eyes cloud over, and his fingers flex and freeze on the door handle, the tattoo on the back of his wrist visible. It's a midnight-black infinity symbol, smaller than a penny. Inside one of the loops, the letter *s* is inked in cursive writing. I bite my lip. S, whoever they are, is very lucky.

He lifts his head. "I like them too."

I smile across the car, my cheeks pushing up into my eyes. Something stretches and tingles inside me, like a new rubber band testing its limits for the first time.

"I'll see you Monday morning, right?"

"Yep. See you Monday, Claire Bear."

He opens the door and walks away into the dark. I swear the ghost of a smirk is visible from the back of his head. Then he's swallowed up in the black blur of the sand and the water.

TEN

"I can't do this."

I drop the yellow bucket and let it tumble onto the sand at my feet. Water splashes back at me, sending drips down my face. I flick my tongue across my lips and taste salt.

It's not my first temper tantrum of the day, and I doubt it'll be my last. My original sand cat was bad. My attempts so far today have been pathetic. Abysmal. A complete joke. Kind of like my dreams of being an artist. Foster clicks his tongue but doesn't look at me. He's otherwise absorbed in his own practice sculpture. He crouches over a row of three uniformly filled buckets, his hands sliding over the tops to smooth away excess sand. I lean back onto the warm, white beach as he releases the sand from each bucket and adds them to the top of a structure he's already completed: a rectangular base with dual levels of cones and cylinders. A basic but structurally perfect sandcastle.

I pick up my bucket and scoop it full again. Foster stands behind me, watching silently. More like silently judging. I ignore him and slam my hands into the sand to make sure it's packed. Then I tip the bucket over in front of me, ready to prove I can make

a stupid sandcastle too. Except nothing happens. The contents of
the bucket stay put, hugging the sides like concrete, no matter how
many times I rap my knuckles on the bottom. I squeeze the bucket
and shake it furiously until half of the sand oozes into a sludgy pile.
The other half sticks stubbornly to the inside of the bucket.

"Argh!"

I rear my foot back and launch it into the bucket, but instead
of the stubborn bucket flying toward the ocean, it skids only a
few inches. Awesome. I can't even beat up a sand bucket
correctly. And now my foot's throbbing.

Foster's eyes follow me as I back away toward the pier
behind us, my bag slung over a shoulder.

"I need a break," I say. Like, a permanent break.

He crouches to pick up his things and walks after me,
because apparently he can't take a hint. We walk to the pier in
silence, me breathing fire and collecting pools of warm sweat as
I march as fast as I can manage. I drop down onto it, sling my
legs over the side, and slump. He sits down a few inches away
and bobs his head toward the white-and-black checked notebook peeking from the bag tucked next to me.

"When are you going to let me look at your sketchbook?"

Heat rises along my ears and neck at the thought of showing
him my work. I shake my head. "Maybe later."

"You've seen my stuff." His chin juts forward. If I didn't
know better, I'd say I'd hurt his feelings.

"That's different," I quip. I'm not sure how, exactly. But my
sketches feel more personal than his sculptures. His art is made
for people to look at and try their best to interpret. It's supposed
to be put on show.

My drawings are each individual beat of my heart inked
onto paper, my most private thoughts splashed across the page.
They exist only for me.

"Okay." He stretches out the word like it's five syllables instead of one.

My head whips toward him. "It is different. Your art is made for public consumption. Mine isn't."

"But it could be, if you wanted."

My eyes roll back, and I dig my fingernails into my palms, a personal warning not to lose my temper again.

"But I don't want to." Clipped. Tight. Furious.

He holds up his hand. "Okay. Whoa. Sorry."

His eyes focus on mine, sending involuntarily tingles across my arms. "But it's not really fair of you to take it out on me when you're just mad about the contest."

I break eye contact as shame washes over me like a cold shower in the middle of January.

I exhale and run a hand over the sand-smoothed wood on the pier. It's just earthy and solid enough to calm my frazzled head.

"My Opa and I were going to go on a trip this summer to all the art museums around. It was supposed to help me figure out where I belong in the art world, what I'm good at."

I shrug and suck in an unsteady breath. "We didn't go on the trip, and now I'm more confused than ever. But I'm pretty sure I don't need any museums to know I suck at this sand thing."

"Was the Little Art Park on your list?" He's got this wistful, wide-eyed look that makes him look like a little boy.

I nod. "Yeah. Have you been?"

He smiles at the shoreline past me. "I've always wanted to go back. My mom took me for my birthday when I was ten. I loved it."

I've never heard him talk about his mom. Or his childhood. This place must have affected him big time. "Maybe I'll make it there someday," I say. Opa did put it near the top of our list, so I probably owe it to him.

"You should. Let's go now." He hops to his feet, extending a hand to pull me up with him.

I stay where I am, my nose wrinkling against the sun in my eyes. "What?"

"Yeah. Why not?" He pushes his offered hand closer, like he's suggesting we start walking to the museum this second.

I grab onto his hand and stand, and then I plant my hands on my hips. Heat from where his fingers touched mine sticks to my palms and makes them sweaty.

"I can think of two very good reasons, and their names are Mom and Dad. They'd never let me go on a trip like this. No offense, but especially not with you.

Foster shrugs, a smile forming around the corners of his mouth. "You'll never know if you don't ask."

———

"Anybody home? Mooom? Livvy?" I swing the front door open and yell into the house.

"Livvy's at a friend's house," Mom calls.

I arch an eyebrow as I meet her near the oven, where's she's staring intently at the blue cartoony whale timer on the counter.

"Don't you mean stuffing her tongue down Evan's throat?"

She snaps her head toward me, mouth pinched. Then she sighs, sending a tiny curl on her forehead flying upward. "I guess it's possible, but she promised she wasn't going to see him every day this summer, and her girl friend did come by..."

Great. Now I've incited fresh panic when I'm supposed to be putting Mom in a good mood.

"I'm just joking. She wouldn't lie to you after she just got ungrounded."

Mom bites her lip. "I hope not," she says. "How was your day at the beach? Get some good tanning in?"

My teeth find the skin on my inner cheek. How can she so casually ask about the beach when I've told her repeatedly how much practice I'm putting in? Does she still not realize how much this means to me?

I guess to her it's still just play, like the rest of my art projects. Just a fun side project, but never impressive enough to be taken seriously.

"Sure. But there's something I wanted to ask you about, okay? Please listen first before you say no."

I twist my hands in front of me. This is my second chance at the summer that was supposed to be.

"What if Foster and I drive to some of the places on mine and Opa's list? Some of them are pretty close by, and it wouldn't take more than a day or two. I think Opa would want me to go still."

My heart pounds in my ears while Mom listens.

"A road trip?" Mom's forehead wrinkles and she tilts her head to one side like maybe she didn't hear me correctly.

I squint, one hand running along the curly baby hairs sticking up along my forehead. "If it helps, you could think of it as a commemorative drive?"

I guess it doesn't help, because the long sigh she lets loose doesn't exude confidence.

"I know you and Foster are good friends, but the kind of trip you're talking about would require you to stay somewhere overnight..."

Her eyes widen, and the crisp silence fills in the rest. Dot dot dot. Fade to black. Etcetera.

It's not like the overnight-slash-possible-hotel scenario hasn't crossed my mind. The idea that something could happen between us without all of the distractions of the contest and our families—it's definitely occurred to me. But Foster and I are friends. Period. I might have a stupid, insignificant crush on him because I'm lucky enough to see him with his shirt off a few times per week while we sculpt, but at the end of the day, we're partners in the most unromantic way possible.

"No, Mom. It's not like that."

Her lips purse, whitish against her annual cherry-red sunburn.

"I swear. This is about Opa."

Her eyes catch on my wobbly lower lip. I swear she has crying detection superpowers. "I know you miss him."

I nod, but I have to pull away to catch my breath and stop the tidal wave of nostalgia threatening to overtake me.

"And we do like Foster..."

My lips clamp shut to hide my growing grin. I've got a real shot here.

She turns from me to slip a mermaid-shaped aqua oven mitt onto her hand. Pulling the oven door open wide, she says, "I'll talk to your dad and let you know in the morning, okay?"

I inhale the aroma of brown sugar and melted chocolate and sigh against the warm gust of cookie-infused air. This trip might actually happen. Even without Opa, this summer could turn out like it is supposed to.

"Thanks, Mom. I promise you won't regret this."

ELEVEN

Foster gets to the house exactly at eight A.M., just like we planned. I'm already on the front steps waiting for him because my plan is to intercept him before my parents can. Under no circumstances would it be safe for him to talk to them unsupervised. Who knows what kind of cringe-worthy things will come out of their mouths.

I figured his parents would drop him off or something, but as usual, he's alone, and this time he's riding a bike. One of those basic black ones that old guys ride around town, hogging up the entire turn lane by going approximately two miles per hour. Once he reaches the driveway, he slows, slings one leg over the side, and hops off. Then he leans the bike along the side of the house.

"Hey," I say, finally standing.

"Hey. Is it okay if I leave this here while we're gone?"

I nod. "Is it yours?" This is the first time I've seen him with a bike.

"I borrowed it from a friend," he says. His hair hangs just past his chin in sun-streaked strands, and it's half-wet.

He catches me staring and shakes his head.

"I woke up late and had to ride over as soon as I got out of the shower." He flips the front part of his hair back just as the front door whooshes open and my parents storm onto the scene.

Dad steps forward quickly to grab Foster's hand and give it a shake. I think I see a hint of pity in his eyes as he glances between Foster and Mom. She's bouncing on her toes while waiting for her turn, ready to pounce.

The smell of flowers mixed with strong soap pummels into me as Mom steers me away and slides in between us.

"So good to see you again. And it's been so nice for Claire to have someone to help her with her little art project this summer. And now this trip."

She's smiling so widely that her eyes disappear into her cheeks. Dad wraps an arm around my shoulders and squeezes. It's his way of apologizing for any damage Mom might do in her helicopter parent efforts. I sigh into his arm and watch the train wreck happen.

Mom's stage whispering now. "Make sure she's driving the speed limit and make sure she stops to drink water and use the restroom."

Foster doesn't move his eyes from her face. He's nodding along, as if everything she's saying is perfectly normal and not one of the most embarrassing pep talks a mother has ever delivered on behalf of her almost-legal teenage daughter. If he did glance over at me, I'm almost positive I would actually die right there on the spot.

"Now, I don't want to make you uncomfortable, but when you two stop to sleep, you'll need to get two hotel rooms. That's something Claire's father and I insist on."

Foster's lips twitch like he might say something (please, no), or maybe just finally let the impending smirk loose, and Mom stops him with a wagging finger.

"Don't worry about the money. We will absolutely take care

of it. We just need you to promise to be careful with our daughter." Her lips make a tight line, and her eyes manage to stay wide and unblinking for far too long.

Foster's head moves up and down, his damp hair sliding along with it, as he nods fervently. "Yes. I promise we'll be careful. I'll have her back tomorrow afternoon at the latest."

Finally, Mom's mouth slips into a smile that could pass for normal, much softer at least than the half-crazed look from a few minutes earlier. She reaches into the purse at her hip and retrieves a blue-and-white credit card and presses it into Foster's hand. Since I'm her daughter and the one who will be driving, I'm not sure why she's not handing it to me, but Foster clutches it so tightly that his fingers burn white.

TWELVE

"It's my turn."

Foster pulls on the cord connecting my phone to the car stereo and switches it out for his own. Then he scrolls to a playlist and a soft rock intro blasts through the speakers.

I shift my eyes toward him as much as I dare while driving, and he grins in my peripheral vision.

I nod at the music. "What is this?"

His face falls. He looks around, his mouth open like there might be hidden cameras revealing I'm pulling some seriously awful prank on him.

"You're not serious, are you? Please tell me you're joking."

My embarrassment creeps across my cheeks, no doubt leaving visible pink streaks of shame. I set my jaw. "I'm serious. I've never heard this before in my life."

He leans back in his seat, hands lacing behind his head. "Well, thank goodness you met me then. It's Pink Floyd."

Obviously, I've heard of the band. Foster's acting like it's crazy I don't know every song by a bunch of old guys, but I'm not completely clueless.

"Oh, yeah," I say. "Dark Side of The Moon, right?"

"Yes!" He claps his hands together like I've just asked him to confirm he's a lottery winner instead of it being a very mundane answer about his favorite band.

The music pounds into my skull like an itch that I can't quite scratch. If I weren't driving, I'd close my eyes and lean into it, feel it more fully, but it's too difficult to divide my attention between the road and the songs, and I'm left torn and annoyed. My GPS tells me to turn right on the next road one second before I've driven too far past it to make a reasonable turn. I try anyway, swinging the wheel so far right that the tires make a sharp screeching sound and my phone on the console between us slips under my feet, out of my reach.

I skid to a stop on the side of the road while Foster turns toward me, eyes wide.

"What happened?"

No way I'm telling him I'm actually getting into his old-person music. I lift a shoulder and grab around under my feet for my phone.

"Oh, hey." Foster's arm reaches across the seat, and he's searching too, both of us feeling blindly under the dark crevices of my seat. My pinky bumps into something cool and metallic and hard, and I emerge victorious, my phone clasped tightly in my palm.

Foster's eyes dart upward. "Nice. You found it."

I nod. "Thanks for helping me look."

He pulls his hand back, bumping it against my phone and knocking it out of my hand again in the process.

We both stare at the phone where it's landed, partly visible, under his seat.

Then I breathe out a small laugh.

And so does he. Giggles tumble out of me until I'm almost breathless and definitely hysterical. But he's laughing too.

He hands me my phone and I set it firmly on the console between us again.

"Um." I take a steadying breath, my face flushed against the cold air blowing from the vents. "Okay, let's get back on track."

And then we're both done laughing, and we don't say anything else until we stop for gas several miles after. But the skin where his hands touched mine after he handed over my phone is warm for some reason.

When his playlist ends, I press the replay button while he's inside the gas station.

———

The first stop on the list is a museum neither of us has heard of. I try to pronounce the name twice and fail before Foster unbuckles and leans over my shoulder. When he speaks, the words vibrate against my back. "After the lake?"

I turn my head half an inch toward him before realizing how incredibly close it brings our faces and shrinking back. He smirks. At my ignorance of Floridian lakes or at how quickly I jump away from him, I'm not sure.

"Lake Okeechobee?"

My nose wrinkles. Of course he said it perfectly on the first try. "Yeah, I guess so." We both gaze upward at the black iron sign sprawling above the whitewashed brick building that reads *Okeechobee Museum of Art*.

"My mom and I used to drive by the lake sign a bunch when I was younger. We looked up how to pronounce all the weird names we saw and memorized them."

He gets this distant, slack-jawed look and gazes past me, out my window. I follow his line of sight, but there's nothing. I guess he's seeing some memory he doesn't want to share.

"That's cool that you get along with your mom," I say. A hint of wistfulness slips into my voice, and his head snaps back to me.

"You don't?"

I make a big show of clearing my throat. "Ahem. You saw my parents that day at the beach. I love them, but they can be pretty dramatic. Especially Mom."

Foster's lips twitch. "I think that's all moms. And even if she's over the top, she probably thinks she's trying to protect you."

I lift a shoulder. "I guess. What's your mom like?"

I search his face, but his only reaction is a tightened jaw. "She's great."

His back-and-forth warm and chilly persona is giving me whiplash. There's got to be some reason for the way he shuts down like this. But for me to find out, he'd have to actually open up to me. Sometimes—like this conversation—it seems as if he's about to say something that will explain everything. And then he closes off and he's stoic, silent Foster again.

"Okay."

I pull my keys from the car's ignition, taking the frigid air conditioning with them, and we step onto the bubbling black asphalt. The parking lot of the small art museum is nearly empty. There are only two other cars, not including mine. One is a beat-up gold minivan and the other is a shiny black pickup truck, and they're both parked right up front like they're poised for a quick getaway.

I speed-walk past Foster toward the heavy metal front door and swing it open without bothering to wait for him. It closes behind me with a satisfying clunk. The huffing breaths I let loose have nothing to do with how fast I'm walking and every-thing to do with how annoyed I am about Foster's reluctance to talk. I've told him plenty about my family, about Opa and Livvy.

Plus, he's met them all. But he won't even give me more than a two-word answer about his.

Once inside, I pause on my heels and turn around the one-room display. Before I can even get a feel for the place, a strong leafy smell hits me. I bring my head up, tilting my face toward the smell so I can drink it in. It's like walking in a forest and coming across a bush full of juicy purple fruit, but instead of eating any, you just shove your face in the bush and inhale.

The door thuds behind me again, and a *hmm* sounds from Foster. Probably trying to figure out the smell too. He stands beside me, and I grudgingly nudge him with an elbow. "What is that smell?"

"Herbal tea, I think. But a lot of it."

None of the peppermint or chamomile teas I've had have ever smelled like this, but it's news to me that other varieties exist, so Foster's probably right.

I breathe in again just as a petite, grey-haired lady wearing tiny gold-rimmed glasses way down on the edge of her nose sweeps in. Her black muumuu runs across the floor as she shuffles toward us from a door in the back corner. The herbal smell increases when she emerges. She must be boiling a cauldron full of tea in that back room.

"Visitors." She clasps her hands together solemnly and nods at us from halfway across the room.

"Hi," I say. I raise my hand in a half-wave, half-salute motion and then pull my arm tightly to my side. A bead of sweat forms on the end of my nose.

She motions around the claustrophobic room. "Welcome. Please let me know if I can help you with anything."

Foster nods. "Thanks. We're just here to look around a little."

She blinks at him and then turns on her heel and swooshes back through the door.

We turn to each other, stifling giggles as soon as she's gone. Sweat pools around my lower back, and I try to position myself near any of the box fans placed in each of the four windows without drawing attention to exactly how hot I am.

The museum is one long row of paintings after another. Each row is divided into different painting styles. One is impressionist, another modernist, some renaissance, and etcetera. It should inspire me to see so many styles all grouped together in such a small space. Instead I count the paintings, filing them away to think about some other time, just like I might for some tiresome homework assignment. Foster doesn't say anything as he wanders a few feet behind me staring at the endless groupings of art. But the repetitive brush strokes and boring colors seem to have the same effect on us because by the time we've both reached the end of the exhibit our shoulders are slumped, our eyes sagging.

Maybe this isn't our kind of art anymore.

Despite never actually drinking any of the flowery warm-smelling stuff, I'm swaying on my feet by the time we move from the museum to the parking lot. My mouth opens in a yawn so big my shoulders shudder.

"That was interesting." Foster side-eyes me once we start driving again.

Interesting, for sure. I nod and rub at my heavy eyes. Hopefully our next stop provides more artistic clarity and a less sauna-like atmosphere.

THIRTEEN

I let Foster pick where we eat for lunch. He's super insistent on something cheap even though we have my parents' credit card. He's all about his job and his own money, but you'd think he'd be glad to have someone else paying for once. Instead, his nostrils flare when I poke him in the back to remind him about the card before we order.

He chooses a food truck that serves only burgers and fries, but I'm not complaining. We order one of each and a side of fries to share. I carry my tray to one of the three black metal tables a few feet from the truck. When I sit, my chair wobbles unevenly under my feet. Foster follows, taking the seat opposite mine.

The napkins included with our orders are the same blue as his eyes. Ever since the first time I noticed his eye color, I can't not think of the ocean when I look at them. That and his love of surfing...in some ways Foster's more connected to the beach than I am.

He pats the stack of napkins on the tabletop between us and grabs a handful. Starting at the top, he makes slow, careful rips that make quick gusts of wind over the other napkins. Once he's done turning the first napkin into equally measured blue strips, he starts on the next one.

"Are you making something?"

His lips smoosh to the side as he considers me, but his eyes— ugh, his eyes. I rip my own gaze away. There's staring and then there's drinking someone in, and I'm about to waver on the latter. Sure, Foster's cute, but he's also infuriating at times, and I'm not about to get myself caught up in all of that.

"I just had an idea." He shrugs.

I lift an eyebrow. "Just like that? You saw the napkins, and an idea popped into your mind immediately?" Where's the skulking around for hours, sketching until your hands are numb, thinking until your brain melts? Art comes so easily to him that I should hate him. But I can't bring myself to feel anything other than utter, sinking disappointment in myself. I bite my lip and try to ignore the rock in the pit of my stomach.

"Don't you ever do this? Just make something out of whatever's around? It's something I've been doing since I was little. It's how I realized I wanted to do something with art someday."

My stomach rolls giant green waves at his words. No, I've never done what he's doing. His hands work quickly as he's talking, and part of me wonders if he's even aware of what he's doing at all. Like, maybe his hands have a mind—and artistic will—of their own.

"So, what's the deal with your grandfather? What do you call him—Opa?"

I suck in a breath. "What do you mean?"

"I just—sorry. I guess I'm just wondering why this trip and the contest and this summer mean so much to you."

"They're all I have left of him."

His face pinches. "Yeah, I get that."

There's a pause when we both pretend to be absorbed in our burgers. I nibble at the cheese peeking around the edges of my toasted bun. Then Foster sighs and swipes the basket of fries aside. Our eyes meet again.

Maybe he's lost someone like I have. Maybe all of the quick answers and silent stares are more than just guarded personality. Whatever it is, I'm starting to think he's never going to tell me. My head turns the other way so he can't see what's written on my face.

"Opa was the one person I could always count on to believe in me. He always knew I could be an artist, even when I wasn't so sure. Without him..."

I sigh and press a palm to the cool metal table top, made slightly damp by the warm summer air.

"I'm trying to keep that belief alive however possible."

Foster nods and sets his creation in front of me. It's a blue paper bird, folded and pinched delicately into a whimsical replica of the seagulls we always see at the beach.

FOURTEEN

We're not going to make it to the next stop. Ninety minutes into our drive along a road that just barely counts as paved, I glance down at the gas gauge and cold dread clenches my arms, leaving tiny hairs standing up as I try to catch my breath. We're supposed to be at a museum north of our last stop with an hour or two to spare before closing time, but it's not going to happen.

We've been relatively quiet since lunch, both of us lost in our own train of thought and Foster absorbed in his music. But now he pulls his headphones from his ears and turns toward me.

"What's wrong?"

"We're almost on empty." I shake my head and point a finger at the arrow on my car ticking dangerously close to the letter E.

Foster leans over, his eyes widening. "Crap."

Exactly.

"I didn't even think about gas after we left the museum. I just wanted to get out of there, but I haven't seen a gas station in at least an hour." My voice cracks, a tiny sound that still sounds like the echo of some deafening thud in my own ears. I can't just break down like this. Foster's still staring at the gauge like he thinks he might be able to fuel the car by sheer willpower. Or maybe he's just searching for the words to chew me out for being the worst road-trip partner ever.

I pull the car over to the shoulder, and we both bump in our seats as rocks and dry dirt jolt under the tires. I put it into park and turn the engine off, collapsing against the back of my seat as soon as the keys are freed. I'm still cold despite the persistent humidity and absence of AC, but no amount of rubbing the skin on my shaky arms helps. My eyes blink closed as I lean my head against the seat.

"Hey, don't freak out. We'll be fine."

Something warm brushes over my arm, softer at first, like an unsure whisper, and then more heavy and reassuring.

I open one eye and squint at his hand on my arm. He's smiling, even up to his eyes. How, I don't know, since we're basically stranded in the middle of nowhere with no plan and it's one of those overcast days so thick with humidity you can smell it. The only worse thing that could come out of this is rain, and honestly, it's probably not far off.

"We won't be fine." I tug my teeth along my lip.

I shake my arm away from him and tuck it against my chest, even though I'm actually a little calmer because of it.

"Worst case we'll have to walk to the closest house and ask for help. Or call an Uber or something."

I almost agree before a pounding sound stops me cold. Wrong. Worst case scenario is this. A rainstorm in the middle of nowhere, leaving us stranded overnight.

Drops patter onto the hood of my car, streaming down in uniform torrents until the air's so thick with rain that nothing else can be seen. I shield my eyes with both hands curved above them, but it's still like diving with no goggles where everything's so blurry you're not sure if that blob in front of you is a fish or a really wiggly rock. Even if I turned my car back on and used my windshield wipers, it wouldn't make a difference.

Silence stings between us until a beeping sound causes us both to look around for the source. My phone beeps again with a warning. SEVERE THUNDERSTORM WARNING! STAY INDOORS OR SEEK SHELTER.

The blood drains from my face as I stare at the message, and my brain flicks through our viable options.

Foster whispers against the torrential rain. "There's that little pink farmhouse a mile back. Maybe they'd let us wait there until the rain settles enough to call someone. Or until we can figure out how to get gas."

I hesitate for a moment, like there's some other option to consider. Turning the keys in the car engine, I start back for the house, driving as carefully as possible to avoid getting stuck in one of the fresh mud pits. I park the car on the road right in front of the farmhouse, and Foster and I look at each other. It's either run for it or risk being stuck in the car for who knows how long.

We both place our hands on the door handles.

"On three, okay?"

Foster nods.

"One...

"Two...

"THREE!"

The last word is drowned out by the pounding rain and our running against the wind. I grab Foster's arm because it's all I know is out there and if I don't, I might lose sight of him altogether.

The distance to the farmhouse is short, but our clothes and shoes are still plastered with mud when we reach it. Floorboards squeak under our feet as we run up onto the front porch. I knock on the pale-pink door, throwing aside all manners and pounding when no one comes immediately to rescue us from the sheets of water falling from the sky.

The door cracks open, and a woman with red hair peeks from behind it, her eyes wide.

"Come on in," she says, ushering us through the front door into her home, like she's been waiting for us all along.

FIFTEEN

Luckily for us, the little pink farmhouse is actually a bed and breakfast that accepts walk-in guests at any hour. Unluckily, Edna's B&B is not for teenagers. It's the first thing I realize once we've paid and are huddled in the sitting room waiting as Edna bustles around looking for our room keys and gathering extremely fluffy pale-pink towels. Still, she makes an exception for us after we explain about the car and that we're hours away from home.

I flop onto a small couch next to the front door with a towel under my legs so I don't get the furniture wet and muddy. Foster's standing next to it, shifting his feet, as visibly out of place as I am. We couldn't have chosen a better place to run out of gas than near a farmhouse bed and breakfast, but, still, we can't be the usual type of guest. Half-drowned teens don't exactly scream romantic getaway like the rest of the guests who are downstairs eating dinner at a cozy wooden farm table.

Now that we're not running for our lives, I have time to look around at where we've landed. It's safe to say pink is Edna's favorite color. In fact, her main decorative theme seems to be just that one color. No inch of the wall space is left untouched.

There are framed black and white photos, framed maps and blueprints of local landmarks, even framed flowers and leaves, preserved to live on forever in a small glass box. Top that off with the usual suspects like white-lace doilies on each table and side table and intricately woven Indian rugs under our feet. One splash of Pepsi or too-full bowl of cereal would ruin this place.

Foster leans across the pillows and whispers. "Well, at least it doesn't smell like a tea factory."

I grin up at him, and Edna turns just in time to glance between us like she wants in on the joke too.

"I'm glad y'all found me. And you're doubly lucky because we've got a generator specifically for storms like these." She eyes the muddy towel under my butt.

I smile at her reassuring words.

Then she says, "I don't usually see many young couples around here." Her smile is as syrupy as her voice. She's probably around Mom's age, but she's not wearing a ring. This business seems to be her whole life. And she thinks Foster and I are a couple.

Foster stares at her, expression unmoving, except for his lips opening and closing at a rapid pace. It'd be funny if it weren't so embarrassing.

My skin flushes warm against my water-soaked clothes. "We're just friends," I say quickly, in a voice that's too high and too rushed to make anything better.

"Oh." She frowns, like she's confused about something.

Foster and I nod, almost in unison, as if our head movements alone will prove how platonic our relationship is.

She considers us and then clicks her tongue against the roof of her mouth. "Well, that's fine. We have an empty room with two beds that's normally booked for families."

My anxiety eases as that weight jumps off my chest. At least if Mom asks—and I can count on her asking—it will be easier to lie about sleeping in separate rooms. Separate beds is basically the same thing anyway. A covert glance at Foster confirms he's thinking something similar. His shoulders ease down, when seconds before they were tight and up by his ears. Instead of more eased anxiety, the tips of my ears warm. It shouldn't annoy me to know he's happy not to be squished into a bed with me. It doesn't occur to me to care at all until I see how visibly relieved he is. Now I kind of want to pinch him.

The room is so tiny I can't imagine how we'd squeeze into a single bedroom if this one weren't available. There's only a foot of space between the two beds to begin with, and part of that space is filled with a small dresser and a bedside table, all in matching antiqued wood.

I edge toward the bathroom, itching to get clean, when I spot two gigantic bathrobes hanging from a hook near the bathroom door. They're pink, of course. I scrub every inch of mud off of me and wash my hair, then I lay my clothes across the side of the bathtub and wrap myself in a robe. I sink into the soft, plush fabric as it hugs my skin like the promise of a bonfire on a cold night. Foster showers next, and I bite my tongue when he emerges in a matching pink robe.

We both collapse into our beds, but even in the dark, Foster's sigh of relief at not being forced to be too close to me niggles at my brain. "Sorry we have to sleep in the same room."

He's so silent I assume he's asleep until I hear a throaty grunt. "What?"

He sighs loudly. "I don't care that we're in the same room. I just wanted us to both have our space."

I grind my teeth against each other even though the gravelly sound makes me want to plug my own ears.

"Yeah, well, you're right—at least we have some space."

He sighs again. "I don't get why you're mad."

If there's anything that gets me fired up, it's being accused of being angry about things I'm clearly angry about but trying not to be.

"I'm not mad. I just don't get what's so bad about sleeping in the same room. Or bed for that matter. I mean, we're just friends."

"Are you kidding? I can't imagine anything worse."

My mouth falls open as I try to incoherently stutter a response.

"No. It's not that... I-I just mean your parents would kill me. That part would suck."

My heart pounds in my ears as a warm rush settles across the whole upper half of my body. "Oh," I say quietly. If that's all it is, it actually does make sense. I sigh a little in relief.

Most of my face is tucked into the crisp white sheets. When I inhale against them they smell like the same springtime-scented detergent Mom uses. Like if freshly cut grass and soap bonded together somehow.

If I looked over at Foster I'd probably be able to see him, barely make him out in what's left of the moonlight not obscured by more clouds. But it's too intimate, especially after all the talk about sleeping together.

"Thanks for coming with me. I mean, it's kind of a bust as far as all the stuff we were supposed to see, but I'm really glad you're here."

I stare at the ceiling from behind the sheets, but I'm listening so intently that I register the intake of breath that comes from Foster's side of the room.

"Um, sure. I'm glad I'm here too." His voice is soft and faraway sounding. I like that he doesn't just brush me off, though, like he sometimes does. He may be a mystery half of the time, but he's still a really nice guy, and right now, I can't imagine wanting to be in this situation with anyone else.

———

The next morning, everything is heavy. My legs are so numb that they practically drag the rest of my body after them as soon as I swing them over the side of the bed. My tongue is sandpaper against the roof of my mouth, and I remember it's been way too long since I've had any water to drink. Mom's cardinal rule. Her thinly veiled instructions to Foster to make me drink water and pee regularly skitter to the front of my mind. I should remind him and jokingly blame it all on his forgetfulness, but we kind of left things on a sweet note last night. Plus, he's still asleep. Groaning snores come from his bed, where only one arm is visible. The rest of him is tucked tightly under the pink-and-white striped duvet, even most of his head. I guess he's pretty exhausted.

I quickly pull a brush through my hair and sigh at the tangles from sleeping on it wet. By the time I've tugged on my still-damp clothes and shoes, Foster's still sound asleep. I tiptoe toward him, which is ridiculous since I have just as much right to be in the room as he does. But I'm still worried I'm bothering him, and there's always the slight chance he wakes up in some post-sleepy haze, totally confused about where we are and why I'm creeping around while he's out.

I stop a foot away from his bed, making muffled slapping sounds with my hands that are no match for his heavy breathing. Next, I step closer and shake the part of the blanket where I guess his shoulder is.

His lips part and a crease lines his forehead. "Ugh."

I move backward as his eyes crack open. "Hey."

He blinks. "Um. Hi."

I edge myself to his bed and plop onto the edge near his feet, sinking into the marshmallowy mattress.

"So, I think we need to go. Last night Edna said checkout is at ten, and it's..."

I glance over at the digital clock between our beds even though I'm very aware of what time it is. Foster's eyes follow mine, and he winces.

"It's nine-fifty?"

He looks back at me for confirmation, and I nod. The blankets around his head slip as he sits up quickly, exposing his bare chest. My eyes find the ceiling. I guess he took off his robe sometime between me falling asleep and waking up. Which is probably a completely normal thing to do, but no amount of rational thinking puts a stop to the icy catch in my breath.

He's oblivious, though. He leaps from his bed and snatches his shirt and shorts from a pile of his things on the floor. For all my efforts not to stare, my cheeks still burn fiery hot as his stomach muscles flex when he moves. There's something very, very different about seeing him in his boxers versus his swimsuit. From over his shoulder as he heads to the bathroom, he calls, "I'll be out in two minutes. Don't worry."

I nod again. The only thing I'm worried about right now is whether or not he leaves the bathroom wearing more clothes than he is currently.

SIXTEEN

After omelets and waffles made by Edna, she emerges from the shed behind her house with two five-gallon gas canisters, one in each hand.

"These should be enough to get you guys to the gas station off the highway."

I could kiss her, but I settle for a hug and a generous tip added to our bill for all the mud she'll likely have to clean from our bathroom.

We're back on the road again after quickly filling up with the canisters and heading to the gas station, where the gas attendant takes one look at the mud-caked wheels and shakes his head. I can practically hear his thoughts. Apparently, only city kids would get themselves stuck in a storm in the middle of farming territory.

I pause the music and turn to Foster. "There's enough time for one last stop before we head home. What do you think?"

He seems to know what I'm thinking. "Let's do it."

The Little Art Park is just as whimsical as Foster promised. We drive off the highway and into a gravel-lined parking lot. To the left of the parking lot is a grass field, and in the center of the field sits a large white awning, like the kind you see at outdoor weddings. Flowers line everything. Wild roses hang from the sides of the awning, dropping down from the top like pink and red polka dots, dotting the sky for anyone who stands underneath them.

Daisies and zinnias stand tall in bright-yellow planter boxes along a winding brick path that circles the awning in a loop. Every few feet, sculptures stand in the grass next to the path. Some are clay sculptures of people or animals. Some are modernistic iron statement pieces. We stop in front of one near the back of the awning.

"This looks like your art." I point to the sculpture and raise an eyebrow at Foster, who's staring at the flowers all the sudden and not the piece in front of us.

I lean closer to the tiny black-and-white tag and gasp. A jolt of excitement runs through me. "This has your name on it!"

Foster finally looks at me and smirks, his eyes crinkling at the edges.

"It's mine." He runs a hand over his hair as I step closer and drink in his work.

It's almost the exact copy of the first picture he showed me at the beginning of the summer. A thick, gold-painted wire runs up through the center of a matching gold sphere. Shapes connected to tiny hooks hang from the wire, like strange Christmas decorations. My heart swells at the sight of art that means something—finally. Even if I'm not sure what it means to Foster, it's more than color splashed on a canvas for the sake of some stuffy exhibit.

"I can't believe you remember coming here when you were a kid." I run a hand across a flower petal and gaze at the sculptures lining the grass. I smile. Inspiration's finally found me at the end of our trip.

Foster looks around too. "My mom loves flowers and the outdoors, and I've always known I wanted to be an artist. It was a really good day for both of us."

"Today is a good day too," I say. The rest of our road trip was chaos, but this makes it all worth it.

And then *he* crosses my mind. Opa would have loved it here too.

———

As soon as I put the car in park after dropping Foster at the beach, Dad is there, standing next to the door. When I get out, his eyes travel to my wrinkled and dirty clothes and up to my forced smile and under-eye circles.

"Is this something we need to tell Mom about?"

"Hopefully not?"

I pull my bag out of the back and loop my arm through his. "The important thing is nothing happened and I made it back on time, right?"

His arm squeezes mine. He pats the hood of my car, checking to make sure I'm telling the truth about both mine and the car's safety. He groans, but the corners of his mouth twitch. "I'll tell Mom you're home safe."

I balance on my toes to kiss his cheek. "Thanks, Dad."

Livvy's lying on her stomach, stretched out on the couch with her phone in hand. She glances up when I walk in, one hand resting against her cheek.

"How was your super-special trip?"

Her vitriol mixed with my exhaustion is more than I can handle and something inside me snaps. My voice turns sugary sweet as I cock my head to the side. "It was great, Liv. Maybe I would have invited you to come along if you actually cared about Opa, even a little bit."

Her eyes widen, and her mouth narrows. Maybe she actually is human after all. Then she shrugs and turns back to her phone. "Funny. I can care about Opa and have a freaking life that doesn't revolve around him at the same time. Wonder why you can't seem to do that?"

I shrink back as her eyes glint. She knows she's struck perfectly once again. None of the retorts hanging on the tip of my tongue ring true anymore, so I suck back the rest of my venom and walk past her to my bedroom, small and deflated.

My whole summer, every year for as far back as I can remember, has been about Opa. What we'd do together, what I'd show him, what he'd teach me. And this summer, even after he's gone, is still his. But what about next year, or the year after that? Something tight grips my chest as I hold onto my bag, hovering over my bed and unable to move my legs to sit myself down. Livvy probably doesn't even understand how close to home she's hit, how true it is that I have no life, no ambition left without Opa to guide me. As wild as she's become, she's the one guiding her own life while I'm stuck in the same loop I've been reliving my entire existence. *Wonder why you can't seem to do that.*

I finally drop my bag at my feet and collapse onto my bed.

SEVENTEEN

"And here we are! This is your spot, Claire."

A middle-aged lady with a chipper voice and a short black hair points to an arbitrary spot of sand on the beach. Sticking out of the sand is a tiny red-and-white flag with the number fifteen on it. I stride over to it and flop my materials onto the ground. I have considerably fewer molding tools than the teams surrounding me, but I'm not too bothered. In our test runs, using these same tools, Foster and I have been able to build sculptures that far surpass my very first sand cat.

The qualifying round of the contest is still two weeks away, but apparently an important part of the process is assigning work areas so contestants can take distance to the ocean into consideration. I'm close enough to the ocean that getting water and wet sand won't take long at all, and I'm in a corner spot, just past the pier and up against the edge of the fenced-off sand dunes, so we can work in private.

The black-haired lady leaves me, and I stare at the sand at my feet for a few seconds. Foster's supposed to be here by now, but he's not answering my texts, and I know he still has data left on his cheapo cell phone. All of the other contestants are busy with their own teammates, making plans. I scan the beach and then the waves, but he's still missing, so I line up my tools and blink at them in the meantime.

"Hey, you're new this year, huh?"

A petite girl who looks way too young to be in the contest marches over to me. Her shiny black hair swings over her shoulder.

I nod over my shoulder, turning to see her. "I'm new to working with sand, period."

Admitting this makes my stomach turn. I'm used to being a veteran in my art classes at school. But I figure I might as well tell the truth and glean any extra information I can.

She puts her hands on her hips and shakes her head. "You're brave."

I nod. "Thanks." I'm not sure what entering the contest has to do with bravery, but sometimes you have to take compliments wherever you can get them. "Have you done this before?"

She sharpens her gaze and frowns. "I'm Carolina Garcia. This is my *third* year in the contest, and hopefully my third year taking first place."

I wrinkle my nose but take a step back just the same. "Isn't the contest only for high-school students?"

She looks like she wants to fight me; all five feet of her body is tensed and her eyes bore into mine.

I frown. Shoot. "Sorry. I-I didn't mean—"

"I'm seventeen," she says. "I just have a baby face."

My mouth forms an O shape. "Oh my gosh. I'm so sorry. I didn't realize..." My cheeks burn, and my feet dig further into the sand. Maybe I can burrow myself underground and escape before she slaps me.

She picks up my longest shovel and digs it into the sand a

few inches from my flag. It makes a sharp dinging sound as it sticks. "It's okay. I get it all the time."

She finally smiles at me, and I breathe a silent sigh. The last thing I need is to make an enemy in the art community here. She leans on the shovel, her arms wrapped around it. "So, I hear you're working with Foster this year? You're Claire?"

My head tilts. How could she know that? How does she know anything about either of us?

She shrugs and shoots me a sly smirk. "Like I said, I've won this competition twice. I do my research. Especially since there's a scholarship on the line for the first time this year."

I nod. Even given the scholarship, it's never occurred to me this was a serious competition. We're working with sand. I'm here because of Opa, because he obviously wanted me to do this. Why, I don't know. To learn something about myself? About my art? Maybe he wanted me to win the scholarship. If he were here, I'd hammer him with questions until it all made sense. Since he's not, pushing forward and trying my hardest is all I've got.

I bite my lip. "You know Foster?"

She studies the dinged metal edges of the shovel, her eyebrows pushed together. "I know *of* him."

"Are you friends? Do you go to school together?" I need to know why she's acting like Foster's some leprous creep instead of the guy who religiously recycles.

She raises her eyebrows, her brown eyes wide. "Um, no, we're not exactly friends. We don't really run in the same circles at school. But I know of him. And he's always at the beach, so I see him around."

Foster's at the beach more than anyone I know. And that's pretty impressive in a beach town like this one. But I've never seen him with any other guys from the high school. I've never seen him spending time with anyone, I guess.

She shakes her head. "I just don't really hang out with guys like Foster. I'm more straight-edge, you know?"

She makes it sound like Foster is some intensely wild party boy, but I've never seen that side of him. If I had, I probably wouldn't have a maybe-crush on him. My mind is swimming, but I force myself to focus on something else for a minute. I don't want to lose out on the chance to pick Carolina's brain about the competition.

"What do you mean?"

She shakes her head again. "I don't want to start any drama. You should probably ask him yourself."

My face flushes. A mixture of nerves and anxiety washes over me and makes my skin itchy and hot. I inhale through the discomfort. He doesn't talk about himself much, but still, the thought of Foster having a secret life is something I've never considered.

"I will," I say. "And, I don't know if this is okay to ask or not, but I'd love to see pictures of the art you've won with the past two years." I'm dying to know what it is about her art that makes the judges love her. I've also never seen a finished sand sculpture other than the generic ones in the contest pamphlet.

Carolina grins and pulls out her phone. I should have expected she'd have her winning shots ready to show off. I know I would if I had placed in any sort of art competition. I hover over her as she scrolls through albums of the past year's contests. Her winner from last year takes my breath away. Chills crawls their way down my arms, creating a bumpy pattern across my skin.

She smiles as she explains it to me. She points to the top structure. "This is New York city. The Statue of Liberty, the Flatiron Building, the 9/11 memorial site. I went there with my dad the summer I turned fourteen."

There's a catch in her throat that makes her pause. I can't

look at her as tears form in the corners of my eyes. I avoid eye contact with Carolina as she tells me about the months after that trip, when her dad died. On her phone, she points to the bottom structure, sand twisted into a pattern that looks like it's being swallowed up in a swirling and chaotic sand pit. Black pebbles line the inside circle, giving off the appearance of an endless hole in the center. She doesn't have to explain that her dreams are being destroyed by this monster of despair. It's true art. And she made it all by herself, with just sand.

"I know how you feel," I say. "I lost my grandfather at the beginning of the summer, and I'm..."

I shrug my shoulder across my cheek, grazing the trail of tears that appear there. "I'm kind of lost, you know?"

She looks up from her phone and nods. "Sorry about your grandfather. The lost feeling never goes away completely, but it gets better."

I run a hand through my hair. People always say it will get better, but they never say how.

"Art helps." She nods again.

I inhale. "Thanks."

My phone buzzes, but a hurried glance at the screen shows a message from Livvy, not Foster. I glance over Carolina's head, but he's still nowhere nearby. My mouth tugs downward in spite of myself.

"Looking for your partner?" Carolina raises an eyebrow, her mouth forming a slanted smirk. It's as close as you can come to saying *I told you so* to a stranger without being a complete jerk about it.

"He's running late," I concede.

Carolina laughs drily. "He doesn't even show up for school half the time. He's not going to take this kind of thing seriously. Maybe you should find a more reliable teammate."

I shake my head. "Your impression of him is wrong. He must have a good reason for not being here."

She shrugs, hands on her hips as she lets my shovel drop to the sand. "I guess I'll have to take your word for it."

EIGHTEEN

"Where were you yesterday?"

Foster meets me when I stop my car in the empty parking lot early the next morning. He's bleary-eyed and groggy, not at all his usual happy-go-lucky self. He's not even giving me laid-back surfer vibes—he's just grumpy. I try to ignore his low groans and shrugs in response to my question and keep talking. When I get to the part about meeting Carolina, he cuts his eyes at me.

"I thought she was coming over to try to scare me off or something, but we actually might be friends after this whole thing is over." I'm still talking just to annoy him at this point. I don't know what his deal is, but his attitude is more annoying than his absence at the stakeout was. Carolina and I already exchanged phone numbers and texted some last night, which I really am excited about. I don't have many friends, and she seems cool. Plus, she likes art, which is more than can be said for any of my friends back home.

"She's definitely not interested in being your friend, especially not if she knows I'm helping you. Everyone at school thinks I'm some delinquent or something." His tone is so matter-of-fact and full of sarcasm that I want to spit at him.

"Don't be a jerk. And why would they think that?" His insinuation that she's not interested in me hurts worse than his gruff tone. I turn on my heel to leave, and he lets me go for a full three seconds. Just as I'm about to drag myself back to my car on principle, he calls after me.

"Hey, wait. Sorry. I'm just exhausted, okay? I was up all night, so..."

I slowly spin back to face him with my hands on my hips. I'm pretty exhausted myself. Dragging any sort of answer out of Foster is proving to be a tiring exercise.

"You know—" I stop to catch my breath. I'm getting sweaty palms and red-faced, and neither of those things has anything to do with the hundred-degree weather. "It's fine if you don't want to tell me why you never showed up yesterday. You don't even have to explain why it was too hard to let me know you couldn't come. But you don't have to be rude."

I wait for him to match my anger and yell back, but he just shrinks. He shakes his head and holds up a hand to shield his eyes while staring at a spot along the beach where the tide is exceptionally low.

"Sorry," he says so quietly that I have to lean forward to hear. "I didn't want to bother you. I don't really like talking about myself."

I bite my lip to stop laughter from tumbling out of me. That's an understatement.

"Well, why are you so tired? Where were you yesterday?" I promised myself I didn't care whether he came or not, but now my resolve is quickly waning. I do care, and it takes more effort to pretend to be apathetic than it does to just feel. His mouth tightens, and lines appear across his face. If someone were spying on us right now, they'd think I asked him to give me a kidney.

"I can't say."

My mouth hangs open. All I'm asking for is a tiny bit of transparency—just a little information. And he still finds it impossible. Tears threaten the corners of my eyes, and my neck stings with heat.

"You *can't* or you just don't *want* to?"

He looks past me, over my head at the cloudless blue sky. Whatever he sees there must be better than giving me the truth because he still says nothing.

"I thought..."

I cross my arms in front of my chest, my hands clutching so tightly that the skin under my fingertips turns white. I close my eyes and summon phantom courage.

"This weekend? Driving together and at the Little Art Park? I thought something happened. I thought that just maybe we could mean something to each other, but now I see how stupid I am."

He's staring at me, eyes wide. "You're not stupid."

I place my palms in front of me and hold them facing outward. "Then tell me what's wrong, Foster. Just answer this one thing, and I'll leave it alone. I swear."

His shoulders make the tiniest of concessions. "I just can't."

I shake my head, and without saying anything else, I turn to go. The sound of him following behind me makes my chest ache.

"Please. Wait." There's so much raw pain in the soft pleading of his voice it could make a sympathizer out of the devil himself.

But I ignore him. I storm off the beach as fast as the slippery sand under my feet will carry me. Instead of going home, I fume in my parked car. But after a few minutes of seething anger at

Foster and what he said to me and his refusal to talk, I'm done. Hot, wet tears drip down my cheeks before I even realize I'm crying. As quickly as I was able to work up a rage over him, now I'm ready to admit I'm more embarrassed than anything. After another minute of red-eyed sulking, I leave my car, standing straighter than before.

I walk down the shoreline with my sandals in one hand and the other hand extended out for balance as I toe the waves. Foster's sitting on a bench near the pier. He doesn't look as surprised to see me again as I expect. His hand raises in a rigid half-wave, but his mouth still sits grim and tight.

"I came back because I need to talk to you about something I heard." I position myself in front of the bench, and he stands to attention as soon as the words leave my mouth.

Foster's holding his face steady, but his eyes give him away. He narrows them like he's scared of something. Scared of me? I hold my hands together in front of me like I learned in last year's speech class. Our teacher told us that hands clasped in front of your body was a universal, professional stance that also hides your nerves. I don't think anything is going to work to hide how nervous I am right now.

"You're hiding something, and I want to know what it is. I'm not giving you a choice this time. Whatever else there is, we are friends, and friends talk about hard things."

He takes a half-step backward.

I shake my head as my heart pounds in my ears. "You can trust me, I promise." I suck in a breath. "I heard from Carolina that everyone at your school thinks you're some crazy troublemaker..."

Foster makes a sound like I've kicked him. He squints.

"I don't understand why they think that. And I'm wondering if it has something to do with you missing the meeting and how we're fighting today." I exhale. "So, what's going on? Are you in trouble or something? Do you need help?" My voice cracks as I spit out the rest of my words.

"It's so complicated."

He wrinkles his nose at the quick breeze floating over us. It's so cool on my flushed skin that I want to pull him away from this awful conversation and drag him into the ocean, like the day in the rain at the pier. I'd even take the surfing lesson at this point if it means we can just move on.

"It doesn't have to be complicated."

He's still not looking at me. A horrifying thought takes hold: I've completely misread everything, all of it, his hands on mine, the almost kiss at my car, how much the road trip meant to him. I've just demanded access to all his secrets, and now I'm preying on him when he's already super vulnerable.

Like a total creep.

My gaze drops. "I mean it doesn't have to be complicated because I want to help. You don't have to hold this in. Whatever it is."

"Yeah, I know," he says. But his voice is distant.

"Sorry—I just thought..." I trail off. What did I think? That I could just swoop in and fix whatever is going on here? That Foster, who has known me for all of half a summer, trusts me enough to spill his guts on the spot?

"You thought what?" There's something almost hopeful in the sharp way he says it. I force myself to meet his eyes. They're not narrowed like I expect them to be. Instead they're his true blue, wide and wondering.

I bite my lip. I can't bare my soul to him just to get shot down again. I shake my head. "I don't know anymore."

Waves crash just a few yards from the bench where we sit. My legs are tucked under my body; I'm rolled tightly into myself like this day's so rough that even my body needs extra protection from the beating my heart is taking. I blink against the blurring skyline, faster and faster to block tears from pooling across my cheeks.

Next to me, Foster inhales sharply. A shaky hand brushes against my leg as his fingers graze along mine, warm and soft. If I were to move my own hand another inch I could grab his, but I stay still.

His voice is gritty and low. "My stepbrother showed up yesterday."

I turn my head, eyebrows raised. "I didn't even know you had a brother."

He sighs. "Last year my mom died of cancer. It was just me and her. I'm her only kid, and my dad has never been around. I don't even know who he is. But she was married to this other guy for a few years, and his son—my stepbrother—still comes around sometimes."

"I wish you would have told me about your mom. I'm so sorry."

I reach my hand forward and slide my fingers along his. My skin warms at his touch. My eyes move to where our hands are linked together, and a hiccup forms in my chest. Somehow the places where we've grasped fit together so well you'd think we were built for this.

"It's hard for me to talk about her at all. But I should have told you sooner." Foster looks at our hands too. His lips form a tiny curve, and my heart thumps wildly against my chest.

"So what did you do? After your mom, um, died?"

It's impossible to even conjure up an image of what it must be like to be without a parent. It sucks that Opa's gone, but I still have Mom and Dad. I've always had someone to depend on. No matter how obnoxious my parents are, it's impossible to even think about a world without them there when I need them. Foster squeezes my hand, just a barely-there pressure, and sighs.

Even though I have no idea what he's about to tell me, my heart sticks in my throat.

"What happened?" I ask. My stomach turns in anticipation.

"My stepbrother. He's twelve years older than I am, and I hadn't seen him for a few years before my mom got sick, but she knew we talked sometimes. She wanted him to have custody of me. We'd never been close, even when I was little, so I thought it was a little weird that he wanted me to live with him. When he picked me up after the funeral, I realized he was only in it for the money. Apparently once he found out I'd be getting monthly payments, he convinced my mom to give him custody in her will. I also got ten thousand dollars, and as soon as he heard that, it was over."

I shake my head. "Over? What do you mean? Like, he stole your money?" Surely his own brother wouldn't do that. The same brother that apparently paid him a visit yesterday and took him from impassable to distraught. Okay, in light of that, maybe he would.

Foster groans and pushes sand around with the toe of his sandal. "Yes. He took all of it, drained the savings account my mom set up for me, and left."

My heart drops. I pretend not to notice the crack in his voice. If there's ever a decent time to cry, it's now. If he does start crying, what do I do? I've never seen someone I like get this emotional. He's still holding onto my hand, squeezing it almost too tightly. Maybe letting him talk and squeeze the crap out of me is enough.

"What do you mean, 'he left'? You reported it to the police, right?" I just can't picture Foster being related to some kind of supervillain capable of evading the police. No one makes off with ten thousand dollars and rides off into the sunset. Foster shrugs and looks past me. Oh boy. "You didn't tell anyone?"

His silence answers my question. I don't know if I should be appalled at his brother, or at Foster for letting his crime go unanswered. But, of course, I'm angry at his brother. I don't always get along well with Livvy, but she'd never do something this bad. If she did....

I shake my head. "Your brother is the worst."

Foster frowns. "He's done some bad things, but he's still my brother. I think he just wasn't ready for the responsibility of taking care of me full time. Or any responsibility at all, I guess."

He runs his hands through his hair, tugging on the ends. "When he and his dad lived with us, I was just a little kid. We didn't have much in common back then either, but his dad—he was mean."

The word 'mean' coming from Foster is such a little thing, but something tells me it's much more than that.

"He hit us—not a lot, but it still happened. When he was mad, he'd just start punching. My mom worked a lot, so she didn't see, but when my brother and I were home, he'd go after us sometimes. Just start whaling on us, almost for fun it seemed like. But mostly his son. Because his son stood up to him and took it for me as much as he could, I think. And when mom found out, she divorced him and took me to a new apartment that night. My stepbrother kind of disappeared for a while, but he wasn't bad, not then."

I close my eyes and suck in a breath. So much pain for one person to hold on to, and all before he's even considered an adult. "Regardless of that, what he did to you is so unfair."

He grins and rolls his eyes. "Your world is so different from mine, Claire. I don't get to worry about what's fair or not. I'm too busy surviving."

It's the truth, but it still stings. I've never seen myself as privileged or spoiled. Livvy definitely, but never me. "Well, what about the monthly payments from your mom? Isn't it enough for you to rent an apartment or something?"

Complete silence again. I'm beginning to hate these telling silences between us. Foster turns his head to watch my reaction. I try to stay calm for his sake. This is my worst nightmare: a terrible thing I can't fix. There's nothing I can think of that will make this better. Nothing I can do changes the fact that Foster has been left or betrayed by so many adults that were supposed to take care of him.

"I'd have to have an address to get the payments. But I don't. Because I live here," he says, motioning to the beach around us.

I arch an eyebrow at him. "Here? As in?"

Foster bows his head. "I live *here*, Claire. I sleep in a tent under the pier." His hands sweep around the beach, motioning toward the sand all around us.

This. Is his home.

My jaw drops. It's not possible. Sick, twisted shock swirls in my stomach. I'm going to vomit, or cry, or something. My voice is small, a tiny squeak. "You don't have a home? You don't have anyone?"

He shakes his head. "It's just me. If I try to use the money going into my account, they'll be able to track me down and find out where I'm staying. Once someone from Social Services discovers my brother is gone and I'm alone, they'll try to put me in a foster home since I don't turn eighteen until next summer."

I get not wanting to be with strangers or ratting out your brother, but I don't understand Foster's intense reluctance to have a real home. I'd take a bed and non-public bathroom over permanent camping any day.

"Wouldn't that be better?"

His eyes widen, and I clamp down on my tongue. Apparently, I've said the wrong thing.

Foster kicks at a speckled shell near his foot, sending it skipping several inches away. "No. It would be worse. I'd rather be alone than with strangers pretending to care about me. I'm tired of people pretending to care about me when they really just want something."

I leave the point alone for now, but I make a mental note to revisit it. Maybe right now he's too sensitive, but surely at some point he'll have to admit living under the pier is not a permanent solution.

"Why couldn't you tell me about this? I wouldn't sell you out." I want to sound casual, but I say the words much too fast and my voice is way too high, and I end up sounding every bit as hurt as his lying makes me feel.

He blows air out in a slow whistle and ducks his head. "If I tell you, do you promise not to take it personally?"

Crap. I have two choices here. I can either lie and tell him that of course I won't take it personally, why would he ever think that, and internalize. Or I can be honest and admit that starting a sentence like that basically guarantees that whatever comes out his mouth next will hurt my feelings.

"Um..." I pause for too long, and my silence gives me away. Foster scoots closer, grabbing for my hand again, sending an electric wave of tingles through my chest.

"At first, it was because I didn't think I wanted to work with you. I didn't think you liked me very much either, so I thought I was doing both of us a favor. But after that first day together..."

I raise my eyebrows. His admission makes sense as much as it hurts. We did get off to a confusing start before we entered the contest together.

"You fell madly in love with me and my amazing sand sculptures and just couldn't stay away?" I finish for him and immediately regret my choice of words. It's an unspoken rule that you don't throw around the l-word, even as a joke. It makes people nervous. My stomach twists in jittery bursts just having said it.

"Exactly," he says.

I squeeze out an unstable smile. What is that supposed to mean? Does agreeing with my—mostly joking—statement count as an admission of love? Probably not. But he doesn't deny it either, so that must mean something.

My heart beats wildly in my lighter-than-air chest. I bite my lip.

"Want to get some lunch?"

NINETEEN

I want to remind Foster what being in a house with a family feels like. I never thought my family, which almost always seems dysfunctional, would be the one thing I could use to help him. But it's the best I've got. When things get tough or scary, I run to the beach house. This time I bring Foster with me. We drive over in near silence, my mind spinning with all the things he just told me.

At a red light, I clear my throat. "Um, so, how do you eat? *What* do you eat? I mean—are you just hungry all the time?"

He stiffens. Maybe it's wrong to ask, but the idea that I've been running home after long days at the beach to home-cooked meals and a freezer stuffed with three different flavors of ice cream while he's potentially huddled under the pier starving...

I force saliva down my dry throat. There are so many basic things that I've taken for granted my whole life.

"I mean—how do you shower, brush your teeth, go to the bathroom?"

His body heaves with an invisible sigh. "I get enough money from selling my trash art to buy food. Mostly fast food and stuff that won't go bad like granola bars and chips."

I nod. But there's still a difference between starvation and being plain hungry.

"What does 'enough' mean?"

He lifts a shoulder. "Sometimes it means I eat at McDonalds twice a day. Other times it means I eat dry cereal out of the box until I can afford something else."

I squeeze my fingers against the steering wheel as the light turns green. "What about my other question? Showers and stuff?"

He lets out a low laugh. "It's probably better if you don't know, to be honest."

Calmly, like he isn't discussing his lack of basic human needs.

I give him a look, because I wouldn't ask if I didn't want to know. He smirks in response.

"Let's just say, I'm an expert at picking the locks they put on the public-access restrooms at night. And I buy cheap soap whenever I can. It's not ideal, but I do what I can not to stink."

My throat tightens again. "I guess any shower is better than nothing."

Though I can't remember ever taking a non-decent shower, and if I had, I definitely would have complained about it as much as possible.

When we get to the beach house, the smell of smoked meats fills half the street. We follow the smoke trail around back to where Dad's hovering over a rack of ribs and thick juicy sausages. My stomach growls in anticipation. When he sees us, he props his pair of metal tongs on the armrest of his nylon camping chair.

"Hey there, Foster."

Foster steps forward to shake his hand, and Dad winks at me over his head.

"We're getting a snack," I call over my shoulder. I lead Foster inside through the back door and straight to the pantry, where I practically shove him forward to choose from the rows and rows of shelf-food staples we have. He does a slow three-hundred-and-sixty degree turn in the small walk-in closet and inhales. Loaves of bread, packages of trail mix, and boxes of artificially flavored Pop-Tarts fill the space. Foster's eyes might bug out of his head.

"This is awesome."

My lips twist slightly for his benefit, but my cheeks burn behind my smile. I've never once thought to be amazed at the food in the kitchen. It's always there, and when Livvy eats the last box of Oreos during a late-night snack binge, Mom goes out the next day and buys more. If the pantry weren't perpetually, magically full, who knows if anyone would even notice. There's always the fully stocked fridge or money for takeout.

He's eyeing a large pack of cookies in the far corner, and I slide them off the shelf and into his hands.

I wave a hand. "Take the whole package. No one will miss them, I swear."

He sits at the table, cookies in front of him. My phone buzzes with a text from Carolina. *Did you talk to Foster?*

One eye on my phone, the other on Foster, I text back quickly. *Yes. It's complicated, but we're good.*

As he's shoveling entire chocolate chip cookies into his mouth, Mom and Livvy walk through the front door and into the kitchen. Livvy doesn't even look at us before slamming her phone on the granite kitchen counter and stomping to her room. The door snaps closed with a loud crack. Mom runs her palms down her face like she's ready to pull her skin off layer by layer to rid herself of the stress Livvy's caused.

Instead she stretches her lips over her teeth in a grimace and blinks at Foster. "So good to see you, hon. Are you staying for lunch?"

Foster nods with his mouth full.

"Glad to hear it," Mom says. She reaches for Livvy's phone on the counter and places it inside a pocket of the purse slung along her shoulder.

"How was therapy?" The question is loaded, but Foster being here means she won't erupt too much, which is a nice advantage.

She puffs out her lips, angrily hissing air through them. "I wouldn't know. She refused to let me come in with her. And then she refused to even tell me how it went." Her jaw is set, her forehead drawn.

"I'm sure everything is fine, " I assure her. Knowing my sister, she wouldn't miss her chance to let us in on the drama if things weren't going okay. Though I'm not sure I'd be thrilled either if Mom and Dad forced me into couples' therapy and then my boyfriend kept skipping sessions.

She lets out another sigh, half-sob this time. "The psychologist wouldn't tell me anything either because of some stupid patient-confidentiality agreement. Can you believe that?"

Foster, who's finished his cookie at this point, shifts his eyes toward me like he's hoping I'll provide an answer.

I reach out and pat her shoulder. "She'll be okay, Mom."

She gives her head a small shake and mumbles something about needing to help check on the meats, leaving Foster and I to raid the pantry again.

Lunch is a silent, drawn-out affair after Mom and Dad try unsuccessfully to drag Livvy out of her room to eat with us. It leaves Foster and me to dominate the conversation, and there are only so many times we can try to explain sand sculpting to them before everyone starts wishing for silence again. Still, Foster eats so many smoked ribs that Dad sends him with a foil packet of leftovers and a slap on the back.

I'm not sure what to say to Foster as we drive back to the

beach. Besides the obvious, "Sorry for my insane family", I'm tongue-tied around him all of the sudden. In the painful silence that follows, he reaches over to touch my hand again. My brain goes fuzzy, and all I can focus on is how soft his fingers are, even in the spots made rough from surfing and sculpting. There are no other cars on the road, and even if there were, I'm so blinded by this moment I don't care that my eyes wander from where they should be.

"Hey," he says. His voice is so soft it almost blends in with the whir of the tires on the road. It's not so much a greeting as a way to fill the silence and get my attention.

"Hey," I say back. I don't mean to match his whisper, but I do anyway.

"I'm sorry for not telling you about all that crap earlier," he says.

I swallow. "It's okay. I think I understand why. It's heavy stuff. And you have a lot on the line if someone finds out. But your secret is safe with me. I hope you know that."

"I do know. I trust you, Claire." His eyes are boring into the side of my head. He's leaning so far into my side of the car that his whispered words aren't soft anymore, and his breath blows across my cheek.

There's a motel with a half-lit sign on the side of the road ahead with a nearly empty parking lot. I signal to turn and pull into the furthest spot in the back. Car in park, I turn my head and lean as far across the driver's seat as I can. Foster's eyes widen, questioning. I have to do this before I lose the nerve. If I'm misreading this, I can blame it on the exhilarating embarrassment of him spending the day with my family. I can say I'm punch drunk or something. I push toward him, and he leans forward even more to meet me. His hands trap my face as he studies me. They're steady and cool against my heated skin. His eyes rove across my features like he's just seeing them for the first time. First my eyes, then my sucked-in cheeks, then my mouth. The hairs on my arms stand on end, but I can't drag my eyes away from him. He inches closer to me. I'm barely in my seat anymore, but I still keep one hand gripped on the steering wheel.

His lips hover above mine, pink and slightly parted. I'm not even sure I'm breathing as I freeze into the moment, waiting.

Then he lowers them to mine.

His mouth moves against mine, slow and warm and persistent. My whole body is on fire, but I only want to burn more, feel more, *be* more. My hands drop and find their way around his torso, gripping his skin through his thin cotton T-shirt. Summer air and spicy body wash sting my nose. The combination sends another jolt to my brain, and I push my lips and body against him harder than before.

Something clicked after I questioned him and he spilled his guts. Things changed, and we've been pushing the limits of the thin line between us in the hours since. Holding hands and now this.

This kiss.

His lips firmly press against my mouth, and my stomach tumbles with the nerves of it all. His fingers lift from my face as his mouth drops. My cheeks spread to form a grin. I've never experienced anything as fundamentally right as this kiss.

TWENTY

Fourth of July tradition demands we visit downtown Old Saint Augustine for their over-the-top display of fireworks along the water. And every year elicits more of the same: insane parking, crowds, and too many heads in the way of the dazzling firework eruptions. Every year, my parents decide we'll give it just one more try in spite of it all. It's one family tradition I don't actually mind because I love the chance to explore downtown. There are so many people, probably half of them tourists, that it feels like we're all part of something big and patriotic. Even if it's just eating as much Cuban food and gelato as possible while we wait for dusk.

My family strolls through the tightly packed, red-stained cobblestone streets. Livvy and I keep with tradition and lag behind our parents. The small streets are loaded with tiny shops selling everything from alligator jerky to clothing made from alpaca wool. The pungent smells of Spanish spices and salty ocean air lace the streets, mingling within the crowds. We wander in and out of the different stores, mostly just window shopping. One of my favorites is a magic shop hidden in the back of a musty building. Everything inside is delightfully random, like the pair of alpaca-covered magician's gloves in the display window.

Today it all reminds me of what's missing: Opa and Foster. Opa loved the Fourth of July. He took just as much pride in these kinds of summer traditions as Dad does and especially loved taking yearly family pictures by the water as the light display went off at midnight. Foster should be here too. He's alone tonight, a fact I stressed to Mom as much as possible without giving away the truth of just how alone he is. But holidays in our family have always been about family time. *Just family*, Mom says. At least he's not hungry though. I made sure to stop by this morning with as much food from the Publix as could fit in my emptied-out art bag. Still, there's a hollow spot in my chest that pangs every time I catch myself laughing at Dad's dumb jokes or shoveling an oversized handful of caramel popcorn into my mouth. I'm not sure I'm allowed to enjoy any of it anymore, knowing what I now do about Foster's life.

There's a band playing makeshift instruments outside of Casa Blanco, the Cuban restaurant we always go to, just like all the other bands stationed on every other corner. Dad slips an arm around Mom as she sways to the music of the trashcan drums. I watch my parents and try to imagine them as a couple. Like a normal couple without kids. I can't picture them as anything other than parents. But every once in a while—like tonight—I get a tiny glimpse into what it must have been like before they got old and Livvy and I ruled their lives. Livvy's watching them too. Maybe she's thinking the same.

We walk into the restaurant and navigate our way around the other families crowded in the front, waiting for the black-clad servers and their stacks of menus. Thanks to Mom's neurotic planning, we give them our reservation name and are seated immediately. As Mom and Dad slide into their seats at the table, Livvy grabs my arm, holding tightly. She angles her head so only I can hear. To anyone else we might look like two sisters sharing a lighthearted secret. I'd be ready to believe it too if this were any other summer.

"I need your help leaving during dinner." Her voice is soft and low next to my ear.

I whip my head toward her, throwing off any plans of discretion with it. Mom raises an eyebrow at us.

"Everything alright, girls?"

Livvy laughs a high-pitched, half-crazed laugh like she's just heard a hilarious joke. I squeeze out a dry chuckle.

"We're good, Mom," she says over her shoulder, her tone bored.

Even though it's been months since we've played off of each other like this, I still know my sister well enough to know she wouldn't ask for my help if it weren't important.

I turn to my parents and screw my face into a sympathetic frown.

"Bathroom. We'll be right back, okay?"

Our parents nod and give us silent waves toward the bathrooms on the other side of the restaurant. We march toward them with Livvy trailing behind me and struggling to catch up for once.

Once we're in the restroom, I fold my arms against my chest. It's pristine white in here, but it reeks of bleach, unlike the mouth-watering smells coming from the rest of the restaurant. Whatever she wants, I'm more than ready to just get it over with.

"What's going on, Liv?"

She bites her lip. "I can't be here tonight." She pauses and then rushes on. "And I know you're going to ask, so yes, it's to see Evan, but it's not what you think. I wouldn't ask unless it was a special circumstance, okay?"

I sigh. "Does it have something to do with your appointment the other day? Mom said he didn't even come."

She sucks in her cheeks. "Yeah, kind of."

My shoulders shrug. "Why don't you just ask Evan to come get you? That's what you usually do."

Her face flashes red. Blotchy spots climb along her cheeks and neck as she shakes her head. Her voice is just above a harsh whisper. "No thanks."

I frown. "Okay. Remember last summer when you tried to be fancy by ordering that gigantic shrimp and steak platter? And everyone told you that much food would make you sick, but you ate it all anyway, just to prove some point?"

She rolls her eyes, but a smirk plays along her pinched lips. "I remember," she says. "You walked in on me barfing my guts up right as we were leaving for the fireworks, but I made you swear not to tell anyone. What about it?"

"Get pretend sick and make sure they know this time. Then you'll have an excuse to leave early while we stay for the fireworks."

"It could work. Except..." Her voice is bright as she plots. "You need to do it too so you can drive me."

I step backward, and my hands slide up defensively. "Why would I do that?"

"Drop me off with Evan, then you can spend the rest of the night with Foster."

An eyebrow arches above her smirked lips as I consider the deal. I have passed most of the trip downtown missing Foster and wondering how he's spending the holiday.

"I don't know, Liv. Mom and Dad want us to be together today."

I shove against the heavy restroom door, and it swings open. Livvy follows me, lip curled.

"I didn't think you cared about family time unless it involved Opa."

I stop mid-stride. "What?"

She narrows her eyes. "I'm not totally clueless. You and Opa were always in his office talking about who knows what. And it doesn't take a genius to see you're not interested in hanging at the beach house now that he's gone."

My mouth moves, but words don't come out. "Liv. I... You're always busy too," I blurt.

She shakes her head and starts walking again. We're almost to our table, where Mom and Dad are pointing to their menus, a teenage girl listening patiently.

"You're so self absorbed when it comes to missing Opa, Claire. You don't think anyone else cares, just because we don't sit in our rooms looking at pictures and crying about him." Her hissed words are sharp, and they hit their target nicely.

I blink, my tongue heavy. "You don't know what you're talking about," I say.

Her voice is low by my side, and there's no venom left. "Forget it. Just help me, okay?"

That's not how I remember it at all, but even if I spent more time with Opa...it never occurred to me that she cared. Mom and Dad are watching us now, so I clamp my lips shut.

We take our seats and my head spins. How much of what she's saying has she rehearsed, just waiting for the perfect moment to slap me between the eyes? How long has she felt like this and kept me in the dark?

"What are you going to order, girls?" Dad narrows his eyes between Livvy and me. She ignores him and watches me.

I sigh and give a tiny nod. She smiles sweetly and orders for both of us. "We'll both have the steak and shrimp platter, please."

Dad points his folded menu at me before stretching it across the table to the server. "Feeling adventurous this year too, Claire Bear?"

I mumble into my glass of water. "Something like that."

Fifteen minutes into dinner, I have to physically clamp a hand over my mouth to keep from spewing chunks of forced-down steak all over the tabletop. My stomach lurches at the sight of the remaining shrimps pushed aside on my plate, each one swimming in a generous pool of pale-yellow butter and chopped garlic. Next to me, Livvy doubles over and groans into the white cloth napkin tucked in her lap. Neither of us need to pretend to be sick, at least.

———

The drive to Evan's house is sticky with silence. Mom and Dad were reluctant to let us go, but after a few minutes of not-at-all-staged almost barfing, they said they'd see us at home. Key word is *home*, where we'd better be by the time they've worked their way out of the downtown traffic maze after the fireworks show.

Livvy pulls a piece of foil-wrapped gum from her purse and pops it into her mouth. The strong scent of peppermint curling around the car invokes Opa like not much else can.

I chew on the inside of my cheek. "What you were saying about Opa—"

In my peripheral vision, I see her raise a palm. "Stop. It's whatever, okay? We both loved him. It doesn't matter that he loved you more."

I shake my head. "He didn't love me more. Maybe we just had more in common."

All of our days spent sketching at the beach, our road trip plans, the application he left for me... I see why she'd feel this way, but it's still not true.

She clicks her tongue against the roof of her mouth. "I said it's fine."

I turn to glance at her, but she's facing the window, her face gleaming off the darkened window, eyes vacant.

At the bottom of Evan's sloped driveway, I lick my lips as she pulls the passenger side door open.

"Thank you. And don't worry. I'll be home before Mom and Dad."

I nod and watch her walk up the steep, curved path to where Evan waits, leaning lazily against the garage door. Funny, I wouldn't have pictured him living in a two-story red-brick house with a tidy green lawn. Maybe he even has a normal family sleeping inside this all-American house.

I text Foster before shifting the car into drive. My phone sits by my side on the console, and I switch my playlist to Pink Floyd on the drive over, humming along to the songs I swore I'd never listen to after the road trip. The second Foster comes into view, butterflies emerge in my stomach. Giant butterflies with wings strong enough to blow over a sizable shrub. Definitely strong enough to make me queasy and knobby kneed. He's waiting for me in the parking lot of the McDonald's across the street from the beach. Lines of cars are parked alongside both sides of the road. There are barely any parking spots left due to the fireworks show at the beach. He jogs toward me as soon as I stop the car. His hand pulls on the door handle, and he opens my door for me, a grin lighting up his face. This is the first time we've been alone since we kissed.

That kiss.

It was a religious experience. Our mouths moving together was the closest I've ever been to pure bliss. It's been replaying in my mind on a constant loop. And now that we've finally snuck away again, my eyes won't move from his lips. I have to fight to keep my hands by my sides and not on his body, where they seem to think they belong now.

"I missed you," I say.

It's only been a day. Less than that, technically. My throat constricts as he gazes down at me. I look up into his eyes and click my car door shut behind me. My back bumps against the window, but I barely register anything as Foster hovers closer and closer.

His hand brushes my ear, sending electrifying shivers down my neck. His eyes zero in on my lips, and I hold my breath. How is it that time can move so fast when I want to hold on to something but not the other way around? I need him to kiss me already.

As if sensing my impatience, his arms circle my waist. Then finally, finally, he ducks his head. I stand on the tips of my toes and crash my lips into his. His mouth on mine is so warm that I might melt from the impact. I tease my tongue with his, out of breath and reluctant to ever come up for air all at the same time.

He murmurs against my lips. "I missed you so freaking much."

The sky above us is midnight black, but in this moment, my world is an explosion of light. This is all the fireworks I'll ever need.

TWENTY-ONE

Foster's sitting on a bench on what I used to call Opa's beach.
It's early enough that he still has his shirt on and it's not soaked
through with sweat yet, but not so early that we're the only ones
here. I can't help but think of this as *our* place now—Foster's
and mine. I wonder what Opa would think about the shift in my
thinking. Foster waves as I walk up, and I nod my head since
both my arms are full.

"Good morning," I chirp. "Before I forget—"

I set my armful of stuff on the bench and slide the grocery
bag toward him. "Eat something first, then we can get to work."

He eyes the bulging paper bag before pouncing on it and
unloading a pile of bananas, granola bars, and sports drinks. He
stops once he gets about halfway. His eyes connect to mine, and
he reaches in and throws his head back with a sharp groan. His
fist emerges, clutching chocolate in a plastic wrapper.

"Thank you for this. Seriously. The other stuff is great, but
this." He holds up the king-size candy bar like a first-prize
trophy. "I could eat a whole grocery bag of just these."

I roll my eyes, the corners of my mouth lifting. "I'll
remember that next time."

He unwraps the candy bar, snaps it in half, and passes one piece to me. I wave him away. "I'm full."

His cheeks are already bulging with chocolate, but he lifts a shoulder and swallows, making room for more.

I shake my head. If this is how he eats when the food is there, how hungry does he get when it's not? I sit down next to him on the bench, our ankles bumping.

"Okay, so, we need to finish our plans and turn them into the judges by the fourteenth, which is..." I wiggle my head from side to side as I calculate. "It's next Saturday." Just over a week away, which suddenly makes it seem like the summer is closing in on us.

Foster finishes chewing the rest of his chocolate, and now he's washing it down with a blue sports drink. "Well, I have a few ideas, but we should decide together." He sets down the empty plastic container with a clunk.

My mouth twists. "I have some ideas too."

I hand him a sheet of poster paper from my bag. Last week after our firework of a kiss, I stayed up to sketch out some ideas when sleep just wouldn't come. I've brought the best one with me today. It's beach inspired, of course. But it also belongs to me and Foster in a way that makes my stomach clench as he pulls the sketch closer with furrowed brows.

He looks up. "From the road trip?"

I nod. My shoulders relax as his lips curve upward.

"Nice idea. Do you mind if I add something?"

I wrinkle my nose playfully as I hand him a pen from my bag. He hunches over the paper and draws. I chew on my lip while I wait.

When he holds it up for me to see, it's like he's added the final piece of a puzzle. All along where I've sketched our plans for the sand art, he's inserted arrows showing where items from his trash art will fit. It's a combination of both our styles, both of our stories.

I stare at it until I'm forced to blink. "It's perfect."

He sets the paper on the bench beside us. His hand drags through the back of his hair as he turns his attention to me. "I don't think this needs to be said, but I'm going to say it anyway."

I inhale when he pauses. My heart beats deep inside my chest, the thundering moving up to my ears and pounding in my head.

"I really like you, Claire."

I lace my fingers with his, sliding my thumb along the inside of his.

My insides expand, like they're suddenly full of helium. It's hard to carry my voice higher than a choked whisper. Our hands intertwined, our voices soft; it's a reverent moment.

"I really like you too. Um, a lot."

His hand squeezes around mine, pumping my fingers like a heartbeat.

We fall back into silence as we study the sketch of our sculpture. His head bumps mine, and a strand of hair falls and tickles my cheek. I glance up. and his eyes are no longer on the paper. He leans down, his lips brushing mine softly—

"Hey there, little brother."

A loud voice near us destroys the moment. Foster's head snaps upward, and he sucks in a sharp, audible breath.

I look up and follow Foster's gaze to see a tall, stocky guy stalking toward us. Foster nods at him, but he whispers under his breath so only I can hear.

"Don't say anything."

My breath catches as I smile through gritted teeth. I'm not as good of an actor as Foster is, and I'm even worse at hiding facial expressions. By the time the guy reaches us a few seconds later, perspiration is already dripping down my neck and the small of my back. I have a pretty good idea who this is. And if it's who I think it is, Foster is in trouble.

Instead of talking to Foster, he walks straight to me. He points one giant finger into my face and chuckles, low and deep in his throat. "You're not with this guy, are you? Are you kidding me, man?" His square face scrunches up and he turns to Foster, whose face is blank. I'm full of enough wide-eyed terror for the both of us.

He whirls on Foster. "I thought I told you to get off this beach. If you're not gonna come with me, you're sure as hell not gonna be sleeping here."

He leans more of his full weight into Foster with each word. I glance at Foster for some subtle sign or direction. Should we make a run for it, or should I call 9-1-1? I've never quite been clear on whether you're supposed to call the moment you feel threatened, or the moment some crazy person at the beach starts to pummel you. Foster won't look at me. He doesn't even blink.

I'm almost positive Foster will hate me for it later, but I do the only thing I can think of in the moment.

"Hey," I say, waving my hands in the face of the near-giant. "Hey, it's not your beach, you know. This is public property. Anyone can be here."

It's a stupid thing to do. And a stupid thing to say, but I'm not quick in situations like these, so I'm kind of proud of myself for even being able to get words out. Foster still won't say anything, but his eyes bug out and his neck flushes red.

My plan is working, though. Because instead of screaming in Foster's face, the guy is back to leering in my direction.

"You gonna stop me from splitting his face open?" He nods in Foster's direction and bares his knuckles, all without breaking eye contact with me.

I want to tell him his threats make him sound like a lame character from *Grease*, but I've already antagonized him enough. I wait for Foster's cue to know what to do next, but it doesn't come. He's completely frozen. This is real. This guy is dangerous, and I'm going to have to get us out of this on my own.

"We're not going to fight you," I tell him. "We're just sitting on the beach, talking." I gesture to the scene around us, where people fill the beach, lounging on towels draped across the sand and splashing through the shallow edge of the ocean.

"And, in case you didn't notice, we're not the only ones on the beach today. So you might want to keep the threats to a minimum."

I use the deliberately calm tone Mom uses when she thinks Livvy or I are being unreasonable. Who knew I could learn so much from Mom's psychological tactics.

He turns to give the beach a quick once-over before he starts to pace between Foster and me. "I need to talk to my little brother. I have every right to."

I raise my eyebrows but resist the urge to look at Foster.

"Johnny, this is not a good time." I jump a little when Foster speaks, because I'm so surprised he's finally shaken off his stupor. Johnny stops pacing to curl his lip into a snarl. I'm getting scared enough to start offering this guy money or something just to leave us alone, but something warm touches me, and I glance down to see Foster's hand covering mine. His fingers tremble against my skin.

Suddenly, I'm standing up and squaring off face-to-face with the guy. "Leave us alone," I say. "Or I'm calling the police." I hold my phone up as proof. He stares at it and then back down at me. His mouth hangs open a little bit, and his eye twitches like he's trying to convince himself that he heard me correctly.

His balled-up hand reaches for my phone. Foster leaps from the bench and darts between us, a blur in my side view. And then there's a *crunch*. The guy's hard fist comes in direct contact with Foster's chin. Blood sprays through the air as Foster's knees buckle to the sand. Screams come from somewhere nearby as other people catch sight of the fight. Johnny steps over Foster and spits in my direction. A blob of spit like a washed-up jellyfish lands inches from my shoe.

"We're still gonna talk," he calls over his shoulder as he strides away.

TWENTY-TWO

"I'm so sorry. I'm so so so sorry."

Foster hasn't stopped apologizing. Which is ridiculous, because my faux bravery is the reason his chin is twice its normal size and black and blue. He also has a small cut on his cheek that's gushing blood like a bottle of ketchup. The doctor at the emergency-care office says it's probably due to Johnny's massive hand size as well as how hard he was hit. A two-for-one sort of thing. They almost didn't agree to see him after we couldn't show them an insurance card, but I slapped down my emergency credit card, only a tinge of guilt niggling in the back of my brain.

"Don't apologize. You didn't do anything wrong." The situation is awful enough without him reminding me how badly I messed up. He should be giving me the silent treatment or yelling at me—or something—since I'm the one who antagonized his brother into hitting him. I didn't even have the foresight to call the police—even though I had threatened that exact thing and was already clutching my phone. Some people are quick under pressure. Me? Not so much.

"I didn't do anything at all. I froze." His hands encircle his head, and he curls into his knees.

"You were scared." I give my head a tiny shake. "I was too."

"Johnny would have come after me whether you were with me or not. I just hate that you had to see that." Foster groans softly as I set an arm around him. Even though his injuries are restricted to his face, he moves his whole body gingerly. A side effect of being in extreme pain, I guess.

I can't let him go back to the beach like this, knowing Johnny is potentially there waiting to beat him to a pulp. And even if Johnny's gone, Foster needs to rest somewhere comfortable for a change, so he can start healing. And I already have a plan in motion—he just doesn't know it yet.

After we leave the doctor's office, I pull into the drive-through of the closest burger place. I order two milkshakes (one chocolate, one vanilla), two cheeseburgers, and two large fries. People are much more likely to accept crazy ideas on a full stomach; that's just common sense. It's a tactic I learned from Dad. He used to take Livvy and me for milkshakes and fries every time he needed us on his side for a vacation choice or weekend plans. Mom pretended to hate that we banded together against her, but I think it secretly made her happy everyone was getting along.

I hand Foster the vanilla milkshake and take a giant slurp out of the chocolate. He eyes me before drinking it. "How did you know I like vanilla?"

I shrug and reluctantly slip the straw out of my mouth. "I have a milkshake theory," I say. I know I sound ridiculous, but I figure Foster should get to know this silly side of me too. He raises his eyebrows and purses his lips. Some people take badly to being categorized, but it never occurred to me that he might be one of them. "Do you want to know what it is?"

He nods. "I'm very interested to hear."

I take another big drink of my milkshake and grin. "Some people, like me, are chocolate. We're sweet, kind of quirky, and we romanticize things."

Foster thinks about it and then nods. "Okay. I guess I can buy that. What about vanilla people then?"

I smirk. I'm enjoying this too much. Maybe it's wrong, but it's kind of fun to watch Foster try to figure out what I think about him. "People who prefer vanilla milkshakes are sweet, smart, and unpredictable." I turn to smile at him. "I knew you were a vanilla guy from day one."

Foster throws his head back and laughs, the sound echoing off the car's window panes. "So, vanilla is unpredictable, not boring?"

I nod. "Maybe people who don't know you well enough think you're boring. But I know you're far from it."

He leans over me and plants a kiss on my mouth. His lips are soft and cold. "Okay, then, what about strawberry?"

I wrinkle my nose. "If someone's favorite milkshake is strawberry, they're just weird."

Foster rewards me with a laugh, and I blush. I'm not used to being the funny one. Weird on account of my obsession with art and reptiles, yes, but never the one people go to for a good joke. It's a good feeling—even if I know he's probably a little biased. Foster nibbles the edge of his burger, winces, and then sets it down, frowning to himself. I eat in silence, and we steal small smiles at each other in between me scarfing down my food. When I'm done and the last of the fries has been devoured, Foster points a finger at me. "Okay, so what do you want?"

I try my best to look offended. It's hard to furrow my brows for too long when Foster's pointing at me like that, though. Maybe I'm not the only one who's good at reading people. "I have a plan." I was hoping to wait until we got to my house to admit what I was planning, but I guess I have to tell him now. "Don't say no yet—just listen."

Foster crosses his arms in front of his chest. "I'm listening, but I have a bad feeling about this already. If it's bad enough to warrant a milkshake and a burger, it must be bad."

I shrug. "A milkshake, burger, and fries," I say. Foster grins. I stretch across the console and invade his seat. I finger the bruised and bloody patches on his chin. "You can't sleep at the beach tonight."

He holds up his hands in silent surrender.

"You agree with me?" I raise my eyes and bite my lip. I had an entire speech planned, but half my work is already done for me. The other—possibly tougher—half will be convincing my parents.

"I'm not stupid," Foster says. "I know when I need to be careful. And after a fight with someone like Johnny, I know lying low is the only way to handle things. Plus, I can't complain about you worrying about me. I kind of like it."

I roll my eyes. I like it too. Even though I wish I didn't have to worry about him.

"What about your parents?"

I start driving toward the beach house. I have a plan for convincing my parents, but I don't say it out loud. It's easier if I just let it happen without thinking it through too much. So I just shrug in response to his question. "They're not evil, Foster. They won't want you out there alone with Johnny anymore than I do."

He doesn't say anything, even if he secretly wants to contradict me. Maybe this will be a good chance for my parents to see why I like Foster so much.

We pull up to the house, and I make Foster wait in the car. He shoots me a look—all wrinkled nose and flighty eyes—that tells me he's not thrilled about the idea, but I'm on a roll with being bossy so I just go with it. The door is unlocked, and I can hear my parents talking through it before I even go inside. For once this summer, they're not fighting. It sounds like they're actually getting along. Maybe even having fun. Mom is laughing loudly. She sounds suspiciously like Livvy, which I normally would not condone, but it's hard to hate the obvious happiness. And Dad is laughing too, in between something that sounds dangerously close to singing. John Denver lyrics echo through the door, and I pause to take in the happy sounds. I know I'm interrupting something special, so I wait. Any other night, I would leave them alone. I'd be thrilled to just let my parents enjoy being together— however weird it is to think about. But Foster needs help tonight.

I knock loudly over the blaring music and then turn the knob. They're sitting at the kitchen table with a tub of ice cream and two spoons between them. Their smiles fade as soon as I step inside, and I try to smile to ease their minds. Too many bad things have happened this summer, and we're all on edge.

"Hey, you. Everything okay?" Mom's out of her chair and in front of me within seconds. The giggling, ice-cream-devouring woman of the last minute alters before my eyes and is replaced by her familiar, more sensible alter-ego.

I nod. "Everything is fine—with me. But, Foster..." I lick my lips and try to think of the best way to say this. And then I just tell them the truth. That I was with Foster at the beach. That someone tried to pick a fight with us, and Foster tried to protect me. And then he got beat up because of it. It's not at all like what I practiced in my head, but it is the story. And it's practically the full truth, which leaves me with at least some sense of accomplishment.

Dad anticipates what I want before I can even formulate the question. He shakes his head as he puts a solid arm around

Mom's shoulders. "What can we do to help? Have you called his parents?"

I study him. The wrinkles around his eyes and mouth. The grey hairs jutting haphazardly out of his ears and his sideburns.

"Dad, he really needs somewhere safe to stay."

My parents exchange confused looks. And I realize my mistake.

"Why won't he be safe at his house?" Mom arches an eyebrow and frowns at me.

Clearly, I should have thought it through more. Telling my parents about how Foster has no guardian and no home could mean certain death to our already quasi-doomed relationship. But leaving him alone to try to hide on the beach or the streets downtown feels just as dangerous. I take a deep breath.

"Foster's mom died last year. He doesn't have a set home right now. He's been sleeping...different places...until he finds something permanent. But I'm afraid his brother, Johnny, will find him if he stays at one of the usual places. He already found him today, and Foster's okay, but his face looks bad."

I swallow back bile at the image of Foster broken on the ground.

Mom covers her mouth with her hand, and a small whimper escapes her. When Dad speaks, it's in a whisper fierce enough to match his flaming cheeks.

"No teenage boys are sleeping in the same house as my daughters. It just won't work. We can give him money or some other help, but that's it."

"He's a kid, Aaron. We can't just throw money at him and ignore the fact he needs help."

Dad's forehead creases with explosive lines. "I'm sorry, Claire. I really do like him. He's a good kid." He looks between Mom and I, eyebrows furrowed before walking into the hall.

My parents' bedroom door clicks closed. The echo of it hangs in the air seconds after he's out of sight.

Eyes brimming, I turn to Mom. I hate making my parents angry, but I made a promise to Foster. I couldn't live with myself if I didn't try to protect him, whether he thinks he needs protection or not.

"He's not some random homeless person, Mom. He's only seventeen, and he's kind of my boyfriend. He's alone, and he needs our help."

My voice wavers, but I bite it back.

It's the first time I've used the word *boyfriend* around my family, and it doesn't escape Mom. Her mouth drops open, and she rubs a hand across her temples when I say it.

"Who's supposed to be taking care of him?"

"It's a long story, but he really doesn't have anyone he can count on," I tell her. Stupid, warm hope bubbles in my chest.

She nods and claps her hands together. "Don't bring him in yet. Let me talk to your dad. I don't want to do anything we don't agree on, but I think I can convince him it will be okay. Tell Foster he's welcome to stay here for as long as he needs."

My arms wrap around Mom's back, squeezing. I inhale against her hair before letting go. "Thank you."

"You're welcome. And we're going to need to hear that story, however long, very soon, okay?"

I go back to the car where Foster is waiting. I expect to find him worried or bored or some combination of the two. I've been gone much longer than I anticipated. But what I find is way worse than anything I could have imagined. Foster is still where I left him, lounging in the passenger seat of my car. And next to him in the driver's seat is Livvy, who appears to be talking his ear off. I stomp over to them and glare at her through the window.

I pound on the glass until she opens the door a crack. "Leave him alone, Liv."

She laughs and looks at Foster. He sees my dagger eyes and doesn't join in. "We were just talking," she says. The sparkle in her eyes tells me that whatever she was talking about was not as innocent as she'd want me to believe. "So, what are you two up to tonight?" Livvy bobs her bouncy ponytail between Foster and me, grin still in place.

I ignore her and focus on Foster. "They said yes. You can stay here tonight. We just need to give my dad a few more minutes to stop freaking out." In a few minutes, he'll probably still be just as nervous, but I omit that. Livvy makes a choking sound anyway. I roll my eyes at her as she clutches her hand to her mouth and closes her eyes, heaving with silent laughter. Everything's a joke to her.

"Seriously?" Foster lets out a long breath. A hint of a smile plays on his lips.

Livvy suddenly stops laughing and turns her head to scowl at me. "Wait. They really said your boyfriend could sleep over? But they won't even let Evan in the house!"

I shrug. "Foster needs somewhere to stay. Plus, he hasn't been arrested twice for selling drugs."

Her face turns bright red, and she shoves me out of the way as she marches up the driveway.

"She's not that bad," Foster says.

I roll my eyes and say nothing. Livvy is good at fooling people, but I'm not in the mood to hash it out with Foster.

After ten minutes of random music on the radio and nervous silence, I fling open my car door. "Ready to go in?" He follows me, his gait stiff. I walk up the driveway with Foster's hand in mine. Here we go, into the fire.

TWENTY-THREE

Family dinners with Foster are a lot like family dinners without Foster.

The first few nights he was here, everyone sat up straighter, made more eye contact. And we all talked more, too. The first night we all ate together ended with Mom spilling an entire pitcher of grape juice over her fancy white tablecloth—the one with the white flowers stitched into the corners. She stood up, bright red juice dripping over everything, grasped the wad of paper towels Dad had dashed to get, surveyed the catastrophic mess, and cracked a smile. She actually smiled. Opa's ghost was probably hovering around the table in the kitchen, his pearly white head rolling with laughter at the scene.

If the same thing happened today, she'd probably scream at all of us for more towels and bleach *now*—Foster included.

He's standing at the counter, cutting potatoes for Mom on a beat-up old wooden cutting board while I set the table when Dad walks in. The shop has needed a lot of attention lately since the new hires are still being trained, and Dad's been gone for far more hours than he likes during the summer. This is the first time he's made it home in time for dinner this entire week. He tugs his tennis shoes off at the front door, kisses Mom in the kitchen, and then turns to Foster.

When Dad gets excited about an idea, he vibrates with it. His eyes light up a brilliant grey-blue, his hair sticks on end from running his hands over it, his hands wave in the air. As a younger kid, the excitement used to be so contagious that I'd get sucked into it every time. Now, I'm a little more wary. Especially when this new idea seems to involve Foster.

"I've got an offer for you."

Foster sets down his knife and handful of potatoes, looking cautious.

Dad pulls up tufts of hair and slaps his hands on the table-top, mouth pulled into a grin. "How would you feel about putting some of your art in our shop?"

Foster's chin lifts, and the corners of his mouth curve. "That would be awesome."

Some tiny part of me beats its green chest, roaring against the hypocrisy of it all.

Here I've been all along, and no one's ever asked to put my art in the shop. The shop my family owns, to be exact. Sure, I may not have any pieces quite ready to part with at the moment. But it's the principle of the thing that matters, and the fact that no one's even thought to ask me, yet they ask Foster after he's been living here for less than a week pricks at my pride.

I pull a stretched smile anyway, letting the stack of plastic plates in my hands clatter onto the table.

"Good idea," I say.

Foster's eyes watch my mouth, like he sees right through my forced happiness. Maybe he does, and the thought of him seeing the jealous monster raging underneath my bared teeth warms my neck.

Dad, oblivious to what either of us is feeling, nods around the kitchen.

"It'll be a good way for you to get your stuff out there and make a little extra money, hopefully. We can figure out the details later, but start organizing some of your work, and I'll take a look later this week."

"I really appreciate it. Thank you." Foster beams up at him before shooting me another look. His eyes go quiet despite the smile he's wearing.

After dinner, I clear my plate and head out the back door —alone.

The click of a door closing from behind me signals Foster's followed me anyway. He unfolds a second chair and sets it next to the camping chair I've dropped into. Instead of saying anything, I run the bottoms of my bare feet along the stubby blades of grass. The air in the backyard hums with such a varied chorus of bugs that my skin would probably be crawling if these weren't the sounds I cut my teeth on.

"I can tell your dad no, if you want."

I lift my head. "That isn't what I want."

If Foster could sell some of his work in the shop, he'd make more money than he is now. He needs money, and I don't. That's not what this is about at all. It's the consistent lack of belief in my talent from my parents that makes my head pound.

He leans his head back against the chair and sucks in his cheeks, giving him a hollow appearance that makes his big eyes look twice their normal size.

"No, I'm sorry. Seriously. I'm being dumb. I shouldn't have taken it out on you." I'm every bit the selfish brat I feel like.

One hand reaches back to massage his neck. "It's not a big

deal. But try having a little more faith in yourself. You're good at what you do. You know that, right?"

"I'm not sure. But my parents have never seen me as an artist either, so it must run in my family." I swipe a dandelion from the grass at my feet and pinch delicate yellow petals off one at a time.

"What about your Opa? He was kind of like your muse, right?"

His eyes seep into me, deeper than they should. If he sees more than I'd like him to of my confused little soul, he doesn't say. The black tattoo on his arm glistens in the dusky light.

My lips curve, which was obviously his plan. I've told him about how Opa still is my muse in a lot of ways. But my eyes are still trained on his arm.

"Can I ask about your tattoo?"

My finger traces the ink on his wrist in soft strokes. The act is somehow just as intimate as all the kissing we've done combined. Ocean-blue eyes watch me, his head hung low over the tattoo and my hand and our mouths inches apart.

"Is it for your mom?"

Above his throat, his Adam's apple bobs. His lips part slightly as he inhales. "Her name was Scarlett." He taps the tattoo. "I got this the week she died. After Johnny and—everything. I was completely alone, and the first thing I did was blow what money I did have on this."

His voice takes on an edge I've never heard from him, tapping into that well of unfair sorrows he's had to endure that he doesn't bother to acknowledge the rest of the time.

My fingers curl around his, squeezing. He ducks toward me, mouth close enough I can practically taste the soft texture of his lips.

"It's beautiful." I free my hand and run my fingers along the ink again. "I'm sure your mom loves it too."

Foster catches my hand in his and pulls it to his mouth. He presses his lips against the back of my hand, his kiss warm against my skin. Something hot and wet falls from his face. His eyes are red, lashes heavy with teardrops. I turn in my chair and throw both arms around his head, cradling it to my chest as he cries for a loss so big all the art in the world can't make up for it.

TWENTY-FOUR

Before the sun is even up the next morning, there's a knock on my door. I slide out of bed and stumble to open it. If it's Livvy, I'll kill her for waking me up this early just to bug me. But it's Foster standing there, not Livvy. He glances at my baggy striped pajamas and flashes a toothy smile. I blush. No one but my family and my girl friends have seen me in my pajamas. Definitely not a guy I'm dating.

"Do you want to head to the beach soon and do one more practice round?" His whisper is hard to catch, and I have to move my head even closer to hear him.

I nod. "Sure. But why so early?"

He shifts his eyes and looks away. I've never seen him look so uncomfortable. And if I wasn't slightly annoyed to be woken up hours before I usually wake up in the summer, it might be cute.

"What is it?" I put a hand on his arm and lean my body against the doorframe to steady my wobbly legs.

Foster meets my eyes and starts to whisper again, his mouth barely moving as he forms the words. He might be equally as afraid of waking my parents up as he is of whatever else is bothering him. "I don't want you to be scared or anything, but Johnny isn't going to stop. I just don't want to risk running into him until he has time to cool down. He's not a morning person, so we'll be safe if we go early."

"Hold on." I hold up a finger. He takes a step back as I shut my door with a gentle push. Still dizzy with sleep, I turn around my room until I find a pair of shorts and a T-shirt from the discarded pile of clothes near my bed. When I come out a minute later, Foster is leaning against the wall with his eyes closed, soft snores sounding from his nose.

"You don't have to be dramatic," I tell him. "I got dressed faster than it took you to pretend to be asleep."

Foster runs his eyes down my wrinkled Guava Guava T-shirt and my tiny cotton shorts with a grin. He wraps an arm around my waist as we tiptoe through the house and down the driveway to my car.

———

We drive in groggy silence for a few minutes before my head is clear enough for conversation. Foster stares out the window, his chin resting on his hand. It's like he's somewhere else. After the emotions of last night, I don't blame him. I try to bring him back by asking the question that's been picking at me since the fight with Johnny.

"Why does your brother care where you sleep anyway?"

I keep my head forward, eyes focused on the road, but I catch him frowning in my peripheral vision.

"It's complicated."

People always say that, but it's rarely true. He has a faraway look as he tangles his fingers in his hair, brushing it to the side.

"Can you just try to explain it? No pressure or anything, but I did almost give my parents a heart attack so you could steer clear of him." I'm not trying to be snarky, but my words come out shrill and quick before I can call them back. I have Foster's full attention. We're at the beach now, so I pull into a far space in the parking lot so we can talk. Getting information out of Foster is like pulling teeth, but I've got to try to understand.

"You're right," he says, "I owe you the whole story. I know you've put a lot of trust in me."

I wait.

"Before, when I was supposed to stay with him but he took my money and left, he still wanted me, I guess. I didn't know what to believe, and I didn't want to go with him after what he did. So, I just figured I'd be better off on my own. But he reported it to CPS as me being the one who ran away. So, they've kind of been looking for me ever since."

Foster rubs the back of his neck with one hand and reaches for mine with the other one. I hook a finger around his pinky, but I don't move my gaze. I put pressure on his hand, slowly.

"What do you mean looking for you? Who is? Like the police? I—I don't understand." I'm trying to keep the mind-blown tone out of my voice. I can't believe Foster kept this from me, even for a day. He should have said something.

He nods. "I'm sorry I didn't tell you. I just wanted to protect you."

His words are the final flame to my already-smoking fuse. The one that's been trailing our relationship ever since it began. It was founded on secrecy, and there are still things I don't know.

"Protect me? Are. You. Joking? You told me you had no other choice. You lied to me about something important."

Foster looks away. Maybe he has nothing to say. Then he rubs his chin and nods. "I know. I told you he ran away, and that was true. But he came back at the beginning of the summer. He's not the best guardian, but family is important to him. He says we're all we have left and that we should be together in Alabama, where he lives. Since I wouldn't go, he's threatening to report where I am to CPS. They might make me go with him, so I've been avoiding him for the past few weeks. Until he found me at the beach."

I bury my face in my knees. Everything feels so twisted and messy and out of control.

"We'll figure it out," I finally say. It's stupid, but I have to say something because even though I'm angry, he's looking to me for some sort of support. "Is there anything else I don't know?" *Please, please, please say no.*

"Well, there's something about your sister."

I grip the steering wheel and raise an eyebrow at him. "What are you talking about?"

Foster squints like he's weighing his answer. I'm not even sure I want to hear it if it involves Livvy, but it's too late now. "Livvy told me she's only dating Evan to get on your family's nerves."

My mouth drops open. My first reaction is to slap his knee, hard. "Tell the truth!"

He takes in my wide eyes and laughs hesitantly, rubbing the spot of impact. "She told me last night in the car that she thought she was in love with him for about a week at the beginning of the summer. But that wore off pretty quickly. I guess she hasn't told your parents yet because she's afraid they'll make her stop seeing Evan if they know he's not going to be their future son-in-law."

I shake my head and let out a low sigh. I'm torn between an odd sensation of relief and jealousy. Livvy told Foster her biggest secret. Just last year, I would have been the one she'd go to first. Before Opa's death inexplicably tore us apart, before she dove headfirst into life with Evan and I found Foster.

"Foster, let's promise to be honest with each other from now on, okay? I can't take much more drama. And I've never been someone who enjoys surprises."

He smirks. "Deal. But you never know—I bet I could pull off a good surprise."

I hold up a palm. "No. No surprises, please."

All I want is for the rest of the summer to go as I planned.

———

Now that we have decided on a sketch for our sand sculpture, we need to focus on making sure we have all of the right tools. One of my favorite things about sand sculpting is that artists of all different backgrounds are drawn to it. We all bring our favorite tools and make good use of them. Some people even bring random things like furniture pads and oven mitts to smooth and pack the sand. Foster and I pool our resources and come out with a few chisels, two paint spatulas, half a dozen buckets, and four shovels. We've decided to do a trial run of our complete sculpture to make sure there's nothing else we might need on the actual day of the competition.

While we start shoveling enough sand for the base of our sculpture in the pink and yellow morning light, the beach starts to fill up more quickly than we anticipated. Carolina wanders past us and then stops and calls my name. I almost don't turn because I'm concentrating so hard on wetting the sand.

"Are you spying on us?" I raise an eyebrow and wave my shovel in her direction playfully. She plants her hands on her hips and rolls her eyes.

"I'm just at the beach for the Food Festival, like everyone else."

I shrug. I have no idea what she's talking about.

"It's new this year. All of the best food trucks in Florida are supposed to be here. They're going to park right on the beach at eleven." She taps her phone and grins at the crowd of people gathering where she pointed. "But while I'm here, I figured a little recon on my competition would be a good way to pass the time."

I like to win, no matter the stakes. Probably another thing I've inherited from Mom. So, when the signs start rolling out for the different food trucks, I can't resist setting down my bucket and chisel. "How about a warm-up competition, then?" I point to a red-white-and-blue plastic sign hanging on the side of the truck nearest us. *Ice Cream Eating Contest. $50 Prize and free T-shirt.*

Carolina sizes me up and then shrugs. "I'll win, but sure. Why not?"

Foster watches us warily. I tend to err on the impulsive, jump-in-headfirst side. He's more the wait-and-see type. Carolina and I line up with a surprisingly small group—for free ice cream I'd have thought there would be a longer line—and start tucking into the assorted flavors. The goal of the contest is to eat a small cup of each of their twenty flavors without throwing up. If there's a tie, both contestants have to eat a large sundae of their choosing. I'm already mentally picking out my sundae flavor when I notice Carolina plowing past me in the flavor lineup.

I hear someone chanting my name, and I look up at the gathered crowd to see Foster, who's evidently left his post at our sculpture to cheer me on. I grin and throw down my spoon to start shoveling ice cream into my mouth with my hands instead. I scoop it out of my individual cups with my fingers and slurp it into my mouth, causing the people closest to me to make gagging sounds. I should be embarrassed, but all I can muster is a small shrug. Five minutes later, Carolina and I are both staring down at an enormous sundae with all of the works. We agreed that to keep the playing field completely level, we would order the exact same thing: a cookies-and-cream sundae with fudge sauce, cookie chunks, three maraschino cherries, and a whipped cream mountain the size of my face.

As soon as the crowd-led countdown reaches zero, we're both a flurry of ice-cream-filled spoons, passing from the bowls to our mouths over and over. Five minutes in, I sneak a glance at Carolina, who's slowly licking the end of her metal spoon like a sick puppy. I swirl my spoon around my bowl and shove one last enormous bite of sweetness into my mouth with a painful and icy gulp down my throat.

Victory.

I hug Carolina afterward, and she pretends to be bummed, but she's laughing. "Text me later and let me know how bad your stomach hurts after this, okay?" she demands.

Foster and I celebrate the entire drive home by jacking the radio up and head-banging at every red light. I slip my prize T-shirt over my head, even though it's two sizes too large and hangs to my knees. By the time we walk into the beach house, we're laughing hysterically at this radio show that prank calls locals and convinces them they're the grand prize winner of a one-cent gift card. It's not even funny, but laughing with him is contagious. I'm delirious from the sun and sugar, and I accidentally elbow a bowl from the long table near the front door and it crashes to the ground with a sharp clang. Mom and Dad run into the living room from their bedroom. They spot Foster and me, and the happiness is zapped from the room.

Mom doesn't yell, but her voice bites, even though her face is streaked with dry tears. "First you disappear this morning without even bothering to let us know. And then some man came here looking for you and Foster and scared us half to death."

I bite my lip to stop the trembling. Don't cry. Not now.

TWENTY-FIVE

Foster freezes.

"Johnny? He was here?"

My eyes go to Mom's thinly set mouth. Dad's arm settled around her waist, and the two of them pull close together.

Dad nods his head. "He was here. We told him he wasn't welcome, and he left pretty quickly."

Mom tugs at the end of her frazzled ponytail. "After how he hit you, Foster, we were so worried when you two disappeared this morning. We thought he'd left here and found you and Claire."

Dad's frown deepens. "We were just about to call the police."

I swallow as goose bumps trail along my arms and neck. "We had no idea, I swear. We were just at the beach. And I didn't have my phone."

Mom nods. "We saw it on your bed. Claire—we were terrified."

I step forward and let her wrap her arms around me. Her squeeze is like a boa constrictor intent on breaking my ribs.

Dad places a palm on my back and pats. "It's alright now,

but I think I'll still go visit Opa's old police buddy and let them know about Johnny. Just to be safe."

Foster's still blinking dazedly, his hands limp by his sides. He's just watching us, like he's some stranger who just happened to wander in on this scene and now he's too frozen to walk away.

I edge back toward him with my hand outstretched for his, but he pulls away, running his hands through his hair instead. He stares at my parents.

"I'll get my stuff and go." There's no catch in his voice, no hesitation.

Dad crosses his arms in front of his chest, his mouth drawn tightly. Mom's lips pull downward.

"No one was suggesting that it's your fault. We just want to take the necessary steps to make sure we're safe. All of us." She sweeps her arm around the room.

At my side, Foster shifts. "You've been great. And I really appreciate you taking me in, but I can't stay here. Not when Johnny's threatening your family."

He finally looks at me, and I step back, almost tripping on my own feet in the process. Why is he doing this?

Dad runs a thumb along his chin. "We'd love for you to stay. You're still welcome to a room as long as you need, just like we promised you." But he seems to know something I don't because he and Foster jerk their chins at each other across the room in some silent understanding.

Hands on her hips, Mom narrows her eyes. "We're worried about you just as much as we are Claire and Livvy. We're not going to let you leave here, knowing you could be in danger."

Foster nods. "I know. Thank you. But I'll be okay. I have a friend I can stay with. He just got back into town."

My mouth drops. He's lying. Why is he lying like this?

Mom walks to him to wrap her arms around his neck, and

then Dad shakes his hand. He looks at me for a beat while I'm still too slack-jawed to stop him, and then he goes down the hall to the guest bedroom.

My feet start working again, and I run down the hall too. Dad stops Mom from following me, his arm a barrier. "Let them say goodbye," he says from behind me. I stifle another sob.

I close the door behind me and lean against it, crumpling at the knees and letting my body slide to the floor.

I suck in a shallow breath. "Please stop."

He's sitting on the bed tucking his few belongings back into his backpack. He crawls next to me on the floor against the door, and I lean my head onto his shoulder.

"What if we found somewhere to stay together? You can't stay at the beach anymore, and I could help you stay away from Johnny." Part of me feels responsible for the way his brother slammed his fist into his face. I can't let him leave without knowing he'll be safe, even if it means I have to leave too. I look up at him with a spark of hope in this completely dark moment.

He still won't look at me. Instead, he sighs into my hair. I get a sinking feeling with every second he breathes over me and doesn't answer. I try again.

"It's a crazy idea, I know, but it could work. There's only another year until we graduate and then we can work full time, and we'd probably have enough money to live wherever we want. Maybe I can convince my parents to help still." I edge out from under his arm and slide in front of him, so he can't ignore me. Our feet touch.

"What do you think? Talk to me." I reach out and touch his knee. He stares at my hand and finally meets my eyes. His are steely.

"No."

I pause a beat because I'm sure I heard him wrong. Or maybe he just doesn't understand what I'm offering.

Then more loudly, he says, "No, Claire. It's not going to work."

He doesn't have to say what he means anymore. I know without hearing the words, without making him explain, that he means 'no' to everything. No to finding an apartment together, no to me moving out, and no to us having a future. I pull my hand from his knee and focus on taking deep breaths. I've never had a panic attack before, but I imagine this is what it feels like. My tight chest, the way everything around me blurs at the edges, the way my hands go to my head, itching to pull every strand of my hair out, but stop because I can't muster the energy to do more than take in ragged, uneven breaths

His blue eyes are duller now. And they're dry, while mine might never be again. I'm grasping to find meaning in anything right now. He stands up and takes his backpack off of the bed. I struggle to my feet too and stand by the closed door. I could use my body to block him from leaving. To push him back into the room and make him stay until he agrees to my plan. Instead, I step aside and let him open the door. He looks at me from the doorway for a second. I can't look at him anymore though. I want to disappear into the tacky blue-and-cream dolphin rug I'm standing on.

"Claire, I'm so sorry. None of this is going to work, though. It's not safe for you. I'm not good for you."

His voice falters, and it takes every ounce of paltry self-control I have left not to check if he's crying. I don't say anything, and he walks away from me and down the hall a second later. I go to my room and close the door behind me. I'm not crying, I'm just numb. Being swallowed up in this nothing-ness is scarier than I could have imagined.

TWENTY-SIX

"You're the saddest person I've ever seen at the beach."

Carolina stands over me as I dig a gigantic trench in the sand. I ignore her. She kicks some sand into the hole, barely missing my head in the process. She's as sick of hearing about Foster as I am of talking about him.

"I'm not sad. Just focused." Focused and losing hope. I haven't heard from Foster since he left the beach house. I've called, but every time, he's sent me straight to voicemail. With the first round of the competition looming closer and me reduced to half a team, I haven't had time to sit around crying. Not that I haven't cried, but it's been less than it would have been if I weren't so busy. I thought I was determined to win the sculpting contest before, but now it's all I can think about. I even dream about how amazing it will feel to win and to get the scholarship, as I emerge victorious, on my way to becoming a real artist. Foster be damned.

Carolina swings her legs over and hops into the hole with me. "It's okay to be sad and focused at the same time. Just let what happened with Foster feed your artistic energy and channel it into your work." She is a real artist no matter what, and she owns it.

"Thanks." I don't move my eyes from my work.

After she disappears to fine-tune the plans for her own sculpture, I pull out a notepad to add some more details to my new sketch. It's still going to be great, just in a different way. A little sand crab worms its way out of a tiny hole in the sand and crawls past me. I close my eyes after it passes and soak in the heat on my skin. There's the shuffling-on-sand sound of someone walking up, but I take my time opening my eyes. It's probably Carolina, back to deliver another pep talk. But when I turn, it's to see Livvy, her arms folded.

I frown. "What are you doing here?" I've barely seen her all summer, between both of us having boyfriends and both of us having something to hide from Mom and Dad. I haven't felt close to my sister lately, but the realization that we both had something in common this summer makes me soften when I look at her.

She shrugs and runs her hand through the damp sand I've just dug up. "I wanted to see how your thing was going." She points at the pile of sand and tools I've accumulated.

Last night at dinner, she announced she had news. She and Mom and Dad sat on the couch in the living room talking soft and low for almost an hour. I only caught a little bit here and there from my bedroom down the hall, but from what I heard she's in a lot of trouble. Still, some of Mom's most recent wrinkles seem to have vanished overnight. So, there's that.

"It's going okay," I say. I know it's not the real reason she's here, but I'll find it out soon enough. "Did Mom and Dad come with you?" She shakes her head, and I exhale. I've been avoiding them since Foster left. Neither of them seemed concerned about me when they let Foster leave and my heart shattered into thousands of irreparable shards. No matter what they say, this makes things worse, not better.

"They dropped me off and told me to check on you. Mom's waiting in the car."

She points to my sketchbook and wrinkles her nose at my drawing of an alligator, its jaws locked around a chicken head.

"That's what you're doing for the contest?"

Livvy has never cared very much about hurting anyone's feelings. I'm too tender right now to care. I need to win this contest to prove to myself, and my parents, that I'm the artist I aspire to be. I'll take any help I can get at this point.

I sigh. "Well, I can't do the same thing I was going to do when Foster was still helping."

Livvy rolls her eyes and groans loudly. "Why not, though?"

I blink at her. "Because he left, Liv. He's not part of my team anymore. He won't even talk to me."

Livvy shakes her head and eyes me with disdain. "Your original idea was way better than this. Don't change it because of some jerk."

I throw down my things and massage my temples with my thumbs. There's no point getting upset at her for calling Foster a jerk. I focus on the tide, moving steadily across the shore, and then I turn my gaze back to my sister. Across the beach, I make out Carolina's form as she shovels sand.

"Want to take a day off?"

———

An hour later, Livvy, Carolina, and I drive down the highway with so many snacks and assorted flavors of drinks you'd think we were escaping for the rest of the month. "So where are we going?" Livvy watches me from the passenger seat while I fiddle with my phone at a red light. A spontaneous day trip sounded fun, but now I'm not so sure.

I shrug. "Maybe just out for ice cream?"

Carolina leans forward from the back seat and tilts her head at me. "No, seriously, Claire. Where are we going?"

I roll my eyes. "Okay, I was thinking we should hunt down Foster. I need closure or an explanation or *something* from him."

Livvy grins and shakes her head. "Let's do it."

Carolina wrinkles her nose.

Livvy reaches for the radio and turns the volume up so loud that I can't hear anything else. I roll down the windows and let the wind stream past our faces to blow our hair. We're so wrapped up in our mission that we don't need to hear any more—we just need to go. Our first stop is the beach under the pier. It's a stupid place to look, but I figure starting small is ideal. Of course, he isn't there. Someone else's belongings are stored under the corner of the pier. My stomach turns at the sight of a different backpack and a faded blue, one-man tent where Foster's things used to be. What used to feel like a safe place now makes the hairs on my arm rise.

Halfway through the day and at hour three of scouring Saint Augustine, our excitement runs low. "He's gotta be somewhere else," I say. I roll my window up and turn down the music. I'm starting to get a headache from too much white noise. Livvy's pretending to sleep in the seat next to me, but I see her eye twitch.

She rolls her head toward me and groans. "This was a bad idea," she says, her eyes still closed. "Sorry I pushed you into it."

Carolina leans forward again. "Are you sure this is worth it? Isn't he kind of a jerk?"

I bite my lip. "I know he can seem that way sometimes, but it's because he's had a bad last few years. And he makes me happy." My cheeks burn as I admit how I feel.

She claps a palm against the seat, leaning back. "Good enough for me."

I'm not ready to give up yet, after all my talk about needing closure. But we've checked literally every place I've heard Foster mention, plus some that just seemed like good hiding spots.

I only have one place left to check, but it's a stretch. I decide to drop Livvy and Carolina off at the beach first and then play my last card. That way neither of them are responsible for me if I'm bummed after not finding him. Livvy wishes me good luck, and I drive to the north side of town, since we've covered virtually everywhere else in Saint Augustine. I pull into the parking lot of the gardening store, but I don't get out of the car. Instead, I wait. I scan the faces of those who wander the parking lot, but none of them are the one I'm hoping to see. There was a pretty slim chance of me finding him here. I knew that going in. But I couldn't have guessed I'd be as crushed as I am to end my search with even less certainty than I came in with. I wish there was some way to turn off the memory of how I felt when we came here together, back when I was falling for him so quickly but still afraid to admit it to myself. And he was playing up the whole beach-guy-surfer thing way too much, but it worked anyway.

It was one day during the first week we'd decided to work together on the sculpting project.

Foster and I pulled into the parking lot of the small gardening store. There were several types of potted plants in the front, along with statues of cherubs and hand-painted signs with sayings like "Home is Where the Heart is" and "Happy People Live Here." We made our way past all of the vegetation to the back where the tools were kept. I knew next to nothing about that part of the process, but Foster seemed to know exactly what we needed. *He grabbed an armful of items and then looked at my empty hands.*

I shrugged. "This is my first competition, remember? I'm new to sand sculpting. And sand..."

He smiled and held up his collection smugly. "Well, then, let me educate you."

Great, *I thought:* He thinks he's educating me, and all he's got is the same shovel I had as a six-year-old.

"See, it doesn't actually matter what we use. That's the secret."

I wrinkled my nose. Some great secret trick of the trade. "I kind of picked up on that when I watched a video of someone's grandma sculpting with a teaspoon," I said. I didn't try to exclusively speak to him in sarcasm, it just happened that way. He laughed because he didn't seem to mind though. It was nice.

"Exactly," he said. "The secret, though, is that the more obscure your tools are, the better your sculpture will turn out." He picked up a spiky-looking thing and pretended to thrust it at me. "This thing will really impress the judges."

"I'm not sure that's how it works," I said. But the idea of using random objects to create an already obscure style of art appealed to me. It's the exact brand of quirkiness I'm into. Kind of like Foster. But out loud, I only mentioned my affinity for quirky art, not my affinity for quirky boys.

That day, I never would have guessed that a few weeks later, I'd spend my free day scouring the town for him, hoping he was sleeping behind an old building or staying with a random friend. But I also never thought we'd happen in the first place, so I've surprised myself doubly.

I suck back impending tears and pull away from the store, driving as slowly as I can without cars rear-ending me when I stop. What I definitely don't need is a trip to the auto shop with a totaled car. I drive around the back of the garden store once more, just to torture myself a little longer, and then I see it. Foster's stupid backpack. And a few feet away, Foster sitting on the ground and leaning against the back of the building with his eyes closed. I almost slam on my brakes, but I catch myself just in time. I whip the car around and park in an empty space next to the back lot. As I march toward Foster, blood pounds in my head, matching the angry music playing in the back of my mind. I stomp in front of Foster, and he opens his hazy blue eyes to look up at me.

His eyes flash as he scrambles to his feet. What I'm feeling now is an overwhelming urge to rear back my fist and propel it into his stomach, just for the pleasure of seeing him double over in pain. It'd only be a fraction of the hurt he gave me. This is the opposite of what falling in love is supposed to feel like. This is a slow-boiling overflow of emotions I want to hold back, but once I admit how furious I am at him, everything comes tumbling out and there's no use trying to put the words back in. My hands are trembling, but I don't care anymore.

"You just gave up on me."

He opens his mouth like he wants to correct me, but I shoot eye-daggers at him and he shuts up. "You gave up on us, just because things got a little messy. And you didn't just give up— you cut me off because you're a coward."

He flinches at the word "coward," but I can't stop now. I'm an avalanche of emotion, and I've just gotten started. I'm crying, but I don't even know why, because I'm not sad anymore. The entire day I've spent chasing him down feels like a waste. I can't even remember why I'm here, yelling at him.

"That's not fair. I was trying to do the right thing."

I stomp my foot as he reaches for me. Backing away, I shake my head again.

"You don't get to decide what the right thing is if it means abandoning me. That's something we're supposed to decide together."

I throw my head back and wipe my tears on the back of my hand. He abandoned me like Opa did, like Livvy did, like everyone else I thought I could count on this summer. Foster's a few inches away, and he reaches for me again, but I hold my hands up, so he backs away.

"You made me fall for you. And the second you saw I was falling, you dropped me."

There's nothing he can say, and he knows it. And now that I've got everything out in the open, I don't what else to say either. We stand in awkward silence until Foster takes a tentative step in my direction. I don't try to shake him off when he slips his arms around my waist and brings his face next to mine, his breath tickling my cheek.

"You're falling for me?" He looks down at me and grins.

After everything I've said, and after I just called him a coward, that's all he says.

It should infuriate me. But I hold my breath and wait. Something warm springs from my chest.

"I'm sorry, Claire. I'm so sorry you thought I dropped you. I thought I was protecting you from all of this." He points at the trash littering the ground behind the building, his torn-up backpack, and the homeless man sleeping a few feet away from us. "But you're right. It's not my place to say what you can or can't handle."

My teeth find my lip as I pull his face to mine. It's only been a week, but the way his lips melt into mine feels like it's been years since the last time we've kissed. My hands wrap around his back and he squeezes me closer to him. We get lost in the rhythm of our kissing until a car full of college-aged kids honks at us. One of them leans out of the back window and cheers.

Foster waves and smiles back at them. Ducking my head, I turn so they can't see my red, tear-stained face.

"I'm going to fix this." He cups a palm to my chin. "I'm an idiot, and I can't ever go that long again without holding you."

I sling his backpack across my shoulders. "Agreed."

We climb into my car and drive back toward the beach house. I'm going to make sure Foster knows he belongs there now just as much as the rest of us.

TWENTY-SEVEN

Mom's pretending to read a book, but her eyes wander in our direction too frequently for her to be actually absorbing any words off the pages.

This is just ridiculous. "Mom," I say, "we're just sketching. You don't really need to chaperone."

She tries to feign surprise, but her frown fools no one. "We're glad you're back with us, Foster." She dog-ears her page and sets her book down on its face. She touches a hand to his hair, and he smiles up at her.

As soon as the sound of her footsteps disappears and her door clicks shut, Foster's hand is on mine. He rubs his thumb in a circle on my skin until I feel like the spot might melt off my body entirely. It's almost impossible for me to make my eyes meet his, but when I finally do look at him, everything else fades. The beach house, the table we're sitting at—all gone. All that's left is the two of us and the heat spreading through my face.

Before I can register what I'm doing, I've left my chair and I'm standing in front of him. He wraps his arms around my waist and pulls me close. I kiss him so hard we both almost fall over, but Foster grabs onto the table. He holds my face in his other hand and kisses me back. There is no too much when it comes to kissing him. The only thing that can stop us is an outside force. And one comes in the form of the front door swinging open.

I stumble backward and quickly turn to the door, fully expecting to see Dad standing there. Miraculously, Livvy stares back at Foster and me. She's red-faced and laughing into her hand as she hurries past us. "Seriously, you guys." She shakes her head and leaves us.

It was enough to bring us back down, though. We've cooled off enough to think clearly, and we both look at each other, thinking the same thing. If it were anyone else at the door, we'd have been caught.

"Want to go get something to eat?" I'm not exactly starving, but I need a distraction, and more than that, I need a crowd of people to help me hold back from Foster. Before we leave, I stop at Mom's room to let her know where we're going. When my knock goes unanswered, I slip the door open slowly to see her sitting on her bed, staring at the quilt.

"We're going to Guava Guava," I say.

She nods before looking up. Tears bead in the corners of her eyes, and I don't know what to do. I've never walked in on her crying before. Actually, I don't know if I've ever seen her look this sad, even at Opa's funeral.

I sit next to her, my arm around her back. "What's wrong?" I stroke the back of her head like she used to do for me when I was younger. It's been years since she's touched my hair like this. Probably years since I've let her near my hair. "Mom, please tell me." Seeing her like this, so small, so fragile-looking, scares me.

"I'm losing you girls," she finally says. The words come out as a whimper, and she closes her eyes as she speaks.

"Mom, you aren't losing us. We're together the entire summer." I know what she means, but I don't want to accept it either. I always saw Livvy as the one who was destined to disappoint our parents, but that wasn't fair of me. Maybe all of us—every teenager ever—is destined to disappoint our parents. We have to grow away from them and become someone they feel like they don't know. Maybe that's the essence of growing up.

She hangs her head and grabs my hand in hers. I give it a squeeze. "You and your sister are growing up. It's just so fast. All in one summer."

"Livvy's trying to grow up too fast. I'm acting like a normal seventeen-year-old." I can't ignore the opportunity to bring my sister into this.

Mom eyes me, probably deciding whether or not to let my comment go unanswered. She sighs. "Livvy's stuff has been hard for me. Especially considering how young I was when I got pregnant with you. I don't regret anything, but I had your dad." She pauses and exhales again. "She dodged a bullet, but I'm not sure she appreciates the fact."

I don't know what to say, though so I squeeze her hand tighter. "I'm sorry."

Her shoulders shake in a light laugh. "You don't have to be sorry, sweetie. You girls growing up isn't the real problem. It's just me. It's such a big change from when you were my little girls." Her smile wobbles.

I return her smile, but I know it does nothing to help. "I can stay home."

She shakes her head. "No, go. But bring me back some fries. The crispy ones, please."

I hug her from the side and walk toward the door. "Just give me a second." I run down the hallway to where Foster's still waiting at the table. He eyes me questioningly. "Um, change of plans. My mom needs me tonight."

Foster nods. "I'll go get something and bring it back for everyone."

I hug him goodbye and turn back to Mom's room.

I stand in the doorway. "Want to watch a movie?" I wait for her to turn me down, say she's too tired or busy, but her face spreads into a grin.

"I have caramel corn I've been hiding from you guys." She holds up a bag from her nightstand. For one more night, we can pretend things aren't changing.

TWENTY-EIGHT

When I get to the pier, Foster's leaning against one of its pillars. His eyes are closed, his face kissing the sun already bearing down on the crystalline white sand. He snuck out early this morning, according to Mom. I woke up to a note in his hand-writing slipped under my bedroom door asking me to meet him here. He's wearing just his swim trunks and standing next to his surfboard. No shovel, no buckets. I get as close to him as I can without alerting him to my presence; it's easy to cover the sound of my footsteps when I'm barefoot and my toes dig into the slip-pery sand. I wait until I'm close enough to smell the saltwater on his skin before I reach out and poke him.

"Boo."

Foster's eyes flash open at the same time as he takes a small jump backward and lets out an adorable *squeak*. His mouth twists from confusion to joy in a split second.

My cheeks swell with my smile. "Sorry, did I scare you?"

His laugh is low as he shakes his head. "You could never scare me." He grabs my hand that's still floating in midair and laces his fingers through mine.

I shrug. "I've never heard someone who's *not scared* scream so loud."

His hands pull to my sides and I screech with laughter. "Not...ticklish...seriously...you're the...worst!" I scurry away from him, back a few feet, until I can catch my breath. "That was a totally unnecessary sneak attack." I tilt my head, eyes narrowed, lips tight.

Foster's eyes gleam. He's completely enjoying this. I may have started it by scaring him, but I'm not going to admit it out loud.

"So, um, where's your stuff?" I point to where his surfboard rests in the sand. I was supposed to meet him to sculpt, not surf. We're supposed to be creative, but a surfboard is too big to sculpt with.

He raises one side of his mouth, turning to glance pointedly at the ocean behind us. I blink back at him. "Are you being weird on purpose? Is this some sort of relationship test? Like if I can't guess what you're trying to say, you dump me?"

He throws his head back and groans. He bends to pick up his surfboard, which he walks over to me, stroking it with one hand. "No. I thought we could take a break from sculpting practice today. And maybe help you earn your status as a reverse snowbird."

I wrinkle my nose. "I can't be a reverse snowbird. Texas is just as hot as Florida. And I already told you: I don't surf." I glare down at his gleaming board like it's a weapon and not a form of recreation.

"Okay, but that was when you were a little kid, right? Maybe, just maybe, you could handle it now that you're seventeen and all grown up?" He says the last part in a baby voice, wearing a smirk that makes me want to punch him. Or kiss him.

Maybe a little of both.

I push my bottom lip out and turn to face the waves. The water's calm today. There's no breeze to cut the thick humidity, the waves are only making miniscule ripples, and there's hardly anyone else here. If I'm going to try it, it might as well be today.

"Okay," I say. "But I have two conditions."

Foster shakes his head. His hair bounces across his face and whips water through the air like a dog after a bath. He must already have been in the water before I got here. "I would expect nothing less from you. What do you want?"

"First—and most important—if I say I'm done, I'm done. No trying to convince me to give it another chance, okay?"

I inhale and wait for him to answer before I go on.

He nods, locking his gaze with mine. Those steady blue eyes I'm positive couldn't lie even if he wanted to reassure me. "Okay, I promise."

"Good. The second condition is that after we do *this*," I point to the shiny board mocking me in his arms, "we do something I want to do."

He shrugs. "Cool. Let's go."

———

"I wanted to borrow my buddy's board for you to use today. He's the one who lets me store my stuff at his parent's house. But I guess they're out of town or something." He rubs a hand on his neck and focuses on the wave behind me as it approaches.

"This is fine," I say. "Sharing a board with you has its perks."

We're scrunched together on the middle of his surfboard, my chest against his solid back and both of us in tight, water-logged swim suits. We paddle out to where the waves are big enough to ride. They're tame today in comparison to what they usually are—thank goodness. Foster had me practice on his board on the sand for a good thirty minutes before we got into the water, just to get the feel for it. Considering the fact that I fell off the stationary board a few times, I'm not sure I got the feel the way he was hoping I would.

He stretches out an arm to point to the incoming wave, and we turn and paddle forward, our arms propelling us through the water in sync.

"Ready?"

I shake my head, but he's already focused entirely on the wave. I grip the sides of the board until my knuckles turn white. Suddenly, Foster's slapping my leg and pointing. He pops up without looking back. I climb to my knees and bend them until I've reached a crouched standing position. Foster turns the board, and we both lean our hips with the water as we glide toward the shore.

But instead of making it all the way in, the waves pick up, and the board shudders underneath our feet. A wall of water beats over me, and I lose my footing in an instant. Warm water fills my mouth as my head is pulled under. I'm screaming, but no sound comes out. It's another full second before survival kicks in and I kick my legs as hard as possible, inching my body upward.

When I break the surface, I cough and sputter until my chest calms enough to breathe normally. My eyes are blurred and sting from the salt water.

"Yeah!" Foster's grinning and flashing me a thumbs-up from the shore, just a few feet away. My chest sinks. All that and I was never even in real danger of drowning. He's already run across the tide in a fit of...adrenaline, maybe? I trudge toward him and sit dumbly on the surfboard he's dragged along the sand, feeling less energized than when we started. He frowns at my lack of enthusiasm and walks to me.

"You okay?"

"That. Was. Terrifying." My face burns even as I admit it. Especially considering he already teased me for being a baby in the water. And he's right. Nearly drowning as a kindergartner shouldn't have a hold over an almost high-school senior.

He kneels next to me; one leg succumbs to the gloppy wet sand. "Did you hate it? Was the wave too big? I tried to start small, but I should have known it would be too much."

I touch his knee. "Please stop." His rambling just makes me feel worse. "It's not your fault. I'm just too much of a wimp for surfing, okay? I tried to tell you." I chew on the inside of my cheek and train my eyes on the hem of my suit.

He tries to pretend like it doesn't matter. His voice is well-practiced, but it's not fooling me. I can sense the disappointment. "Okay, well we had a deal. What did you have in mind?"

———

"Here." I tear a sheet of paper from my sketchbook and slide it over along with a pen. We're sitting on the bench closest to the parking lot. Foster's hair is gold in the shimmery midday sun, and I wish I had more than my oldest pens with me to do it justice.

He raises an eyebrow. "What are we doing exactly?" We'd changed into dry clothes, and I had come back from the beach bathroom with my activity—the pens and sketchpad I keep in my car.

"We're drawing each other. Practically sketching 101." I tap my pen against the sheet of paper in my hand and consider him.

He rubs the back of his neck. "Just a warning: I'm awful at drawing. I have no talent whatsoever."

"You're telling me you're creative in every other aspect besides drawing? I'm not buying it." I shake my head as I start sketching an outline of his face. First the shape of his hair, the parts that dangle just past his ears, and then the shadowing on his eyes.

"You'll see," he says. He's absorbed in his drawing too. I sneak a look out of the corner of my eyes and see him studying me intensely, his face tight and solemn. Butterflies flutter through my stomach. I'll never get over the fact that he seems to be just as into me as I am to him. When we're together, it's like he actually sees me. He's not just looking at my face, but staring through all of my walls. And better yet, he likes what he sees. His cheeks flush pink when he looks up and sees me.

"Are you trying to cheat?" He snatches up his paper and presses it against his T-shirt. His eyes widen in mock indignation.

I roll my eyes. "I'm not cheating. I *was* thinking how cute you are, but you kind of ruined it." I scoot away from him just as he tries to lean over for a kiss. I tap my pen against my paper and point a finger at him. "Set a timer. Sixty seconds."

He raises his eyebrows and does as I say, setting his phone timer to one minute. We both focus on our pens and draw as fast as we can while still watching the other person. When the clock runs down, we set our papers on the bench facedown, our pens to the side.

"You go first." Foster toys with a corner of my paper but trains his eyes on me until I nod my approval.

"Okay, but it's not my best work." It's not—it was a shaky rush job, but I know he won't mind. It's more nerve wracking to show him one of my sketches than it was to be squeezed together on a surfboard in the middle of open water. My hands shake a little as he flips it over and brings the drawing closer to his face.

"It's perfect," he finally says.

I slump my face into one palm and watch him from my uncovered eye. "Really? You don't hate it?"

He laughs and wraps an arm around my shoulders. "I don't hate it. It's so good. I mean, I knew it would be good, because it's you, but when I look at it I can tell you really get me." He slaps a hand onto the sketch. "This is the same me I see in the mirror every morning."

It's the highest compliment someone can give an artist. Which is technically cheating, since Foster is an artist himself, so he knows exactly what to say to feed my ego. Still, I blush and lean into him, inhaling the smell of warm sunshine.

"Okay, now I'm ready to see your sketch." I don't wait for him to turn the paper. I grab for it and hold it away from him while I look.

It's me, but it isn't. He lied about having no drawing skills; how typical. I recognize my slightly wavy short hair, the too-serious look I'm often told I wear, the tank top I've recycled too many times this summer. But the eyes are wild. They're big, and even in black and white they appear to be sparking with color and way more full of life than mine. Everything about the girl in his sketch is fiery and fierce. I'm neither of those things, but I guess no one told him that.

"You hate it." It's not a question, but a statement. Like he's so sure I'm angry that he's already apologizing.

"I don't," I say. "I'm just confused and slightly flattered that this is how you see me."

He kisses my cheek, just a gentle press of his lips against my skin. "If I were a better artist, maybe I could convince you it's how everyone sees you."

I can't think of a single thing to say to that. Maybe it's exhaustion from the ocean or maybe it's the wild look in the drawing's eyes. But I'm feeling more reckless than usual. Something's swelling deep within me, and Foster at my side is drawing it out.

"I know it's getting late, but do you think we have time to catch one more wave?" I swallow, nerves piling up at the mere thought. But I'm feeling braver now than before. Like I can do anything. I can be the girl in the drawing—if I want.

TWENTY-NINE

"Are you sure you can't come with us?" Mom is not above begging, but I still shake my head and shoot her a look.

"Mom. I can't miss the qualifying round. It's mandatory. But tell Becca I say hi." As if there weren't enough nerves surrounding today, now I have to convince my parents for the third time this week how important today's contest is.

She sighs, her shoulders dropping. "And you'll stay the night at Carolina's house and only come back here in the morning?"

I nod. "Yes, that's the plan. Don't worry."

Next to me on the couch, Foster nods too, for extra measure.

Livvy rolls her eyes back in her head and groans way louder than necessary. Visiting Becca, Mom's best friend from college who lives a few hours away with her twin girls, is not Livvy's idea of a good weekend. But she has to go because my parents don't trust her without an adult around. Me, on the other hand, they trust enough to leave for the whole weekend. I'm not sure if it's that I'm older or just that they'd never expect me to do anything wild, even though their being gone leaves me alone with Foster.

Becca just had knee surgery, and her doctor husband has a

hard time getting away from work, so Mom volunteered to come up and help for a weekend. And then Dad and Livvy got dragged along. It just happened, and then it was perfect, for me at least. Time to myself for an entire weekend is just what I need to de-stress from all of the family drama this summer.

I wrinkle my nose at Livvy and turn to my parents, eyelashes batting and voice dripping with honey. "I'll miss you guys, but everything will be fine here. Besides, you deserve a fun trip."

Mom puts a hand to her chest, like my words have pierced her soul. Dad raises an eyebrow. "Are you sure you'll be alright? You stay at Carolina's every night, okay? No sleepovers at the beach house." Dad leans over for a side hug, and I nod into his chest. I'm pretty sure he's staring Foster down over my shoulder.

"Yes, absolutely. You guys have fun, and we'll see you Sunday night."

Mom hugs me until I'm forced to peel my body away from hers. She follows Dad and Livvy out the door and calls over her shoulder. "Good luck at your sandcastle event today, you two."

We watch from the window as their car pulls away from the driveway and turns down the street. Home free. I plop back down onto the couch and let my head rest against the back cushions. Foster collapses next to me. As much as I love my family, space from them is nice.

Foster and I go out for breakfast. We have plenty of time to sit and contemplate our waffles before we need to sign in at the beach. We've been preparing for weeks, but I feel sick when I think too much about what's at stake. The scholarship, the bragging rights. But especially Opa. He wanted this for me, and that's enough to make it important.

"We've got this," Foster says. He nods at me over our plates, both of which are swimming in blueberry-flavored syrup, but it isn't convincing enough to settle my upset stomach.

"We've got this." I've been repeating everything all morning because I'm too distracted to think up my own words. "I'm so nervous." Strangely, it feels nice to admit out loud.

Foster nods and reaches across the table for my hand. "I know, but we've put in the time. And our sketch is really good." He's right. I've never been as prepared for anything in my life. But I'll still be glad when it's over.

Carolina meets us at the sign-in table. She's carrying a big white box of doughnuts, and she offers us one after we fill out our forms. I take a chocolate-iced doughnut even though I'm still full of waffles. I'll need all the sugar I can get if I'm going to make it through the work we have ahead of us. Foster takes a vanilla-iced doughnut, and I grin. Does he remember the conversation we had about milkshakes? He winks at me and takes a big bite of frosting. Carolina side-eyes him before walking away, shaking her head as she goes. After doughnuts, it's time to get to work. We pass a lot of teams I recognize from all the hours spent prepping on the beach this summer. Besides Carolina, there are only two other teams made up of just one person. Not having to split the scholarship money would be nice, but the hours in the sun with no one to trade off isn't worth it. Not to me.

Foster starts digging a hole for our sand supply while I lay out our tools and tape our sketch to a big poster board. I also tape a stick to the poster board and shimmy the stick deep into the sand next to our numbered flag. Now we can look at our vision and execute it perfectly, or at least that's the idea.

The first hour goes by so quickly that I wouldn't have realized it if there weren't judges walking around, reminding contestants of the time every fifteen minutes. The next hour consists of building the bottom level and prepping for the next level. The first step is making sure the basic shape is there. Then we can move on to the detailing. Detailing will take the longest, but it earns us the most points on the judges' score cards.

"We're making good time," I say. Foster is so focused that he doesn't hear me, and I have to repeat myself. When he finally responds, it's only with a barely discernible nod. For all his talk of not being very nervous, his hands sure are shaking a lot.

"Crap. Crap. Crap." Foster turns to me with wide eyes. "I forgot all of the detailing tools."

I glance at our stash laid out on the sand and confirm that, in fact, there are no detailing tools. Just a wide variety of shovels and buckets we use to smooth and pack the sand.

We stare at each other as precious seconds tick past. My heart sinks into my stomach at all the work that will be lost if we don't think of something.

"What if we just use this?" Foster holds up a small gardening shovel. He points to the narrow rubber tip on the end of the handle, eyebrows up, hopeful.

I shake my head. "It's still not thin enough. It will make everything look too sloppy."

One of the judges walks past us and reminds everyone else that there's only one hour left. We're doomed.

"One hour to etch our design in this four-foot sculpture?" I put my hands to my head to drown out the noise. How can we save this? My fingers brush up against the bobby pins I've haphazardly stuck in my hair to keep the bangs I'm trying to grow out of my face. This is the biggest miracle of the summer thus far. I pull them out and hand one to Foster. "The best artists improvise." His face breaks out into a grin, and we almost trip over each other racing to get to work as the clock ticks down.

My wrists burn from the tiny motions necessary to create a gigantic statue. But by the time I'm done, there's still ten minutes left before the official competition time ends.

Foster steps back from the side he's working on and considers me.

"Did we do it?"

I nod. It's a proud moment, even though the judging hasn't even begun. We wrap our arms around each other, and Foster whispers "Good job," into my hair, arms stroking my back over my tank top.

The judges gather together and announce the official ending of the time limit. Including the judges, everyone on the beach wanders through the maze of sculptures. The nerves set in, and at first, we sit down next to our sculpture and wait like proud parents. Thirty minutes go by, and my stomach is starting to ache from the anxiety of doing nothing but waiting. When we finished, I was sure our sculpture was the best in the contest, but every minute that passes is another minute I doubt my work. So, Foster and I decide to leave our post and check out the competition. I want to head straight for Carolina's top-secret project, so I can finally see it completed. From where I'm standing across the beach, I can tell there's a big crowd surrounding her sculpture.

"Let's make our way around," I say. Seeing the amazing sculptures is both inspiring and daunting. The more sculptures we pass, the more my confidence plummets. The basic structures I was expecting are missing. Instead, each sculpture we pass is more intricate than the previous. One team has even erected a nearly perfect likeness of Guava Guava, complete with the signature dancing guavas on their sign.

By the time we've made it to Carolina's sculpture, I have a pit in my stomach. I inhale loudly when I see her sculpture up close. This contest means as much to her as it does to me, and it shows in her work.

"This is beautiful." She's sculpted a mermaid sitting on a

rock, basking in the sun. In one hand, the mermaid holds an easel, and in the other, a completed painting.

"I think we gain creativity in the arts by consuming creativity," she's saying to the people gathered around. Foster nods, agreeing with her.

I eye both of them as an epiphany hits me. All of my favorite artists: Frida Kahlo, Andy Warhol, Joan Mitchell, they all dedicated their lives to pursuing art. None of them ever woke up one day and decided to become a great painter, paintbrush in hand, never having studied another artists' work. All the years I've spent drooling over the beautiful paintings hanging in museums and filling the pages of textbooks, and it's still never occurred to me that they did anything more than inspire me. Consuming other artists' creations is almost as important as creating my own pieces. Mind blown.

And just like my idols, I've spent the summer so far in pursuit of my own brand of art. Foster's trash art, the bland paintings from the museum, and Carolina's sand creations: they've all led me to here. The feeling that I'm close to being a real artist itches through my wrist, screaming to be let loose to create.

"You deserve to go on to the next round," I breathe.

She smiles and waves a hand at me. "I'll tell you if I think you're going to move on after I check out your sculpture."

Foster and I share a look behind her back. The thought of Carolina seeing our work makes my stomach turn, but she'll see it sooner or later, no matter what.

"Okay, but you have to tell us the truth. We can handle it."

Carolina shoots me a look that says, "Don't I always tell you the truth?" Which is true—she doesn't sugarcoat things.

Foster leads the way to our station, and I lag behind. It's hard to imagine her loving it like we loved hers. He and I step back and let Carolina take it in. She stares for a minute and then turns back to us, one eyebrow raised and her mouth scrunched up. This is where I'm supposed to say something deep and meaningful like she did. Too bad my brain's one big blank canvas at the moment.

We've pulled off the masterpiece we planned for, but just barely. The base of the sculpture is thin coiling sand packed tightly and supported by a background block of sand in the shape of a large rectangle. Verging off from the coiled base are five offshoots, each one different. There's one in the shape of a glass bottle, a giant swirled conch shell, a sand dollar with a chipped corner, plastic bottle rings, and a newspaper. Pressed into the sand are real pieces from Foster's collection—the brightest pieces of sea glass and plastic we could find. It's as close to a jumbo-sized copy of Foster's art as we could get, and every time I glance over it, my heart swells and my head gets all light and funny.

"It was a team effort." I nod toward Foster, who shrugs. He couldn't care less about impressing her.

Carolina squints at us and grins in the bright sunlight. "It's really unique. Good job, guys."

"Thanks. You did a great job, too. It's just a relief that today's over. Either way the judging decision goes, there's no more stressing for a while." I let my body take the break it's aching for and drop down onto the sand. The next second, I feel someone standing over me.

"Is this your sculpture?" The voice looms above my head, and I scramble to my feet. A girl not much older than me holding a small notepad and a megaphone peers at our sand sculpture with pursed lips.

"Yes." Foster and I respond in sync.

She frowns and scribbles across the page with speed before handing a small rectangle of paper to me. On it are a number and a date for next month. "Congratulations. You will be moving on to the next round. Details to come."

We've barely begun to thank her and squeal with absolute excitement before she trudges on to inspect the next sculpture. I stifle a giggle at her lack of enthusiasm. Everything seems funny right now because I'm slaphappy, too full of glaring sunshine, sugar, and stressful, sleepless nights to think straight. Later, when the high has worn off, I'll have less to laugh about. Now, I embrace it.

I lean back against Foster's chest. It's warm and solid, and I could fall asleep in a millisecond if I didn't also want to make out with him right this second. He slips an arm around my shoulders and presses his lips to my cheek. I wish we were alone instead of surrounded on a crowded beach.

We follow Carolina back to her display and learn that she's moving on to the next round as well. It's not a surprise, but we cheer for her too because the euphoria is contagious. A sour pang of guilt plagues me when I walk past a few artists who are packing up and watching the cheering groups with wistfulness I know well. Not everyone can win. And only one group can win the next round. If we don't bring our A game, next time we could be the ones walking away with nothing. No way I'm going to let that happen.

THIRTY

"We should be celebrating." Foster frowns through a mouthful of fish taco the next day at lunch.

I point to the tray of tacos between us on our table at Guava Guava. I guess we have different definitions of the word.

"We *are* celebrating. What did *you* have in mind?"

Foster grins, and I think I might regret asking. "Well, I took the liberty of picking Livvy's brain the other day, and she let me in on a little secret."

I definitely regret asking him. "I don't like where this is going," I say. I shovel another taco in my mouth so it looks like I'm just starving and not so nervous that my neck's working up a cold sweat.

Foster thumps his hands on the tabletop like a drum. He makes a trilling noise with his mouth. I wrinkle my nose.

"What are you doing? Stop."

He stops and rolls his eyes, letting out a low whistle of a sigh. He hasn't known me long enough to understand how much I truly hate surprises. The only thing worse than surprises are drawn-out surprises, which is where this looks to be headed.

"Just tell me, please." I'm actually desperate for this to end.

Foster puts his hands down and studies me. "You look like you're being tortured. Is my drumroll that bad?"

"Actually, it is. And, while we're being honest, I just thought you should know I'm not the kind of girl who enjoys surprises. I like knowing what's going on. The idea of being led somewhere mysterious while wearing a blindfold is basically my worst nightmare."

Foster chuckles and ducks his head. "Okay, fair enough. I'll throw away my blindfold. But do you think you trust me enough to let me have one small surprise? I promise it won't be anything awful."

I groan. He's trying to be sweet, and I'm ruining things, per usual. If he's trying so hard, I guess I can try a little, too. "Sure," I say, "of course I trust you." We finish our lunch and walk back to my car. "Where now?"

Foster shakes his head. "This is only going to work if you let me drive."

This plan is getting more involved by the minute. But in the spirit of trying to be fair, we switch seats, and I stare at him, waiting for the answer. This better not just be his ploy to get a turn driving.

"I can't tell you where we're going because it will ruin the surprise, but I can tell you that you'll love it. I think."

I bite my lip and slump into the passenger seat. Foster starts driving and he's going slower than Opa used to. "You know you're driving like a grandpa, right?"

He turns toward me when we stop at a red light, and his mouth is open wide. It's hard not to laugh at his expression. "I do actually know that," he says. "I'm driving slowly because I know you'll kill me if I crash your car. Safety first, Claire."

"Oh yeah. Good idea." I smile to myself as he putters along and the other Florida drivers lay on their car horns as they zoom past us. It's a nice feeling to have someone other than my parents care about my safety. Even if I'm tempted to duck my head anytime someone passes us.

When Foster makes a right on a familiar country road, my stomach jumps. When he turns the car into a parking lot with a giant green billboard over it, I almost leap out of the moving car.

"The Alligator Zoo?" I'm practically squealing as I reach across the seat divider to squeeze his arm. "Livvy told you about this?"

It's hard to imagine my sister doing something so nice, but there's no other explanation. I can't even think of any ulterior motive she'd have for telling Foster how much I've always wanted to visit the zoo. The Alligator Zoo is a farm out in the country with various species of alligators in a fenced-in swamp. It's located in the middle of nowhere off the highway, right between two stands that sell fresh Florida oranges. Every summer of my life, I've begged my parents to take us to see the alligators, and every summer my mom refuses. They took us to the regular zoo, the aquarium, the wax museum, but the Alligator Zoo was off limits because Mom insists just the sight of alligators makes her physically sick.

"This is the first good surprise I've ever had." I lean across the console to kiss him. He grins with his lips pressed against mine. Our breath comes together in short, fast puffs of air.

"I'm glad. You deserve it. You did awesome at the sculpting contest. We're a perfect team."

I blush, and I can't think of anything else to say. I smile back at him until I have to look away or we'll never make it out of the car and into the zoo. We hand the tickets Foster purchased in advance to the zoo employee and head through the entrance gate.

There are several exhibits of small reptile breeds at the beginning of the park, and I walk slowly past them, eagerly staring. Ever since I was a little girl, I've been fascinated by all animals, but especially the green and slithering ones like lizards and snakes. My mom's been trying to talk me out of my interest for about as long as I can remember. The fact that Foster brought me here is the best thing ever.

We walk along paved pathways that wind around different water enclosures. Each enclosure holds small families of alligators, grouped together according to size and sex. In the very middle of the zoo, located directly under a swooping bridge, is the main attraction. There's an informational sign explaining that this is the home of Big Benny, the second-largest alligator in captivity in all of Florida. Foster and I huddle together to read it and then turn to each other with wide eyes. He tugs on my hand and leads me closer. I don't even have to say it out loud because Foster understands I can't leave the zoo without seeing Big Benny up close.

We join a crowd gathering in the center of the bridge and peer down into the water. There are several gators swirling around in the murky green-brown gunk, but it's impossible to tell whether or not any of them are the famed alligator. Minutes later, someone in the still-growing crowd points at the water, and we all follow his focus. A massive green-and-tan tail whips up, and a trickle of water lands on the crowd watching from above. Everyone screams.

A handler appears at the edge of the bank down below. She probably took one of the narrow paths from the bank while the rest of us were distracted by trying to find Benny. I take in a sharp breath. I love watching the gators, and I'm dying to see the big one, but I know I'd never be brave enough to risk standing feet away from their powerful bodies. Feedback echoes from a sound box, bringing everyone's attention to the handler. There are more gasps and murmuring from the impressed crowd. The handler's face gives no reaction. She taps the voice piece hooked on to the side of her ear before speaking into it.

"Hello there, y'all. Welcome to feeding time at the Alligator Zoo. As you can see, our very intelligent alligators here know their lunch is on its way."

She pauses as we all look toward the swirling alligators below us. "I'll begin by feeding the smaller ones, and then we'll end with feeding Big Benny."

She reaches to her side for a bucket of small, wriggling fish. She waves two of the fish high up in the air, and a small alligator jumps from the water and snatches them from her outstretched hand. The crowd goes silent as we're all reminded how dangerous these animals can be. She empties the bucket two by two, and with every alligator fed, their sizes increase. Finally, she holds up the empty bucket so everyone can see that the fish are gone. Then she holds up her other hand, producing a second bucket. She pulls out a chicken. Dead poultry stings at my nose and taints the air.

It's not alive, but it is fully beaked and feathered. The way it hangs limp in her hands makes me want to turn away, but I'm too invested in seeing Big Benny emerge to leave now.

"I'll need complete silence for this, please," she says into her voice piece, scratchy and urgent. I can't tell if I'm imagining things, but her voice seems to be shaking a little.

I reach for Foster's hand and slide directly in front of him, his chest behind my head. The handler raises the chicken in the air by its legs. We wait. Three seconds later, an enormous creature leaps out of the murky water and attaches its powerful jaws to the butt of the chicken, yanking it out of the handler's hands. Water sprays in a rainbow pattern as his tail slaps the water. As the gator dives back under with its food, the handler sways on her feet, knocked off her balance by the monster that is Big Benny.

"There you go, y'all," she says. "I'm going to get out of here while these guys are eating, but thanks for watching feeding time. We'll see you for the next meal at 5:00."

I can't stop talking about Big Benny on the car ride home. "Could you imagine being that close to an alligator so big that he almost knocks you off your feet?" Foster nods at all the right times, but I'm not sure he's as into all of it as I am. I grin back at him. "Thank you. That was so amazing, and it means a lot to me."

He eyes me while he drives. "I had fun too."

It's getting late, but the sun doesn't set until after nine during the summer, so it's still light outside.

"Should we stay up and watch a movie?" I don't want him to drop me off yet; the day has been too perfect.

Dad's programmed the TV remote in the living room so it's almost impossible for anyone but him to use. While Foster makes popcorn, I run to the bathroom and change into a spare pair of pajamas to get rid of the alligator smell. We sit on the sofa while we watch one of the Fast and the Furious movies on my laptop which is on the coffee table. I'm not really sure which one it is. I let Foster pick the movie since he saw the alligators for me, but these kinds of movies aren't my thing. Foster loves cars and action movies, but he's not paying attention to any of it tonight.

Instead, he's running his hands over my back and bumping his legs against mine every chance he gets. I'd rather kiss him than watch the movie anyway. I pull his face toward mine and kiss him, hard, until I'm forced to come up for air. His lips are salty from the popcorn. My hands wrap around his neck and trail down his arms and along velvety tan skin. He touches my face, his hands running through my wild hair. Everywhere he touches tingles with warmth.

"Should I take you to Carolina's now?" His voice is low and breathy.

I shake my head and whisper, even though there's no reason to. My heart beats into my chest as soon as I get the words out. "Not yet."

Foster stretches across the space between us to kiss me again and everything is warmer and faster than before. I stop kissing him back and try to catch my breath—and clear my head. He pulls away, and we stare at each other, breathing hard and eyes wide.

"Are you okay?" he whispers with his nose against mine. I breathe in the coconut shampoo from the guest bathroom.

I nod.

He untangles his arms and legs from my body and leans back against the couch. I stay perfectly still until he reaches for my hand again and squeezes. I join him and lean on his shoulder.

"Thank you for today," I say.

I snuggle my head into his chest where his heartbeat drums wildly against my ear.

THIRTY-ONE

My body is so stiff and sore when I first wake up that I'm sure it's the middle of the night. One squinted glance at the room around me, and I'm completely lost. Light pours through the windows and fills the room with dancing spots of yellow and white. Foster's arm flops over my stomach...and then I remember with a flash how tired we were last night after the movie. I told myself I'd just close my eyes for another minute and then I'd get up and have Foster take me to Carolina's. Apparently, that was a terrible plan.

I shake Foster's shoulder until his eyes drift open. "Foster, wake up." My voice is softer than I mean it to be and my face warmer. I don't know why I feel shy about it; it's not like we planned on spending the night together. But we did, and somehow it feels like a big deal.

He glances around until he comes to the same realization. "We fell asleep?"

I nod. "I guess we were more tired than we thought."

He sits up and rubs his eyes, and I sit back down on the edge of the couch next to him. "What time is it?" His voice is husky and groggy and adorable.

I glance at my phone, noting I have a handful of texts from a worried Carolina. "It's only seven." The Florida summer sun rises early.

Foster drops his head, eyes closed. I laugh. When he doesn't open his eyes, I drape the blanket back over his legs as his soft snores fill the room again. I guess he wasn't pretending to sleep.

I'm never going to be able to fall asleep again after the surprise of waking up next to him, so I leave Foster and make myself some hot chocolate. I save half of the hot water I boil in case he wants something to drink, too. Bright sunshine glares through the windows of the kitchen and makes rainbows on the silver spoon I'm using to stir my chocolate. I've always loved mornings, and this morning in particular is one I'll remember, I'm sure of it. I smile to myself as Foster's snoring escalates, echoing through the entire house. One minute, he can be the best at driving me crazy, and the next, I'm obsessing over the way he sleeps.

Foster's eyes are still closed by the time I drain my mug. I'm drowsy and warm as I crawl back into bed with him. As soon as my butt hits the cushions, Foster reaches around me and pulls me against him, like a baby with a teddy bear. He snuggles his head against mine, and seconds later, he's breathing deeply yet again. Short puffs of air tickle my neck, lulling me to sleep along with him.

When my eyes crack open next, the spot beside me is cold. My hand grapples through a sleepy haze to find Foster, but he's sitting on the end of the sofa out of reach. His head is ducked and cradled in his hands.

I crawl to him, still wearing the T-shirt and cheeky shorts I changed into before the movie last night. Before this morning's happy accident. He seems closed off though...and it's starting to worry me. My chest is tight and heavy. I raise a hand to his back but let it hover before dropping it by my side. My voice falls quietly through the thick air.

"Hey. What's wrong?"

Foster sighs and rubs his thumbs across his temples. He's still facing away from me, his shoulders tight. Whatever he wants to say to me is hurting him, but I can't imagine it's worse than what he's doing to me by shutting me out.

"I have to go."

The words hang in the bright morning air before they bounce against my reluctant ears and slam into my heart. I shake my head like I can't hear him.

"Go? Do you mean because of my parents' rule?" Words rush out of me like maybe the faster I talk the quicker I can fix whatever's bothering him. "Don't worry about that. I can go to Carolina's now and come back later. It was just an accident, anyway. We're fine."

"That's not what I mean. I'm leaving Florida."

A sharp breath escapes me, pulled from somewhere deep in my chest.

Foster exhales into his fist, turning to look at me. "Someone at Child Protective Services found out I don't have a guardian. They got in touch with Johnny and then with me. We're going to Alabama, just like he wanted."

This cannot be happening. The yo-yoing on my heart is stretching it to the point of breaking.

"We're supposed to win the sculpture contest together." It's a dumb thing to say. Why would I think he'd still be interested in doing the contest even if he were staying? He's leaving me, which means he doesn't care.

But I say it anyway. Anything to try to get him to listen. "What about the finals?" My voice is as small as I feel. It's not about the contest anymore, and we both know it.

"I can't think about that." He shifts his feet and lifts his shoulders one at a time. "There was this mediation appointment where me and Johnny met with this lady. I didn't tell you about it because living with Johnny is something I've been running from for so long. And I didn't think anything would come of it."

I inhale a squeaky breath. "But something did?"

"Yeah. We talked a lot. He remembered stories about my mom I hadn't thought about since I was a little kid." He holds up his phone, a short text message from Johnny filling the screen. "And it's all settled now, just like she wanted from the beginning."

"I know you miss your mom." I smile weakly.

"I do." He's quiet.

I bet Foster's mom was kind, like he is. As wild as she drives me, life without my mom is incomprehensible. Like suddenly waking up one day to find your right hand just disappeared and now you're expected to go on living life like everything is fine.

The same way I feel without Opa.

"But why would you trust him again?" I can't comprehend giving another chance to a person like Johnny, relative or not. Even though my heart is shattering into sharp, pointy shards, I don't want Foster hurt again.

Foster shrugs. "I don't trust him yet, but he's family. I owe him another chance." My fingers itch to touch him, squeeze his hand, and tell him how much I hope he's right. But his words are a barrier, and they make it impossible for me to reach out, even though he's right next to me.

"What if he doesn't deserve a second chance?" Sour words twist my mouth.

His hands run across his neck and through his hair, tugging at wayward strands. "My mom always said family was important. It's something I heard her say all the time growing up. I can't just ignore that when Johnny's trying to make things right."

I stare at him, and it's like watching a stranger. My mind

swirls with images of kissing him, and milkshakes, and the Alligator Zoo—it's hard to believe how good everything was last night.

For a moment, it looks like he might actually reach out to touch me. He raises a quivering hand but then drops it. I'm torn between an ache to show him how I feel and the need to erect a fence around my already raw heart. He's leaving anyway, so there's no point in trying to fix things now.

"Johnny called this morning. He's waiting at his hotel. I just wanted to tell you before I leave. I know I owe you at least that much."

His voice breaks as he stands, hovering over the couch.

"I'm sorry for how everything turned out. We tried, but this relationship just won't work."

I shake my head, standing to follow him. "We could have tried harder." *He* could try harder instead of giving up on us.

He blinks at me but says nothing. And I can't think of anything to say either. He goes to the guest room and shoves his things into his backpack, and I stand in the hall watching. Bitter bile rises in my throat, and I swallow it down until my stomach feels heavy with it.

I'm running my arm along the beads of moisture collecting at the corners of my eyes when the front door swings open. Mom, Dad, and Livvy crowd in, talking and laughing until they come to the hall where we are. They look between Foster and I with raised eyebrows and come to some horrifying conclusion, apparently.

"What is going on here?" Dad's glowering where he stands, his eyebrows raised so high that there are wrinkles past his hairline. Livvy scans the scene with an impressed smirk. Mom cocks one eyebrow, hand on her hip.

My parents' gazes take in my shorts and loose T-shirt. I have a feeling my choice of pajamas isn't doing much to help my cause. Apparently, being comfortable is a crime now too.

"I know this looks bad, but a little trust right now would be great."

Livvy makes a choking sound, silently laughing into her hands. Of course, she thinks this is hilarious. Mom and Dad ignore her and continue to stare between Foster and me. I guess they're waiting for some mind-blowing explanation, but all I have is the truth.

"We fell asleep last night watching a movie before Foster could take me to Carolina's. This was a complete accident, and now—" I raise a shaky finger and jab it at Foster. "He's trying to run away again."

Their heads turn to him, and he squares his shoulders and bows his head. "My brother and I worked things out. I think this will be good for us. But I'm glad I get the chance to say goodbye to you guys."

Mom sucks on her bottom lip and slips an arm through mine. "Honey, it's his choice."

I shake my head. "No." Trying to win this argument is like climbing up a mountain of loose sand. It's pointless and exhausting. My heart pounds in my chest. I look around, hoping someone will take my side, but Dad and Livvy avoid my gaze. "No," I repeat.

Foster swings his backpack over one shoulder and tugs on the strap with his other hand. Then he looks at me. Really looks at me. For just a few seconds, it's like everything else fades away. My family disappears, and the beach house transforms, and we're back on the beach together with nothing but the sculpting contest before us. If I close my eyes, I'll smell the ocean and feel his arms around me, taste his lips burning against mine.

With a slight jerk of his head, the moment ends, and all my delusions are shattered.

He moves toward the door and nods at my parents. Mom hugs him and slips something into his hand, maybe money. "You've always got a place here, if you change your mind."

Dad slaps him on the back. "Good luck to you, Foster. Make sure you call us if you need anything, alright?"

Foster's eyes go squinty and red as he passes through the front door. "Thank you. I'll miss your family a lot."

I squeeze my eyes shut so I can pretend he's talking to me and only me.

Dad shuts the door behind him. The click hangs in the silence.

My legs propel me past them to follow Foster, but Mom catches my arm as I'm grabbing the doorknob. "Maybe it's for the best if we let him go. He deserves a chance at family again."

I tilt my head. She doesn't get it. None of them do.

"*We* were his family, Mom. We're still supposed to be."

My head swivels as they each avoid my drawn mouth and wide eyes. Don't they see the mistake they're making? I claw at the door again, and Dad grabs me this time. Time freezes as I pull away from the door and push past Livvy and Dad toward my bedroom. My feet are lead as I fall onto my bed, crashing facedown into the cool fabric of my pillowcase. Dad follows me, planting himself in my doorway, his forehead deeply furrowed. I stare past him until he's replaced by empty space, and then I lie in bed and pretend none of it happened.

THIRTY-TWO

To whom it may concern on the Flagler admittance board:

This summer, my grandfather died. He was my first and biggest cheerleader when it came to my art. It's because of him that I first became interested in enrolling at Flagler College. I've always been inspired by artists who break the rules, use new mediums, and turn the definition of art on its head. Thanks to my grandfather, I was able to step outside of my safe version of art and become immersed in something new: sand-sculpting.

At first when my grandfather left me with an application for the sand-sculpting contest, I was nervous about such an unconventional medium. I've always seen myself as a sketch artist, maybe a painter, but sculpting never crossed my radar. Almost as soon as I began working with sand, I started to feel like a true artist for the first time.

This summer has changed me in more ways than one, but most importantly, it's proven to me that art can be found anywhere, in many different forms. I hope to pursue sculpting as a future career, thanks to my experience with sculpting sand. I would be honored to study at Flagler College and continue to learn in the place where I first dreamt of being an artist.

. . .

Sincerely,
Claire Haynes

Mom tries to talk to me after a few days, but I still can't bring myself to say anything about what happened. She and Dad take turns hovering in my open doorway, their mouths pinched as I type away at my essay and prepare for my interview.

Today, her shadow covers the floor as I work. "Claire, baby, we're here to talk if you need to vent. I know you're upset, but we're here for you. We love you."

I glance up, and she offers me a smile. I look away again. *Tap. Tap. Tap.* I'll wear out the keys on my computer before I talk to my parents about what happened. Venting is for people who are mostly happy. People who have hope. I don't have anything except another scar from someone I love abandoning me.

"Are you going to keep ignoring me?"

Mom's hands are on her hips now, and her tone is no longer sweet and pleading. I didn't sign up for another fight, so I shrug. She stares me down until I feel compelled to say something to end the harassment.

I drop my hands. "Mom, I don't want to talk about it, okay? Please. Just give me time to be upset." My voice is scratchy from underuse.

She lowers her gaze and moves like she might walk away. But instead, she marches over to my bed and sits beside me. It's impossible to squirm away when she puts her soft hands over mine like some sort of gentle trap. I sigh and give into her gesture.

"I'm your mom. I can't just let you be upset. I need to feel like I'm helping you." She gazes at me while continuing to pat my hand. It's ridiculous, but I can already feel some of the weight I've hung on to slip away.

"Foster's in trouble."

Her eyebrows raise, and she moves her hand in a circular motion in the air, gesturing that I should keep talking. I close my eyes and tilt my head back. I'm trying to think of the right words to describe how I'm feeling without breaking down and letting her see how I really am doing. Letting my mom in a little bit is okay, but letting her in completely just can't happen.

"His brother is just going to hurt him again, but I guess Foster wants to give him another chance. He basically chose him over me, and that makes me feel..." I can't finish the sentence without getting throaty and red-eyed. Thankfully, Mom doesn't push it and nods her way through the silence of my unfinished sentence. "I understand."

And I don't know if she really does, but it's nice of her to say. Even better is the fact that she's letting me talk without interjecting a helpful suggestion every other sentence.

"Thanks for letting me vent."

"Sure." Her eyebrows tug down. "I just wonder..."

I should stop her. I'm not sure either of us want to know the answer to her question. But for some reason I let her keep musing.

"I wonder how Child Protective Services knew where he was. It's not like they're the FBI. If it wasn't Johnny who told..."

We stare across from each other for a beat before either of us speaks again. Now that the mystery has been planted in my head, I don't know how to shake it out. And the more I think about it, the guilty party has to be someone close to home.

Someone in my family told CPS where Foster was.

Mom arrives at the same infuriating conclusion I do. Maybe

we're thinking of the same person, because she won't meet my eyes anymore.

"Mom."

"Hm?" She's tapping her fingers on the wooden footrest of my bed so quickly that I feel like we're trapped in an episode of the Twilight Zone just before the twist at the end. Before things turn awful.

"Mom, look at me." My voice is thick. She's been staring at an empty spot on the wall, but she inches her face around toward me. I can't handle the suspense any longer, so I burst the bubble in one fell swoop.

"I'm sorry. But I deserve to know, Mom. Did either of you tip CPS off about Foster? Were you guys trying to get rid of him?"

"The truth is, Claire, I don't know about Dad, but it wasn't me."

My stomach sinks. She wouldn't lie to me, even if it were to protect Dad. I have to believe she's telling the truth, which means I can't heap blame on my parents just yet—no matter how badly I want to right now.

Her moment of hesitation speaks just as clearly as her words do. "Your dad and I had a conversation after Johnny paid his first visit to the house. About how we could make sure everyone was safe. And Dad mentioned letting the authorities handle it, but we never made a final decision."

I bite my lip and nod. I can picture it now. He pretended to be okay with Foster's past but he was secretly scheming. Dad has been the more reluctant one from the start when it came to Foster living here. I'd been too blissed out earlier this summer to notice anyone else's doubts about Foster and me. In retrospect, maybe I should have listened. If I had, I wouldn't be spending the rest of summer break weighed down in heartbreak. Mom sighs and throws her hands up in the air in front of her. They fall to her face and cradle it.

"We both like Foster a whole lot. But it wouldn't surprise me if Dad would go to questionable lengths to make sure you girls are safe. He'd do anything to protect you two, you know?"

I narrow my eyes. Not out of anger anymore, but an aching wound. The deepest and rawest betrayal comes from those you trust the most. I know my dad wants the best for me, but can something that wounds this deeply really be the best thing?

"He would risk Foster's safety and my trust just because of one measly visit from Johnny?"

Mom leans against me, and her hands go around my neck. My arms hang limply at my sides. "I don't know that. I shouldn't have even said anything. We don't know anything for sure. But, if he did, try to understand where he's coming from. Where we're both coming from."

I try to understand. I take the next few minutes of silence to work through the myriad of emotions this revelation brings. My parents' near stifling love. How Foster leaving was ultimately his choice. It all hurts. And I'm left with this hollow chest. A heart beating along as each day passes, but nothing to fill it.

———

Carolina and I meet the next day for some serious research before the interviews with Flagler. Outside of the contest, we both have scheduled interviews as the next step in our application process. The second round is different from the qualifying round in that we won't have the chance to plan a project in advance. Instead, teams are assigned a project idea and are expected to come up with something creative in the given time frame. There's a lot more pressure. And this time I'm doing it alone.

When I get to Guava Guava for breakfast, Carolina is running late. I sit down and pull out a notebook to sketch with. When someone slides across from me in the booth, my eyes don't even lift to greet her as I furiously scribble the last of my idea. Carolina understands being lost in a creative moment, so I know she isn't offended.

Except when I look up, it isn't Carolina.

Livvy is hovering over the seat, crouching into it but not really sitting. She's positioned in a way that makes it easy to escape. Her big eyes are swimming with tears that she's trying to silently choke back.

I stare at her. "What are you doing here?" Livvy's always finding some new way to corner me.

"It's my fault," she says. It sounds like she's choking as she spills out the words. "I called CPS about Foster. I heard you talking to Mom. I was mad. At you for leaving me out of everything with Opa. And at Mom and Dad for smothering me until I snapped. Just mad at everyone, okay? But I'm really sorry. I know that doesn't make a difference now, but I'm so sorry."

"You? *You* called them?" The words are so soft I'm sure only I can hear them. I should be screaming at her. Where's all that rage from yesterday when I thought Dad was the one who turned Foster in?

She sniffles. "It was weeks ago, before I even really knew him."

Somewhere behind us the restaurant's phone rings. The family in the booth next to us laughs as their baby blows spit bubbles and widens her own eyes in surprise.

I look anywhere and everywhere but at Livvy. I'm numb. I can't even tell if it's because I'm that angry or if I don't care anymore.

She slips a sticky note from her pocket and slides it across the table. It's a seashell sticky note from Opa's desk. He used to leave them around the beach house all summer with notes like, "Going out for a morning walk. Be back after sunrise." or "Headed to the grocery store. Call me if you need ingredients." He'd stick them in the most bizarre places, like on the lid of the guest toilet seat or on a spoon in the silverware drawer to make sure we saw them before eating, or peeing.

"I don't have time for this. I have an interview to get ready for." I stand and walk toward the door, Livvy's note clutched in one hand. Blood pounds in my ears. I'll have to text Carolina and cancel because I can't meet her like this. *Don't look back at Livvy*, I tell myself. *She just wants attention, but she doesn't deserve it.*

My eyes focus on my sister anyway. Livvy watches me with wide, wet eyes. She hunches over the table like she's trying to recover from a nasty hit. She shouldn't look so devastated. I'm the one she hurt. Still, the image of my little sister sobbing alone in my favorite restaurant blinks across my brain until it's stamped there in permanent ink.

I don't unfold the sticky note until I reach my car. I expect some type of apology, but there's none. Scribbled in purple glitter pen in wide precise letters is a street name and number. Under that is Foster's name. I watch Livvy leave Guava Guava and walk alone down the street toward home, head down. I drive past her to the beach house, my vision blurring.

THIRTY-THREE

I smooth my sweaty hands over the hem of my black skirt for the tenth time in just under five minutes. I sit alone in an oversized office lobby in tight, unforgiving clothes. Last night, Mom told me she would help me pick something to wear for my interview, but her help consisted of her pointing to a pencil skirt and a gauzy blouse with an and-this-is-final look. There was a receptionist sitting at the desk when I first walked into the room, but he disappeared just a minute after I took my seat. I slip my phone from my bag, where I have it hidden and silenced, to check the time. It's two minutes past the official slot for my interview, but I feel like I've been waiting hours.

"Claire?" The receptionist reappears from literally nowhere. Apparently, he shares a skill set with my sister. He stands behind me and points to a door near the back.

Great. They've filled all the spots, and they've decided to do us all a favor and kick me out right away. I stand and trudge toward the door, avoiding the receptionist's gaze and wide smile. It's annoying to be smiled at so much. Everything is getting on my nerves all of a sudden; it's difficult to hold a smile of my own when I'm on the verge of a defining moment like this one.

"They had to switch interview rooms because the air conditioning went out on this side of the building," he says as he speed-walks ahead of me, arms pumping wildly by his sides.

A different room? Is that all? At least I have an excuse for my melty appearance, even though I'm still not sure my sweat is from anything other than awful nerves. I scamper behind him and practice taking breaths like a normal human being. In and out, or something like that. It's hard to think clearly about anything when I'm so aware of the fact that the next fifteen to twenty minutes will define the rest of my life. *Please don't epically fail, Claire.*

The receptionist points to a door at the end of the hall, and I pause outside of it. He disappears back down the hall and leaves me standing alone, one hand hovering over the door knob. Deep breaths, shoulders back. Don't mess this up.

I turn the knob and sail into a room so small it's almost ridiculous. Three judges, two women and one man, sit at a long table along the back wall. In front of them is one lone chair. I tell myself to stop stalling and walk to the chair.

The judge in the middle, the youngest woman of the group, calls my name. "Claire? How are you?" She nods toward the chair, and I sit.

"I'm doing well, thank you." The words sound too stuffy in my mouth. Even as I say them, I wonder if I'm saying them wrong. Words are hard when they're worth everything.

The man speaks next. "Please start by telling us about yourself."

I smile automatically. In my brain, I'm chanting the memorized responses I've practiced all summer long. *I'm an artist who enjoys working with all mediums. I love spending time with my family. This is my dream school, and I would consider it a great honor to attend classes here.* But when I open my mouth, none of those words come out.

"My family and I come to the beach every summer." I focus on the youngest woman, who winks at me encouragingly. I take a deep breath. "This summer I entered the sand art contest because of my grandfather, even though I didn't want to at first." I pause to deliver a wry smile. Each of the judges smiles back. The older woman raises her eyebrows, in disapproval or interest, I can't tell. "And, I didn't expect to, but I fell in love with sand as a medium. I realized I love art in almost every medium. And then I fell in love with a boy who also loves art and who helped me see the world in a new way. Challenging myself by learning something new was the best decision I've made. If I'm admitted to the art program, I look forward to challenging myself more and working with more new mediums. I want to be an artist in every sense possible." I clasp my hands in my lap and await more questions. None come.

All three judges ignore me and scribble on their notepads. Then the young one nods and claps her hands. "I'm satisfied," she says. "What about the rest of us?" She turns to look at her friends, who both shrug.

The man chuckles slightly. "Well, what about the boy? The artist who showed you more of the world?"

I blink at them and feel flustered again. The ladies nod and look to me for an answer. "Um, ha. Well, this isn't part of the interview, right?"

The young interviewer smiles kindly. "Just a personal question, if you don't mind."

I nod. It's actually very personal, but I don't want to upset these powerful adults. "It didn't work out. Um, romantically speaking, it didn't work out. But we still keep in touch. It's, um, kind of complicated."

Wow. Where did the girl who just delivered that amazing interview answer run off to? Way to make an awkward question even worse by butchering it.

"That's too bad," says the older woman. The younger nods sympathetically. The man, who seemed so interested moments ago, shrugs and says nothing. They stand one by one, and I do the same.

The man taps my resume and cover letter and nods. "Good stuff right here. You'll be hearing from us soon, I think." The two women glance at him and then roll their eyes at each other before smiling at me.

"It's been a pleasure," the youngest says.

I bob my head up and down until I feel dizzy from the effort. "Yes, thank you. Thank you all very much." I walk out of the room exhausted. A seed of hope wriggles its way into existence.

But as I exit the building and find my car, the man's voice rings in my ears. *What about the boy?*

THIRTY-FOUR

The family gift shop is only open until noon on Fridays, but I stop by at 12:30 anyway. I know there's a good chance my parents will still be there, taking inventory or helping a last-minute customer. I ignore the "We're Closed" sign, push open the door, and walk to the back. Mom and Dad are sitting back-to-back in a pile of inventory sheets and receipts scrawled over in the world's tiniest handwriting.

"Is this Opa's stuff?" The only explanation for why they would deal with this level of chaos is that it must be inherited.

Mom groans and pushes herself to her feet. "Yes. Your grandfather was never a packrat, but apparently he was an overzealous bookkeeper."

Dad nods and stretches his hands behind his back before grabbing another stack of papers. "We've been sifting through everything all summer. The worst part is it's almost impossible to tell what's actually important and what's just random notes and lists."

They exchange a look and shake their heads. The sight of the hundreds—maybe thousands—of documents makes me grateful I decided against working here this summer. I'd have been stuck behind the counter, reading grocery lists instead of honing my art skills.

"This is crazy," I say. It's insufficient, but they agree with me.

"So, what are you doing here? I thought you were spending all your time at the beach, getting ready for your big contest." Dad tilts his head, anticipating the worst, I'm sure.

I nod. That's exactly where I should be, but I've got something else on my mind. Something I'm pretty sure my parents will not be excited about.

"I need to see Foster."

Dad leans against a shelf and looks at Mom. They do that thing where they somehow silently communicate without either of them moving a muscle. It never fails to impress and mystify me. This time I hope it also works in my favor.

Mom exhales and turns back to me. "You can't go alone," she says.

I swallow my excitement and agree. "Yeah, totally, but what if I take Carolina and we make it a road trip?" The phrase "road trip" does nothing for my case, and I bite my lip as soon as the words leave my mouth. Mom and Dad both narrow their eyes at me. I shake my head. "A speed-limit-driving, singular-purpose, there-and-back kind of trip." And magically, they agree, as long as Carolina can come with me.

———

"Please, please, please." I hate begging, but if it gets Carolina to agree to come with me, it's worth it. She rolls her eyes so hard I almost get dizzy.

"Fine. But I'm picking the music, and I'm not sticking around to watch you stick your tongue down Foster's throat, okay?"

I wrinkle my nose. "That won't happen," I say. "This is not that kind of trip, I promise."

Carolina pulls her hair over one shoulder, running it through her hands. She levels a hard look at me, lips pinched. "He's lied to you a lot, you know. Are you sure you even want to get back together with him? If you say he's nice, I believe you. But I worry he's going to hurt you *again*."

I blow out a breath. "He has legit reasons for keeping secrets, but if he wants to get back together in the future, I'm not going to make it easy on him. Right now, I just need to see him. Nothing else is going to happen."

She rolls her eyes again, but this time she smiles. "Whatever. Fine. I'll come."

———

We leave early the next morning. The sun isn't even up yet, and the air has a rare chill to it. After kissing my parents goodbye and swearing on my nonexistent art career that I'll be careful, I pad out to the car in my grey Flagler sweatshirt, the one Opa bought me a few years ago. As I'm programming my phone GPS with the address Livvy gave me, my sister appears at the passenger door. She waves through the window, her eyes still red from last night and her hair an uncharacteristically frizzy disaster. Did she even sleep?

I don't wave back. She pulls the handle and opens the door just a few inches. Her voice is raspy. "Mind if I come too? Dad says it's up to you."

I stare back at her through the crack in the car door, blank-faced and thin-lipped. "You can't come."

Her face falls. She bows her head and looks away like she's going to leave. Then, softer than before: "Please?"

She's crying again, but her hands are covering her eyes.

They're red and wet, just visible between her fingers. I'm never going to speak to her again. She blinks at me through the window. Like I'm supposed to take pity on her. Like she even deserves it. Even Dad knows this is one thing Liv won't be able to talk her way out of. Last night when I finally told my parents why I've been refusing to be in the same room as her, Dad didn't even try to convince me to be nice to her. Because it's obvious to everyone who isn't Livvy that she's really messed up this time. You can't just come back from this kind of betrayal.

"Claire, please. Let me come with you. I want to make it up to you."

My eye twitches at her whispered pleading, so reminiscent of our childhood. When we were littler, she would beg to be invited to play with me and my friends from the neighborhood. We would stick our tongues out at her as we clutched our Barbie dolls close and ran away, faster than her small feet could carry her. She's always been tough, and she didn't usually let it bother her. But sometimes the sting of being the baby sister was too much and she'd burst into tears. One time, she'd been so upset by our teasing that she had collapsed into a tear-filled puddle on the sidewalk. I'd shushed my friends with my best withering look, inherited from Mom. After they scampered away, I let Liv hold my mermaid Barbie she'd been eyeing all year and we sat in the backyard together eating cookies from the package. After that I tried to include her more often, and my friends stopped teasing her as much.

But that closeness all stopped as soon as Liv decided she was cooler than me. Now here she is, falling apart again because I'm not including her. I don't owe her anything, not after what she did, but whatever genetic force prompted me to share my dolls years ago nudges me now.

"Fine. You can come, but you have to ride in the back. Carolina already has dibs on the front seat." I point my thumb to the backseat. Livvy stops sniffling and nods eagerly. She opens the door and climbs in. Our eyes meet when I glance in the rearview mirror, and she flashes me a hesitant grin. I give her a half-grimace, half-smile. I can't pretend I'm happy with her, but I am strangely not mad she's coming along.

After we pick up Carolina, I almost run over a group of surfers walking to the beach with their surfboards held up high over their heads. Surfing obviously reminds me of Foster, and I wonder how he's holding up in Alabama with no beaches and no waves.

Carolina keeps her promise to be our deejay and starts blasting a mix from her phone the minute I pick her up. I'm more of a Taylor Swift kind of girl, and Carolina's taste is so eclectic it doesn't make sense, but the beat fills the morning silence well and pumps us up for the long drive ahead. Mom insisted on packing snacks, so we have a full cooler in the back and we won't need to stop for food if we don't want to. I'm surprised it's all coming together so well, but I'm nervous about seeing Foster again. Above all else, I'm terrified he'll be angry at me for going all this way to see him. When he walked away from me that morning, he kind of made it clear he wasn't interested in anything else happening between us.

Carolina turns the volume down to a whisper and eyes me. "Can we talk about the real reason we're driving six hours down the interstate?"

Livvy says nothing, and I don't look at either of them. I face forward and keep my gaze on the road in front of me. My heartbeat echoes in my ears. If I inhale too deeply, my car smells like Foster: coconut shampoo mixed with just the right amount of sweat so it's not gross.

"I just need to see him."

And that's it. There's no driving reason for me to drop everything and see Foster immediately. Except for the fact that I still think he made a huge mistake leaving Florida—leaving *me*. And my interview with the admission board from Flagler reminded me of how important art is not only to me, but to Foster as well. Maybe I'm not his girlfriend, but I feel a sense of responsibility for him. He doesn't have anyone else to propel him forward, so it has to be me.

Carolina clicks her tongue but says nothing else. She doesn't have to because her judgment fills the silence.

Livvy's gazing out the window. I have to lean back and hold my breath to even hear her when she starts speaking. "I broke up with Evan."

Carolina raises her eyebrows and nods. I chew on the inside of my cheek. I had no idea. But I've spent most of the summer avoiding my sister, so I guess I shouldn't be surprised.

She's watching me now, waiting for a reaction.

"Sorry it didn't work out, Liv."

We both know I'm not really sorry, but I've been through enough this summer to know it's what she needs to hear. We drive without conversation, just the incredibly loud dubstep now blaring from Carolina's phone. I don't know what Foster will say when I appear at his new house or how I'll convince him to come back to Florida where he belongs. But if he doesn't listen to me, if he stays with Johnny...

Livvy's moved on from her summer fling, maybe I'm supposed to do the same.

The landmarks on either side of the road blur into one another. I've never been able to focus on the individual signs and billboards for long without getting a headache. But all the sudden something familiar catches my eye.

"Livvy, do you remember the summer Opa brought us here?"

I point to the sign and slow as we pass it. The only other car on the road honks and swerves into the other lane to pass us.

Grandma's Treasure Trove. The miniature billboard with loopy cursive letters hovers over a building so small it could be called a shack if it wasn't decorated so well. Wooden boxes filled with wildflowers line the rickety porch like gumdrops dotting a gingerbread house at Christmas. Yellow trims the door and the window boxes and round stepping stones lead up to the entrance in a whimsical trail.

"Aw. It's that little antique store. I totally forgot about that." Livvy clasps her hands under her chin and pouts her bottom lip.

"He let both of us pick out one thing, and we both picked those homemade bath bombs they had at the front counter. Oh my gosh—so relaxing, do you remember?"

Livvy's beaming, and it gives me a warm feeling deep in my stomach.

No one speaks for a minute. Carolina looks out the passenger window and drums her fingers on the armrest in rhythm with the music blaring from her phone's speakers. I stare straight ahead and tighten my hands on the steering wheel. We're passing through middle-of- nowhere, Florida. We've been stuck on back roads and small towns with nothing much to see for hours now, with no sign of anything interesting appearing anytime soon. The tiny main streets with cafe signs and cotton fields are cool for the first little bit, but after a while, they all start to look the same.

As soon as we cross the state line, we pass a sign for the world's largest peanut statue, and Livvy and I both point to it at the same time. We laugh, and the corners of her eyes fade into her cheeks when she smiles. "How big do you think we're talking here? I mean, how many statues of peanuts can actually exist in the world?"

I shake my head at the thought of anyone making art centering around peanuts, but then again, I never thought before this summer that my medium of choice would be freshly packed sand. "Have you ever been to Alabama?"

Carolina shakes her head firmly. "Nope. I never thought I would either. But it's kind of fun, right? Sweet Home Alabama and all that." I nod. Leave it to Carolina to make travelling one state over a big adventure.

"Why are we really going, Claire?" Carolina turns to watch me while I fumble for an answer. "Because, like I said, I'm not dumb. I'm here, so you might as well tell me why you decided to run off to see Foster, if it's not to beg him to take you back."

I click my tongue against the roof of my mouth. "I don't think Johnny really cares about Foster, but I swear that's why I'm going. I just want to help him."

Carolina groans. "Just promise not to let Foster break your heart again. I'm not sure we can deal with that."

I shoot her a sideways glare.

"Seriously, though. I liked you two together. I just don't know if he's capable of being in a healthy relationship with all his family stuff going on. But, I'll admit, you're a cute couple." She glances at Livvy, who shrugs.

I shake my head. "Look how that turned out. I'm too scared to even tell him we're coming because he'll probably tell me not to bother." Turning my head away from them both, I grimace briefly.

"I'm just going to warn Foster, and then I'll let the two of them work it out." I say it with so much confidence that I almost convince myself it's what is happening here.

"Is that why we came all the way to Alabama? So, you could tell him something easily explained over the phone?" Livvy leans forward, her voice sharp.

"You gave me the address, Liv. What did you think we were doing?" It takes all my concentration to not snarl at her. I'm working on forgiving her, but it's hard to forget how much damage her stunt did.

She lifts her shoulders, unfazed. "If you seriously believe the only reason we're driving this many miles is so you can tell him something he already knows, you're delusional." She shakes her head. "Stop lying to yourself."

Hot shame peppers my face. Livvy's known me my whole life, so of course she sees through me. Sees through what I don't dare admit out loud. I curl and uncurl my fingers against the steering wheel. My teeth grit in my mouth until I taste chalky bone.

"I just miss him," I say finally.

Livvy and Carolina are silent, but I press my foot harder onto the gas pedal. *Hurry.* The sooner we get there, the sooner I can ease the cracking, dying thing in my chest.

THIRTY-FIVE

When we pull up to the address Livvy gave me, I can't move. My brain refuses to send the signal to my legs to work and get me out of the car.

"Why did we come here? This was such a bad idea."

I stare at the steering wheel as spinning dots pepper my vision. My stomach lurches like I might vomit any second, and I clutch a hand to my mouth. Carolina makes an annoyed sound and steps out of the car to stretch her legs. I open my door, but I don't join her yet.

She glances at me over her shoulder. "It was a terrible idea, but we just drove six hours and Foster already knows we're here, so get out of the car before I kill you."

I check the back, where Livvy is sleeping under a blanket of her own luxurious hair. I glance up at the trailer and see Foster standing in the doorway. His face is wrinkled up in supreme confusion. I think I see a hint of a smile playing on his lips, but I tell myself to ignore it. Absolutely ignore it. We're not here for some sort of happy reunion. This is strictly business. And that means getting out of the car, doing what I came to do, and ignoring the hopeful feelings bubbling up in me. I definitely need to swallow those feelings and just get it over with. I walk toward the door with Carolina hanging back. She whispers something about tough love and handling things on my own. I glance behind me and see she's retreated back to the car and is now pretending to hide from me in the comfort of the passenger seat. I deserve it for being such a scaredy-cat.

Foster blinks at me, his eyebrows twisted. "This isn't what I expected when I gave your sister my address."

I want to step close enough to close the gap between us. I want to touch his floppy blond hair and feel his warm sun-kissed skin under my hands. But I force a laugh instead.

"Yeah, sorry for just showing up like this, but your cell provider said your number was disconnected."

The muscles in his jaw tighten, and for a moment, I think he's going to start yelling at me for some reason. Then his face relaxes, and he nods his head in Carolina's direction.

"She still hates me?"

I smirk. "She's warming up to you, I think. But she mostly just came along for moral support."

He stands on his toes to inspect the inside of my vehicle. "And your sister is here?" He arches an eyebrow. He's wondering, I'm sure, what on earth could have prompted the three of us to drive this many miles together.

We stand in painful silence for another minute. My skin prickles at the memory of him. My hands still ache to reach out and touch him. I stare at the ground, at my feet, at the long, scraggly weeds sprouting up in every part of the yard. Foster directs his gaze at the air above my head and doesn't waver until I clear my throat.

"So," I say, "the reason I drove all the way here is to tell you something I thought of while I was at home trying to forget about you." My wry smile doesn't do much to cut the severity of my words.

The word "home" makes both us of twitch. Me because the beach is only my home part of the year and him...why does he? Because he knows it's where he should be? I can only hope.

"Oh yeah?" He sighs and bites his lip.

But his offhand tone isn't fooling me. I nod. "Yes. I drove all this way because you need to hear someone tell you you're wrong."

"I'm wrong?"

"Yes. You're wrong if you think coming here and giving up is the right thing to do. You could have fought harder or told someone else about your brother. But you decided to run away with him instead, leaving behind your possible art career. Because it's easier. Do you care about your future at all?"

I shift my feet as I wait for him to process what I've said.

"You think I should come back to Florida? And just finish out the sand sculpting competition tomorrow? Like it's that easy."

All of the hesitation is gone from his voice, and it's the first real glimpse of Foster I've seen since we got here. He's stronger, filled with something like anger but with more purpose. I'm almost happy, but his words are all wrong. I pause and wrap my arms around myself. I'm not scared of much, but confrontation is my kryptonite.

Foster moves his arm like he might put it around me, but then our eyes meet. He steps back and shoves his hands into his pockets. "If this is about the contest, I'll take care of it, don't worry. I'll call Flagler and explain that I bailed on you."

I step back too. My lips tug down. My eyes burn, threatening tears.

"I don't need you to save me, Foster. I'm worried for *you*." I can feel my cheeks burning red because it never occurred to me that Foster would think I drove all this way to beg him to take care of me. The idea of him thinking of me as weak and helpless burns through me with a mixture of embarrassment and scarlet shame. I shake my head and turn away from him and the front porch.

"Never mind. I came to tell you what I think, but I can't make your decisions for you. If you want to stay here and hide behind your white-knight status, that's up to you."

He waits a long beat before exploding. "Are you serious? You honestly think that's what I meant? I just want to help. It's the least I can do after taking off with no warning and dropping out of the contest."

I shrug, my mouth tight. I can't listen to any more of whatever he has to say. My whole body aches with the energy it takes to stand in front of him after he broke my heart for the second time in one summer. I'm slowly poisoning myself even being in his presence. I need to let go.

"It doesn't matter anymore." I lift a hand to wave goodbye as I walk down the porch steps toward the car. This has to have been the worst idea I've had. And I've done a lot of dumb things this summer.

Foster's steps sound behind me, but I keep my back to him.

"Claire, if you think I see you as someone who needs saving, you're crazy."

I frown. More insults from him isn't really what I expected. He lets loose a low groan. He obviously knows he's not making things better.

"You're the one who's been saving me all summer. You convinced your parents to let me sleep at your house, you tried to stand up to my brother, and you shared your art with me. I owe you everything."

I cross my arms in front of my chest, but I still turn to face him. I inhale, searching for a response that makes sense. I look back at Carolina and see Livvy next to her, blinking like she's just been elbowed awake. They stare me down expectantly.

And even though there are people around us and so many unanswered things still hanging between us, it feels like the right time to tell Foster what I've been building up to all summer. If anything will change his mind, these words can.

"Foster, I lo—"

A booming sound from behind us drowns out my words. Someone is yelling now. I twirl to find the culprit and so does Foster. The yelling is coming from inside the trailer.

And everything gets worse from there.

THIRTY-SIX

The trailer door bangs open, and Johnny appears in the doorway. The flimsy black metal door shakes as it slowly swings back toward its proper place. Johnny catches it in his hand before it hits him. Foster quickly turns toward his brother just as I take a leap backward.

"Get off my property!"

I recognize the words as the same he was yelling seconds earlier, now that the sound is no longer muffled by the door. I look at Foster to see if he'll speak up for me, but he's wide-eyed and silent. Carolina and Livvy are both ready at their respective car doors, hands poised to push themselves out and toward us if need be. I don't want this to turn into some sort of backcountry brawl, though. I just want Foster to come back with us.

I turn to Johnny, who's a bigger, older, and meaner version of Foster. They share the same bright blue eyes, tall stance, and shaggy hair, but knowing what I do about the two of them, my brain refuses to acknowledge the fact.

I swallow. "I'm here to talk to Foster."

Johnny eyes Foster, silently challenging him. "Oh yeah?"

I nod. "Foster belongs in Florida. His whole life is there." I point to my car where Livvy and Carolina wait. "We're his friends. We can take care of him when he gets back. You won't have to worry if he's okay or not."

At my side, Foster makes a throaty coughing noise. Johnny looks between the two of us. His lips pucker. "So you got it all planned out then, huh?"

I ignore him and turn to Foster. Put a hand on his arm and try to block the whole thing out. Because what it really comes down to is the two of us. If I can just get him to forget about his stubborn belief in creating a family with Johnny, he'll remember what matters. Art, love, the Florida sun—which is admittedly the same in Alabama, but without the beach that has such a hold on both of us. I can be his family.

But he won't look at me. He just looks past his brother and me. Johnny smirks, and if it weren't for his hands balled into tight red fists at his sides, I might believe he was actually amused by all of this. By me trying to take Foster away from him.

"We'll take care of him," I say again.

Johnny sneers, distorting his features. "We're family. Whatever you've got can't beat that. The kid doesn't want to go nowhere."

Foster breaks his silence by turning to his brother. "We'll just talk for a minute."

Johnny turns from us and walks inside, slamming the door behind him with a thud that echoes over the ensuing silence between Foster and me. Foster's scared of his brother, but now he can say whatever he wants. I'll find some way to make sure Johnny can't hurt him or manipulate him anymore.

"Do you have everything you need?" I point to the backpack around his shoulders. He must keep it close to him out of habit. He's so used to running he doesn't know how to stop. But once he sees how nice boring, normal life can be, he'll have to settle down. He'll want to.

"No."

I raise an eyebrow. "Are you okay going inside? Do you want me to go in and look for stuff for you?"

Foster sighs. His whole body seems to heave with the weight of the breath he releases. It's got to be hard to leave family behind, no matter how evil they are, so I let him have his moment. Then it's time for tough love.

"Come on," I say. "It's better if we go now. He'll probably be over it by the time we're back in Florida." I nod toward the house, where Johnny is undoubtedly skulking by a window.

Foster shakes his head. He finally meets my eyes with his, which are now a clouded blue-grey. Even before he's opened his mouth, I know what he's going to say.

"I'm staying." He looks at me, eyes wide and begging to be understood. Begging to be forgiven for what he's doing to me *again*.

I can't forgive him, though. After everything his brother has put him through, from never being there when they were growing up to stealing his inheritance to this, how can he choose him over me? Not just over me, but over art school, and over any kind of future. It doesn't make sense. But more than anything, it hurts. I try to inhale, to stabilize myself, but my lungs have suddenly run dry. All I come up with is a heavy groan that vaporizes as soon as it reaches my lips.

"Why are you doing this?" My arms flail helplessly in the air, like I'm trying to grab hold of the wisps of hope that haven't yet evaporated.

Foster catches my wrists. His hands are warm and strong on mine. "This isn't about you."

I blink.

"Not everything is about you, Claire. This isn't another summer activity you can list on your resume, okay? Saving some local boy you found sleeping on the beach might be a good head-line for you, but this is my life."

He's breathing fire, panting, his eyes practically shooting sparks. I open my mouth and close it again, but he's not finished. He's not going to stop until I go.

"It was stupid to think this thing between us could ever work. It was a dream—a nice dream for a few weeks—but this has to stop."

He sticks a shaking finger in my face. "Leave. Please leave."

"You are such a coward, Foster." Now I'm trembling. "You can't pretend this whole summer meant nothing. You can't just throw it all away because you want someone to call family. It doesn't work if he doesn't actually love you!"

A beat passes between us as I'm struck by the full weight of what I've done. In my desperation to convince Foster to choose me, I've said the one thing that will alienate him forever. I've gotten too close to the truth of it all, and in one fell swoop, I've burnt the only tie left between us.

It's over.

He shakes his head, tears swimming in his narrowed eyes, and turns away from me. I watch as he puts one foot after the other—each step another dagger—until he disappears inside the trailer, leaving me standing amongst the weeds.

———

I'm too shell-shocked to drive home, so Carolina volunteers. I think she's been secretly itching to drive anyway because she immediately adjusts the seat, cracks a window, and runs her hands over the steering wheel. I'd roll my eyes if they weren't drowning in tears. I held it together until we drove away from Johnny's trailer, but a second later, the crying started. I may never stop. The drive home feels twice as long. It was late afternoon by the time we left Alabama, so half of the drive is beneath moody night skies. The crisp summer air should make me feel alive, but I'm hazy and sore. Just a shell.

"You're strong enough to move on from this," Carolina says. She pats my shoulder awkwardly. I don't meet her eyes, but I give her a half-nod. I don't feel strong enough for anything. She drives to her house and gets out, promising to text tomorrow to check on me. I assume my place in the driver's seat, but I can't move. We sit in Carolina's driveway for too long, with only the radio playing a song so quietly I can't even make out the lyrics.

Livvy whispers from the back seat. "Let's go home, Claire. We're almost there."

It's meant to be encouraging, I'm sure. But I don't want to be encouraged. I want Foster. And now I'm mad at the world. Or at least I would be mad, if I could feel any emotion at all.

I ignore Livvy's plea to drive and lean back in my seat. "So, I have to ask." My voice is hoarse from choked-back tears. But I've thought about Foster so much in the past hour I can't bring myself to talk about him.

Livvy eyes me, one eyebrow cocked.

"When you told everyone you wanted to marry Evan, was that real, or...?" I let myself trail off because the alternative is too hard to ask out loud. Liv alone at the court house in some cheap white gown. Some awful statistic and legally trapped in a life with a sleaze ball like Evan. My current state of mind isn't the best, but at least I haven't reached that level yet.

"It was a false alarm."

But she's too quiet, her answer too quick. "Really, Liv. What happened?"

I'm still facing away from her, but I hear her shift in her seat. She's probably compulsively tucking her hair behind her ears like she does when she's upset during a conversation. "I lied. I made the whole thing up." She sighs. "I just got tired of

Mom and Dad treating me like a baby, and I figured if they thought I was going to run off with Evan they'd take me seriously."

I frown. "That's the dumbest thing I've ever heard." Maybe now's not the time for complete transparency, but I'm too exhausted to filter. "Seriously, that's so bad, Liv."

She shrugs. "I know. Mom and Dad are never going to trust anything I say ever again. They've already planned out the rest of my life at this point."

I force a smile. Livvy's not as unbreakable as she would have us all think. "I thought the hardest thing we'd have to deal with this summer was losing Opa," I say, my voice cracking as I think back to the first day at the beach house.

There's silence, and I think the sharing might be over, but Livvy surprises me again. "I miss him too, Claire. Opa, I mean."

Something catches in my throat. I've been so busy chasing other people this summer that I've forgotten to remember Opa the way I planned. Something brushes my arm, Livvy reaching toward me from the backseat. She rubs the inside of my arm in soft strokes for a few seconds until the lump in my throat subsides and my eyes clear. It's something Mom would do. Neither of us say so, but Opa would have loved to see the two of us getting along, united in thinking about him.

THIRTY-SEVEN

The next morning I drop Livvy off at the beach before meeting Carolina for a pre-competition breakfast. I half-expect Livvy to saunter over to Evan, even though she said they broke up. But as I sit and watch from the car, she wanders over to a shaded spot with one of the wide umbrellas and lies down in the sand, sunglasses slipped over her eyes. She's changing, that's for sure. A bit of sisterly pride washes over me while I spy on her, lounging on the shore like nothing's bothering her while her ex-boyfriend's eyes roam the beach.

I've always wished for a little more of my sister's attitude, but I could use it right now more than ever. Sure, it gets her into trouble a whole lot more than I'd like. But it also gives her resilience and a fire I'd kill for. Also, her hair. I was actually kind of pleased with the way mine was growing out, with little wispy curls that frame my face. But then a little girl at Guava Guava stage-whispered to her mom that I had hair just like her older brother. Carolina snorted into her smoothie with such force that she had orange/mango-flavored stuff coming out of her nose for the next five minutes.

So maybe I'll never have hair like Livvy, but if I could just channel some of her I-couldn't-care-less-what-anyone-says attitude, that would be nice. It's getting harder by the hour to pretend that I'm not devastated by Foster's betrayal. Even though he texted me from his new phone number late last night, it still feels really, truly final this time. No "Sorry you came all the way up here for nothing" text from a new number is going to change anything. If he was really sorry, he'd be here, not with his donkey-face brother.

Carolina smirks when she sees me. "Are you ready for this?" She wiggles her eyebrows, and I laugh.

The truth is I don't know if I'm ready. But the fact that I've made it here to the end of the summer and the final competition is kind of a miracle. Between the drama with Livvy, grief over Opa, and all of the baggage I'm carrying around from my failed relationship with Foster, the past few months have been exhausting. I've barely had time to remember why I joined the contest in the first place. It wasn't even about the scholarship money or the interview to Flagler. It was Opa. I guess he knew what he was doing. I started out convinced the contest would help me find the closure I needed, and it did in a way.

But then I met Foster, and I fell in love for the first time. It turns out love sucks just as much as everyone says it does. And even though Livvy is still as wild as she was at the beginning of the summer, I think we're making progress. We're at least talking again.

Carolina taps her fingers on the table, signaling that she wants me to order so she can eat already. I glance at the calm blue waves and the pink morning sunrise outside the restaurant's windows.

"I'm ready," I say.

———

"In Three. Two. ONE!"

A judge in a white polo shirt embellished with the Flagler logo blows into the whistle hanging from his neck. I watch him seconds after the whistle sounds and everyone else around me starts to run to and from the water to fill buckets. If you would have asked me in May what kind of artist I wanted to be, I would have quickly walked you through the history of sketching, the pros and cons of sketching with pencil and pen, and a thousand other boring and useless facts. Useless now because sketching is no longer what drives me. Sculpting, specifically sculpting with sand, is where I feel most at home in the art world. It's why I have to win the competition. The scholarship money would be nice, but I belong at the beach now more than ever. Turns out Opa was right. If I'm going to go to art school after high-school graduation, I want to do it right. And that means securing a spot at Flagler for the next year.

"CLAIRE!"

Carolina's shrill screech snaps me back to the present. I quickly turn away from the judge, who's eyeing me with pursed lips, and face Carolina's death glare. "Sorry."

She points to the row of empty buckets we lined up in preparation and thrusts one into my hands. I shake my head quickly and sprint to the ocean, where all the other teams are also gathering water to pack their sand. It's common for there to be a daily afternoon thunderstorm in the Florida summers, but this week has been unusually dry, which means the miniscule white sand crystals slip through my fingers and crumble when molded. If I don't mix enough water into my sand, my whole sculpture could fall apart within hours of assembly, which would definitely put me at risk for a bad score.

I scoop water until it just barely risks sloshing over the top of my bucket and run back to my station. I dump the water into the pile of sand I've dug, and then I run back to the ocean with two buckets this time. Once I have enough wet sand to begin working, the creative process can begin. I've decided on a sand version of the Flagler grounds. The old red Spanish-style architecture is difficult to replicate, but if I can pull it off, I have a real chance at impressing the judges and winning. It's not exactly my style, but a little sucking-up is necessary when it comes to stuff like this.

My plan is digitized on an app on my phone, but the screen is too small and too difficult to see in the bright sunlight. So, I've also sketched it onto a poster board set on an easel jimmied deeply into the sand. Before I go back for a second round of sand, I start scooping up the current sand into the shape of the base.

The judge from this morning, the one who blew the starting whistle, stands in front of my barely begun sculpture. He eyes me and then my sculpture in turns, says nothing, and walks away. Carolina watches from the next station over, eyebrows raised.

"Was that good or bad?"

"I'm going to go with good," she says.

I'm almost finished with detailing a particularly ornate stained-glass window on the administration building when I see the judge from earlier in what looks like an argument with two other judges. All three of them are pointing toward my station while they steal glances in my direction. They stop arguing and move toward me. Something is wrong, but all I can do is ignore their grim expressions and focus on detailing.

The original judge clears his throat until I turn.

"I'm sorry to tell you that you can no longer compete."

"Me?" I jab a thumb at my chest. My head swivels, looking all around, like someone else will be hiding behind me and that's who they're really talking to.

It can't be me. I haven't done anything wrong.

There's a beat when no one moves. I'm pretty sure I don't even breathe. Then the judge inhales, meeting my eyes.

"Yes. You've been disqualified."

THIRTY-EIGHT

"I don't understand."

I squint against the late morning sun and frown. I can't be hearing this correctly. Someone has made a mistake, or they have me confused with someone else, because I can't be disqualified.

The judge steps closer and produces a clipboard. He jabs a finger at my name, typed in small black ink right next to Carolina's. Beneath our contact information and scores from the qualifying round, someone has scrawled a note under my name. *Reports of cheating.*

I stare at the words, reading them over and over as I try to make sense of them. It's like trying to read a foreign language. I shake my head as heat rises to my neck and cheeks.

"I haven't cheated." It's lame, but what else am I supposed to say? I have no idea why I'd be accused of anything like this.

"Someone's come forward. Another contestant saw you and your former partner using unmarked tools during the qualifying round. As you know, all items must be checked and cleared with the judging panel prior to the competition."

The bobby pin. The stupid bobby pin that saved us, the whole reason we'd been able to qualify for the final round.

"It was just a bobby pin. It's not like I snuck in a mold and tried to pass it off as my own work."

The edge in my voice slips through before I can rethink it. I should be backing away gracefully, not making a scene. But I'm angry. I deserve to be in the competition. I can win this. Except now I can't even compete.

The judges exchange glances again, frowning even more now. They're probably worried I'll start flinging sand at their heads.

"I'm sorry, but we'll need you to step away now until the end of the contest."

I look to where the judge points, a shady spot near the pier where friends and family members, along with a few curious strangers, gather to watch. I'm officially banished. Carolina's eyes burn into my back from where she's supposed to be working on her own entry. I nod to her, hoping to quickly and quietly convey everything that needs to be said. And then I trudge to the sidelines.

I shouldn't stay to watch, but I can't imagine going home and facing questions.

And then Livvy scampers toward me with outstretched arms. "Oh no! Is it over? Did we miss the whole thing?"

Apparently, I'm not doing a decent job at pretending I'm okay because she stops questioning me and swoops close enough to whisper, "Are you okay?"

Her blanket of hair covers both our faces, and I allow mine to fall under its cover.

"I don't know what happened, Liv." My voice is small and shaky.

I let myself fall into Livvy's arms as she leads me away from the rest of the crowd. She sits me down on a bench on the outskirts of the crowd and squares my shoulders under her arms.

"Okay, talk."

I hiccup through the entire story, but I finally get it all out. "They said I cheated. They disqualified me because of something dumb and insignificant that happened last time. I didn't think it was even a big deal. But someone saw and told the judges."

I'm blubbering into her shoulder, tears I can't control forming a wet spot on her shirt. I should be embarrassed. At the beginning of the summer, I'd have rather died than have a complete meltdown in front of her. But something has shifted between Livvy and me, and I'm not embarrassed to be crying like this with her. At least there's that.

"Let's get you home," she says. "We can figure out what happened later, but you don't need to stay here. Mom and Dad are looking for a parking spot, but I'll go tell them to pull around."

She glances toward the area where the rest of the teams are putting finishing touches on their masterpieces. Where I should be right now. I follow her gaze and shudder. She's right. I can't be here anymore.

I squeeze my eyes to stop the rest of the tears and wipe my face on the shoulder of my T-shirt. "Okay, but I'd like to go alone. I'll see everyone later. And thanks, Liv. You kind of saved me from everyone seeing my meltdown."

She grins. "Well I still kind of owed you."

———

My phone rings less than ten minutes later as I'm driving back to the beach house. I jump, and it slides down under my feet, next to the gas pedal. I thought the distance from the contest would calm my nerves, but the closer I get to home, the more my heart rate rises.

By the time I pull into the driveway at the beach house, my paranoia still cripples me enough that I stay in my car for another few minutes before I remember my phone. I fish it out from below my feet and slump back into my seat. I tuck my feet under my body and check my missed calls. They're both from Foster, and as soon as I see his name on the screen, I breathe a sigh of relief, despite my complicated feelings for him. If anyone will be able to talk me down from what just happened, it's him.

I press *call,* and he answers on the first ring. Which should be my first sign the conversation is not going to go well.

"Claire." He says my name and then spends another five seconds panting on the other end.

"Foster, what's up? Is something wrong?" A rhythmic beat sounds behind his heavy breathing. "Are you okay?" It's hard to contain my rising panic at the weird phone call. More seconds pass before I hear him breathe into the phone. What is happening?

"Yes. Hold on."

I clutch my phone to my ear with sweaty palms and trembling fingers. It's stupid, but I push my finger down on the lock button in my car to lock all of the car doors. It doesn't make me feel any better though. Foster's ragged breathing and the pounding sound from earlier start to match the rhythm of my heart beating in my chest. In all the confusion, I've almost forgotten what happened at the beach and spurred this panic-fest. That is, until Foster speaks again.

"It's Johnny," he says. It's a soft whisper compared to his earlier words, but it causes chilled goose bumps to appear on my arms, even though it's a typical scorching and humid summer afternoon.

"What? What about him?" It's impossible to contain my voice.

I screech at him, but I'm only met by gulping-for-air sounds. Foster groans loudly, and the sound plays on my already fragile nerves like a harp. I scream at him out of impulse, but I'm met with complete silence. I pull my phone away from my face to see that the call ended. And then there's a banging on my car. It takes my terror to a completely new level. I turn in the direction of the noise and let out my most high-pitched scream. A face is pressed against my window, directly in front of me. I scream again and fumble around with my hands to remember where I put my keys. I find them on the passenger seat next to me and quickly turn to the ignition.

There's another pounding on the window, and I'm one split-second away from peeling out of the driveway.

"Claire, wait! It's me!" Foster's voice outside my car reels me in, and I stare at the face in the window in confusion. It's definitely Foster. He's wide-eyed and looking more scraggly than usual. I probably would have recognized him sooner if I wasn't already in full-fledged panic mode. I put a hand to my chest and gulp air into my lungs. Then I open the car door. Foster stares at me.

"I thought you were going to run me over."

I throw my head back, letting it thump against the headrest. "I thought I was too. Where did you even come from?" He points to the passenger side of the car, and I nod. Once he's opened the door and taken a seat, he leans back and rubs his temples. I lean farther back. I'm still trying to catch my breath.

"I ran here from the beach. I took Johnny's truck and drove after you an hour after you left Alabama. I tried to tell you on the phone, but I couldn't run and talk at the same time." He ducks his head.

I furrow my brow and sigh. "You scared me to death. I thought you were hurt or being chased by someone or something."

He frowns. "I wasn't being chased by anyone—yet. But, Johnny will probably want his truck back and come looking for me at some point. I parked it at the beach for now."

I shake my head. "You better have a good reason for showing up like this because I just lived out a real-life horror movie because of you. I don't know if I'll ever be able to answer my phone again."

I look down and cover my eyes. I can't have this conversation right now. I need longer than the requisite minute to get over what's happened in the past hour. "I got kicked out of the competition," I say, remembering suddenly.

"Yeah, I know." Foster reaches for my hand, but I don't give it to him. "That's why I ran here. I saw Carolina at the pier, and she told me what happened."

What Foster said about stealing Johnny's car suddenly registers, and my blood roars in my head. "Johnny's going to kill you! Why would you take his truck when you know how crazy he is?"

Foster glances down at his empty fingers and shakes his head. "He's probably pretty angry, but I'll be fine."

I lower my head to my hands and groan into my palms. Everything is so messed up right now. Foster's here, just like I begged him to be, but it's all wrong. The competition and my chances of a spot at Flagler are ruined. Whatever Foster and I had is over. All that's left is the ensuing mess. "Why are you here, Foster?"

He studies my face, searching for who knows what. "Carolina told me about the competition. I didn't know what you were thinking, but I just wanted to be the one to tell you it wasn't me. I didn't try to sabotage your chances by saying you cheated. I wouldn't do that."

I frown. "The thought never even crossed my mind." I'd

accused Foster of a lot of things in the past week, but being a saboteur is not something I would ever attribute to him.

"I have no idea who got me kicked out, but it's not important right now." I straighten up and knit my eyebrows together. "You shouldn't be here. We're not together anymore. And you're just causing more trouble for yourself."

He turns away from me and faces the window. His face is red, and his fists are balled into tight knots in his lap.

"I know." He still won't look at me, so I crane my neck to peek at his face. His eyes aren't narrowed in anger like I thought. His bottom lip is puckered out, and he's not crying, but his eyes look wet and droopy.

"We're just not good for each other. You were right." My hands sit in my lap, and I stare at them, tracing the lines on my palms with my eyes.

"I came back for you. I know I'm too late, but I'm here now."

I blink. I force a nod. "Yeah, well. It *is* too late."

If only things would go back to the way they were before he left to live with his brother. But I can't take him back, because I really don't trust him anymore, no matter how much I wish I could. I can't magically make things the way they were before everything got complicated.

"I guess I didn't really give you a reason to trust me," he says. "Maybe I'm more like Johnny than I thought."

I close my eyes and turn away. "You're not like him." I whisper it into the steering wheel, but I know he hears me because his face relaxes slightly.

Next to me, he draws a breath. "Claire, I love you."

The words I would have done anything to hear just a few days ago. Now, they feel like an insult. A sharp stinging slap in the face of everything that's happened between us.

"Don't say that," I hiss.

His jaw tightens. We sit in silence until my parents pull into the driveway. They wave, and Foster goes to say hi to them, feeding them some lie about being in town to pick up his belongings, before striding down the street, back the way he came.

THIRTY-NINE

I wake up early the next morning. The sky is still black, but today is the day I have to figure out what went wrong with the competition. If there's some way to salvage my chance at Flagler, I'll find it. Somehow, I have to get everything back on track. So I scrawl a note for my parents and make the drive to Flagler in the cool and hushed morning air. But first, I stop at the beach.

Just as I suspected, Foster is sprawled out on the damp sand a few feet away from where I stand under the pier. He's either in a coma-like sleep or he's not breathing. I hold my breath and edge forward to nudge him with the toe of my sandal.

He rubs hazy eyes and looks around the empty beach. "Claire?" Purple circles his right eye, and there's a trail of dried blood staining his puffy bottom lip. He props an elbow behind him and tries to sit up, but a sharp groan escapes him.

The skin on my arms prickles.

"What's—" I stop because my voice is so raspy that the words stick in my throat. I clear it and try again. "What's going on?" Foster blinks back at me for so long I wonder if he even heard me. I try again. "Did you sleep here?"

"It was either spend the night here or go back to Alabama to face my brother. Unfortunately, he found me anyway." He gestures to his mangled face as a low moan escapes him again.

I take a deep breath and extend my hand. He glances at it and flinches, like he's afraid that I might hit him too. "Come on," I say, nodding toward my outstretched fingers. "This has gone too far. Your problems are next on my list."

He grins and grabs my hand. Together we work on hoisting his body up as carefully as possible.

———

I instruct Foster to wait in the car while I go into the administration building at Flagler to sort out the events of the day before. He refuses. Instead, he follows half a step behind me as I power-walk up to the desk of the same secretary who'd led me to my interview. That interview feels like it was years and not weeks ago. He smiles up at me, no recognition in his eyes. "Name?"

I sigh. "I don't have an appointment." A fact I refuse to let hold me back from speaking to someone this morning.

The secretary plasters on an even brighter smile and nods. He clicks through the computer system, following the screens with his eyes. "Okay, let me read you the available appointment dates, and you can set one right now if you'd like."

I match his demeanor. Smiling through my teeth, I say, "It's an emergency. I need to see someone as soon as possible, but don't worry, I can just wait right here." I point to one of the two empty seats in the waiting area, and Foster quickly follows me with a flustered frown.

The secretary stands, his practiced politeness breaking at my defiance. "You'll need to come back when you have an appointment."

I step closer to explain once again that I'll be waiting here all day if necessary, but a voice interrupts me.

"Did you say your name is Claire?"

Poking her head out of an office behind the waiting room is an older lady with flaming red hair and a carved-into-her-face smile. I blink back at her as she shuffles her way toward me, clapping her hands.

"I just left a message with your parents," she says, looking far more ecstatic to see me than I think my demands warrant. Especially considering the way I was thrown out of the contest. But maybe she doesn't know about that. "I'm glad you're here. Come into my office so we can talk."

She points to the room she just came from and waves me forward. I can't resist flashing a near-smirk at the secretary who's watching us with his mouth hanging open. Foster nods to me and sits down, signaling he'll be waiting for me. Once in the office, I'm not sure whether to sit at the chair opposite her desk or stand against the wall and hope I'm not in for any more trouble from the cheating accusations. I settle for standing near the chair. She slides into her own leather-studded seat and shuffles a stack of papers before drawing one from the top.

She slides it forward across her desk, and I lower myself into the chair, so I can reach the paper. Before I read it, I arch an eyebrow in her direction. "What is this?"

A hand flies to her mouth to cover a round of giggles. "Well, first of all, I wanted to apologize on behalf of the judges and all of the staff here at Flagler for the terrible business that happened in the middle of your contest yesterday. It was a combination of a contestant's overprotective parent and a slightly overzealous judge."

I look up at her, eyes wide. There's a bubbling warmth as her words sink in. An apology is far from what I was expecting.

"You should not have been eliminated for something so inconsequential, and we are sorry it happened."

I exhale. It doesn't change the fact that I was kicked out of a contest I spent my whole summer preparing for, but it does take some of the weight off. I straighten my shoulders as if there was really something there that's been lifted.

She points to the paper again. "And the second thing I wanted to discuss with you is this letter. We received it from your grandfather's lawyer yesterday. You should read it."

I skim the words on the page until I pass the legal jargon and hit on something I understand. Something that makes my heart race and my palms sticky with sweat.

My client leaves for his granddaughter, Claire Haynes, a trust fund in the amount of $15,000 to be used for school expenses. This trust fund can only be accessed for school funds when Claire has completed the creative challenge of participating in a sand sculpture contest held by Flagler College. Enclosed is the account information.

"So, the contest was some sort of test? Opa planned it this way?" It turns out Opa did know what kind of art would make me happy all along. After all my doubt at the beginning, I wouldn't take sand sculpting back now—even if I could.

She nods, lips curved. "It seems like it," she says with a small shrug. "Either way, you've earned it, it seems. And we'd like to further apologize for the contest mishap by extending you an invitation to join us at Flagler for your freshman year. Your interview and portfolio really impressed our judges."

"Thank you so much. I can't believe it." Still in shock, I stand and shake her outstretched hand. She holds up a finger and slips me another small paper. I wait until I'm in the hallway between her office and the waiting room to inspect it. My breath catches when I see Opa's tiny scrawl on both sides of the familiar seashell sticky note.

Dear Claire,

If you're reading this, that means I've finally kicked the bucket.

Don't be angry with me for sending you on a little summer scavenger hunt via the sculpting contest. I know you live for those stuffy museums and dead painters, but I thought it would do you some good to shake things up a little. If it didn't work— you're still not allowed to be angry with me.

I hope you let this summer happen. You tend to unleash your charms on the world if everything's not going the way you want. Be patient. Things always work out better than you expect.

My lawyer has instructions to give this to you after I pass. I know you miss me. Our summers together have been a highlight, always something I could look forward to when getting old got to be too depressing. But a teenage girl obsessing over her grandfather isn't healthy. Don't forget me, but don't hang on to me either. Be happy without me.

I've always told you that you are an artist. Even when you were too small to responsibly hold a paintbrush on your own, you made magic happen. I hope you did that with this contest. Made beautiful art. Expanded your talent. Most of all, I hope you had fun with it.

And when the competition is over, please accept this trust fund in your name. I put this money aside for art school for you a long time ago.

I only wish I were there to see you take the art world by storm.

Love always,

Opa

I'm conflicted whether to laugh or cry. It's so like Opa to get everything about this summer right. It turns out he didn't even need to be here to know what's going on in my life. I spy Foster staring at the ceiling of the waiting room, and his eyebrows shoot up, causing him to wince. He's going to be so confused about all of this. But first things first. I point to him and set my teeth.

"Your thing next."

———

I think Foster would rather me go in with him, but I refuse. I sit in the car and wait in the parking lot of the square, brick government building. He didn't want to go in at all, even after Johnny's latest abuse, but I talked him into it.

His body shakes as he slips open the passenger door and sits next to me. "I did it. And they believed me. They said we could work something out so I don't have to live with him anymore. I can stay here." He's lighter, less adult, more teenager already.

I let my head drop against the back of my seat. "I'm so proud of you."

It would be the perfect moment if there wasn't all of this awkward tension between us. We've both conquered our fears, solved our mysteries. All that's missing is what I want so badly: Foster.

FORTY

It's been almost a week since I've been to the beach. That's a record for me, especially during the summer. It's time to take back my beach. I stand in the parking lot and stare at the pier, watching the people come and go. They're laughing and talking. Exhausted kids, pink from the sun, wear sand-covered clothes. Surfers shoulder wet boards and suits. Old couples walk around me hand in hand with bags of seashells to store in jars in their guest bathrooms. It's like coming home.

I slip off my sandals and hold them in one hand as I stroll across the sand. I weave in and out of the warm water, splashing my own feet as I go. I pass by the underside of the pier. It's empty, but I'm not ready to go over there yet. Someone waves at me from across the beach and I squint into the sun.

"Claire!"

I recognize Carolina's voice immediately and sprint toward her, almost losing my balance in the process. We grab onto each other as we meet and laugh. "Congratulations on your third win in a row!" I exclaim.

Her face pulls down. "I still can't believe we didn't get to battle it out."

I walk a little ahead of her so she can't see my face. I'm brave, but I'm not immune to being sucked into the reminder of how awful that day was for me. Now that the trauma of being accused of cheating is over, my safe place feels that much safer. I shake my head. "It's fine. And we can battle it out at Flagler next year since we both got in!"

Carolina smiles and squeezes my arm. "You're awesome. I don't know what I would have done if it were me. At least it worked out, though."

I shrug. I don't want to talk about it anymore. I'd texted her to give her the update after the crazy turn of events. Now I never want to hear about it again. "Do you want to keep walking?" I point toward the setting sun and turn in its direction.

Carolina shakes her head. "I already told my parents I was heading home. I just saw you and wanted to say hi." She walks in the opposite direction, and I wander toward the far stretch of the beach. But the pier still catches my eye, and I hesitate, motionless.

I clutch my shoes to my side and make my way toward the spot under the pier, where my summer began and ended. Where I thought life might end at seventeen. I graze my fingers along the old wood. It's just wood, just a fixture on the beach. No one else sees anything out of the ordinary. But I'm suddenly vindicated. I wrap a hand around the post and exhale.

Something to the right of the pier catches my eye, and I walk toward it carefully. It's just sand smoothed out into a pattern. For all I know, some little kids were building sandcastles, the same thing I've seen a hundred times before. I take a step backward to try to make sense of the shapes carved into the smooth area. Shells are swirled in a circle around the structure— they look like the same small white seashells Foster found the day we went swimming. In the center of the circle is a sand sculpture in the shape of an alligator.

My breath catches at the sight of painted-over bottles and pieces of glass adorning the alligator's back in place of scales. Foster's work has such a distinct look. Even if the alligator hadn't clued me in, the recycled beach trash is an obvious tell. I crouch next to the sculpture, letting my eyes pass over each miniscule detail. A gleaming green bit placed in between the eyes catches the light, and I reach for it. It's an emerald-green miniature alligator figurine. I'm pretty sure it's something from the gift shop at the Alligator Zoo.

I hold it in my open hand for a moment before pushing the alligator into my back pocket. He wasn't being subtle, that's for sure. Foster knew I'd come here, and he wanted me to see this. But why? We're not so compromised now that we solely communicate via sculptures, right?

I sigh. Whatever it's supposed to mean, it will take more than an alligator charm and some sand to fix our relationship.

———

I pack my bag with the papers I need and head toward the school administration building after lunch. I need to meet with the counselor who's going to be helping me with my enrollment next year and ask for a small favor. There's one thing I've been meaning to do for a while, and today is the perfect day to get it off my chest. After an hour of sorting things out, I thank her for her help and drive back toward the beach.

Foster is standing at the bottom of the pier. It's hard to forget that this beach was the first place we met, where we kissed, and also where we said good-bye. My stomach flip-flops at the exact moment he spots me and grins. I wave, and butterflies beat against my chest, even though there's nothing left to be nervous about. Nothing is going to happen, I remind myself. I asked him to meet me here, but I still react this way whenever I see him. The alligator sculpture thing was sweet, but it can't fix everything that's happened between us just like that.

"Hey. I was just gonna come find you." Foster rubs a hand through the back of his hair. His other hand rests in the back pocket of his swim trunks, the only thing he's wearing after what looks like a day of surfing. I focus my eyes on his. Better to not tempt myself with his wet, tanned skin anyway. It would be so easy to fall back into a pattern, kissing him, wanting to be close to him. I can't lie and say I don't still care about him, but it's complicated now.

"Oh, yeah? I kind of did something sneaky." I laugh, and shakiness rumbles through my chest. Surprises have been hit or miss with the two of us. This, I think he will like.

He shifts his eyes. "Oh boy. What's going on now?"

I suppress a grin and pull an envelope addressed to him from my bag. He turns it around in his hands before sliding a finger under the fold and opening it. I bite my lip and wait for his reaction while he reads.

"I don't understand." He drops his hands and looks at me, a smile of half-confusion, half-wonder on his lips.

I shrug. "I had an interesting conversation with the Flagler admissions board. They kind of owed me still. And something happened during my first interview that made me realize I can't let you give up on something you love. Something you're really good at."

He's still staring at me with open-mouthed awe.

"So, I talked to one of the judges. I showed her pictures of your work. And I explained everything that's been going on, and when she heard how much you've been through and how amazing of an artist you are, she agreed that you needed to be in the program." I rush through the last sentence because he looks like he's going to say something, and I don't want it to be a no.

"Claire."

I hold up a hand. "Foster, I'm sorry, but I had to at least try. You deserve this, even if you don't think you do."

He shakes his head and smiles at the ground. "I can't believe you did this." He points to the letter. "I have an interview next week?"

I nod. "Just one interview, and then you're in. And I have some pull, since they felt so guilty about the way the contest turned out." I can't help it, I'm totally beaming.

"How did you know I still wanted to be in the program? I thought I had you convinced that I was done with art."

I laugh. There's no way he could ever convince me he isn't an artist, or that he could ever be done with art. "You're an artist. We're never really done with our art."

"You really need to stop saving me."

I roll my eyes. This must be how the knights in old fairy tales felt. Like they would save the princesses one hundred times over if they got the chance. Except this isn't a fairy tale because neither of us is a knight in shining armor or a princess in distress. We take turns saving each other. And I'm looking forward to my turn being the princess because I'm freaking exhausted.

"I refuse to stop saving you," I say. It's supposed to be a joke, but the humor in my voice falls flat, and it comes out as a whisper. Almost everything worked out this summer, after all. And the parts that didn't...maybe they weren't meant to be in the first place. Maybe—

Foster interrupts my inner monologue by wrapping one arm around my waist. My skin burns through my clothing. I'm so starved for his touch I practically melt into him. He's holding me so close that the saltwater from his hair falls onto my cheeks in small, persistent drops. I tilt my head to watch as he puts a hand to his hair to brush it back.

He catches my face with one palm and holds it in place

while I blink up at him. I'm convinced my heartbeat is louder than all of the crashing waves combined. If I moved forward one centimeter, our lips would meet. But maybe that part of our relationship is over for good. Maybe it should be.

"I'm sorry for all the crap I put you through," he mumbles against my hair.

I'm paralyzed by how close he is, and all I can do is shake my head. I want him to kiss me so badly I can already taste the memory of his mouth on mine. We stand inches apart as minutes tick by until I can't stand it any longer.

His eyes meet mine as I dart forward and almost close the gap between us. Our first kiss, for the last time. Finally. Our lips crash together and a wave of happiness spreads through me. When I'm forced to come up for air, I lean my head against his chest and sigh. He plants a kiss on top of my hair, my cheeks, my forehead.

We walk with our hands clasped tightly. We stop every few minutes to press our lips together and giggle about nothing in particular. I pause and stand on my tiptoes to kiss him again.

"Don't ever leave me again." I don't care that I'm being demanding. I just care that this is finally happening. After he left this summer, I never thought I'd be this happy again.

"Deal," he says.

I pinch a strand of his hair and give it a gentle tug. We have more summers and more beaches ahead of us. I can feel it.

ACKNOWLEDGMENTS

If I'm going to start at the beginning, I have to thank my mom for spending hours reading with me as a young child. Mom, you passed your love of words on to me, and I'll always be incredibly grateful for that. Thank you to my dad for buying me books of poetry. You shared your love of learning with me, and that love sparked my desire to write.

To my husband, Mark, who has believed in me from day one when we were just a year out of college and two kids deep into parenthood. Thank you for buying me a computer after I woke up on a random weekday and announced it was time for me to start writing. Thank you for all the support and love and proof-reading. Most importantly, thank you for all the chocolate.

Thank you to Brielle Porter, who read early chapters and gave great feedback. To the best CP ever, Jordan Green: Thank you for putting up with me! Your critiques constantly push me to be better.

Stuart White, for creating Write Mentor and for being an all-around inclusive cheerleader for writers everywhere: I'm so grateful. And to my mentor, Brandy Woods Snow, I learned so much about writing and storytelling from you. You helped make this book what it is today.

Thank you to Brookie Cowles at Literary Crush Publishing for seeing something in my words and for being an incredible support along the way. To Arielle Bailey, thank you for your amazing editing skills.

Thank you to my in-laws for the endless support and enthusiasm.

Lastly, I'm so grateful to every one of you who read this book. I hope Claire's and Foster's journeys spark your inner artist.

ABOUT THE AUTHOR

Haleigh Wenger has been writing and reading her entire life. The first book to really break her heart was *Little Women*, which she remembers staying up all night to read in the fifth grade. From then, she was hooked on the rush of being so emotionally invested in a story she could not sleep. She was determined to create her own story that made readers feel big things. She graduated from Brigham Young University in 2009 with a degree in Communications. In her free time, she bakes and goes on walks with her family. She can most often be found with her head buried in a book, flour dusting her clothes, and at least one kid sitting on her lap.

Website: HaleighWenger.com

CPSIA information can be obtained
at www.ICGtesting.com
Printed in the USA
BVHW071643050819
555095BV00014B/1908/P